A PLACE
CALLED
MORNING

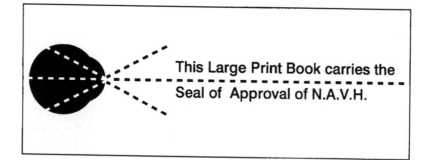

This Large Print Book carries the
Seal of Approval of N.A.V.H.

A PLACE
CALLED
MORNING

Ann Tatlock

G.K. Hall & Co. • **Thorndike, Maine**

DU BR
LP
TATLOCK
A

Published in 1999 by arrangement with Bethany House Publishers.

G.K. Hall Large Print Inspirational Series.

The text of this Large Print edition is unabridged.
Other aspects of the book may vary from the original edition.

Set in 16 pt. Plantin by Rick Gundberg.

Printed in the United States on permanent paper.

Library of Congress Cataloging-in-Publication Data

Tatlock, Ann.
    A place called morning / Ann Tatlock.
      p. (large print) cm.
    ISBN 0-7838-8683-7 (lg. print : hc : alk. paper)
    1. Large type books. I. Title.
    [PS3570.A85P58   1999]
    813'.54—dc21
                                                    99-16635

To Bob
who made all the difference

Prologue

1977

It had happened on an ordinary day, the first minutes and hours of which offered no suggestion that, when the day was finished, it would not be lost to memory like so many others, one small forgotten link in a chain of years.

The morning had simply followed the pattern of her daily routine, beginning with her awakening before dawn, stretching her stiff limbs between a set of floral-patterned sheets, and giving herself over to a generous yawn. That done, she sat up and let her legs drop over the side of the bed. In the still-dark room, she searched the throw rug with her bare feet, then wiggled her toes into a pair of open-heeled slippers. She groped with one hand toward the foot of the bed and, finding what she was after, slipped a green quilted robe over her pink cotton nightgown. Leaving the rumpled bed behind, she trekked across the creaking hardwood floor, the soles of her slippers swishing against the wood as she shuffled sleepily toward the bathroom. Just as she crossed the threshold, the automatic coffee maker in the kitchen began to sigh, and the scent of French Roast drifted between the rooms in the large turn-of-the-century house on Humboldt Avenue. It would be another half hour before she got to it, but she liked to find a full pot of coffee waiting for her when she entered the kitchen for breakfast.

She switched on the bathroom light and twisted the hot and cold faucets in the shower. The water pipes groaned, and after a moment the shower head reluctantly spat water into the tub. She removed her robe and nightgown and hung them on a hook on the back of the door. Tucking her hair into a shower cap and leaving the slippers on the bath mat, she stepped into the invigorating surge of warm water.

"Make me know thy ways, O Lord." Her lips moved, but there was no sound. It was as habitual as the fluttering of her eyelids at five o'clock, this prayer from the Psalms. It had followed her through childhood and adolescence into young adulthood and middle age. "Teach me thy paths."

There was more, but she paused as an image from the previous day interrupted her thoughts.

"I know it all by heart now, Mother Mae," the little boy in the hospital bed had announced. "You want to hear it?"

"I sure do, Alfie." She gently sat down beside him on the bed and took his hand. His clear blue eyes were the only childlike feature of his worn and ashen face. Beneath his lower lids hung dark and heavy half moons, and the crown of his head

8

was as smooth and hairless as an old man's.

" 'The Lord is my shepherd,' " he began, and as he recited the Twenty-third Psalm, she struggled to hold back the tears. She had been visiting the children's hospital for years, had long been known as Mother Mae to staff and patients alike, but she had never become inured to seeing the little ones suffer and sometimes die. It was the hope that she could bring them some comfort and joy that brought her back to the hospital week after week.

" 'Even though I walk through the valley of the shadow of death, I fear no evil; for thou art with me. . . .' "

He's only eight years old, she had thought. *If only you would spare him, Lord. He's hardly begun to live.*

" ' . . . and I will dwell in the house of the Lord forever.' " He looked up at her and smiled.

"That's wonderful, Alfie," she congratulated him. "You said it all exactly right."

"Yeah, I finally got it," Alfie remarked, "after saying it about a million times. I had to ask my mom about the 'He restores my soul' part. I didn't really understand it, but I guess I do now."

"And what did your mother say?"

"She said it means I might not get fixed up on the outside, but God will make sure I'm always all right on the inside."

"That's right, Alfie. Our true self — what's inside of us — is always safe with God."

The little boy frowned. "Mother Mae?"

"Yes, Alfie?"

"Do you think God will fix me up on the outside?"

"I don't know, honey. I hope so."

The boy paused a moment, deep in thought. "If He doesn't," he said quietly, "Mom says I'll go to heaven, and she says heaven is a beautiful place."

"It is, Alfie. More beautiful than we can imagine."

The boy shut his eyes, as though content with the thought. After a moment, he said sleepily, "When I get there, I want to play with the stars."

Mae stroked his cheek tenderly. "You will, Alfie," she said, "if that's your heart's desire. You will play with the stars."

Mae sighed as she remembered Alfie. She would visit him again the next afternoon, but she wondered how many more visits there would be after that. Probably not many. "Take him gently, Lord," she prayed, and as she lathered up the soap between her hands, she thought of her own small grandson and felt suddenly thankful for his life and health.

She was glad her daughter and son-in-law lived nearby so she could spent lots of time with Sammy. Lately Ellen had been dropping Sammy off on her way to a photography class at the community college. After the class, Ellen put in a few hours at her part-time job and didn't return until early evening.

Sammy, at two years old, was a nonstop bundle of activity and chatter. He loved to sing, to color, to turn somersaults across his grandmother's queen-sized bed. He especially loved to ride the rocking horse his grandmother had bought for his visits to her home. He rode like a wild man, one hand clenching the handlebar, the other waving an imaginary lasso as he pretended to be the Lone Ranger, whom he'd seen in reruns on television. Back and forth, back and forth, the rockers digging creases into Mae's throw rug. Sammy's head bobbed on his slender neck and his blond curls tossed as he rocked. "Hi-ho, Silber!" he yelled. "Hi-ho, Silber, and away!"

To add to Mae's joy, a second grandchild was on the way. In another two months or so, Sammy would have a little brother or sister to play with, and she would have another grandchild to love and coddle.

Her only nagging sorrow was that her husband wasn't here to share the gifts of life's middle years. He had died of a heart attack some three years earlier, on the first day of spring in 1974. Now that was a day she would never forget — the day she became a widow at the age of forty-four. When she stood beside the fresh grave, the grass at her feet tender and new, the mound of earth like a swollen wound, she thought she couldn't bear the loss. For months afterward she held long conversations with George in her mind, unwilling to let him go. But that changed with time. She adjusted. The inward conversations dried up along with the tears. She became accustomed to living alone for the first time in her life. And as the months passed, she found to her surprise that she was recovering from her loss. *"We were created with an amazing ability to heal,"* her mother had sometimes told her, and she discovered it was true. She missed her husband still, but the intense pain had dwindled to a manageable ache. Besides, new life was springing up in the form of grandchildren, and in that she found a sense of purpose again.

"Thank you, Lord, for Sammy and for the little one not yet born," she said, slipping into the spontaneous portion of her morning prayers. She went on to pray for her son, Mike, who lived in California and was negligent about keeping in touch. She diligently wrote to him and sometimes called, but she felt it was her prayers for him that kept them most closely connected. She prayed for her friends, for the shut-ins of the church, for the children at the hospital. "Oh, and watch over Roy and protect him," she continued, thinking of one of her dearest friends. Roy was older than she, and yet so innocent and childlike in his ways that Mae always thought of him whenever she was praying for children.

The hours before noon were quiet that day, and because so much of her life was busy, she relished the moments of solitude. They were a welcome resting place in between the hours of baby-sitting and family events, volunteering at the hospital, sitting on church committees, visiting the invalids of the parish, and socializing with her friends. She loved all the activities that filled her days, but she also loved the quiet hours and the soothing company of books and music and even silence. She was thankful for the structure of her life, that she was free to do what she enjoyed without having to work to support herself. Both her husband and her father had been good providers and had made sure she would be taken care of even after they were gone.

Mae dressed in a casual sweater and slacks, then fixed herself two poached eggs and wheat toast, which she ate while reading the morning paper. Later, when the breakfast dishes were washed, she put clean sheets on the bed in the guest room downstairs where Sammy would take his nap. These chores done, she wandered to the living room window to check on the weather. The clouds were tossing out a sparse array of snowflakes that undoubtedly wouldn't amount to much. She and Sammy would be able to take their walk after lunch. For now, she curled up in a chair with an old hard-cover copy of Dickens and a cup of steaming coffee while a symphony of Beethoven played on the stereo.

When Ellen and Sammy arrived, she greeted them both with hugs and kisses. Ellen breathlessly chattered for a moment, running through the list of items in Sammy's tote bag.

Mae eyed her daughter's bulging coat with a mixture of joy and concern. "How are you feeling, dear?"

"Just great, Mother, really," Ellen assured her.

"I hope you aren't overexerting yourself —"

But Ellen only laughed at her mother's unnecessary caution. She had heard it all before when she was carrying Sammy. "I'm fine, Mother. Don't worry so! See you around six-thirty, all right?" She kissed her mother and her son, then rushed off to class.

Alone with her grandson, Mae peeled away his heavy jacket and mittens, pulled his feet out of his rubber boots, and tied on the sneakers she found in the bag. They shared a lunch of peanut-butter-and-jelly sandwiches, then Sammy hopped aboard his horse and rode off to places unknown while his grandmother cleaned the kitchen. As she wiped bread crumbs off the table, she heard "Giddyup, horsey, giddyup!" and she smiled as she pictured him on his horse in the guest room, one hand clutching the handlebar, the other thrown recklessly above his head.

Then she bundled him up again and put on her own winter garments for their afternoon "Icicle Walk." This was the first winter of Sammy's life that he could put a name to all the fascinating things in the world around him, and for the past several months grandmother and grandson had been taking "Icicle Walks" and "Hoarfrost Walks" and "Snowman Walks."

That afternoon the plan was to scope out all the icicles hanging from their neighbors' roofs, and to pick out the largest one. Mae and Sammy pressed mitten to mitten and walked together along the salted sidewalks of the neighborhood, their eyes turned upward in search of the longest funnel of dangling ice. Sammy thought the icicles looked like the teeth of the dragons in his fairy-tale book. He wanted to break off the biggest one and keep it to play with. Pointing to the chosen icicle with one oversized mitten and stomping his boots on the sidewalk, he cried, "Take that one home, Grammy! Take that one home and keep it!"

"Oh no, Sammy," Mae explained with an amused chuckle. "You can't keep an icicle. They melt, just like the ice cubes that we put in your lemonade to make it cold. You have to keep them outside and look at them from a distance. But we'll come out and visit all the icicles again."

Satisfied, he let her take his hand, and they walked against the chill wind toward home.

All of this happened on the day of the incident, but later she would not remember any of it. All those hours of that March day were gone, relegated to the place where lost hours are buried because they are too routine, too unimportant to be remembered. Those forgotten hours were the foundation upon which the pivotal moment rested, the moment that changed her life, but they had been only a quiet prelude to the mad song that followed. It was to one incident that

15

her mind would be drawn again and again. A single incident that would tug on her mind like an irate child yanking his mother's skirt, demanding her attention.

Sammy was curled up in bed in the downstairs guest room, finally settling into sleep after insisting on the same Dr. Seuss story twice. The door leading into the hall was left open so that his grandmother could listen for him should he call out for water or cry out from a bad dream. She sat in the overstuffed chair in the living room, her slippered feet tucked up beneath her, her recipe book open on her lap as she tried to decide what to make for dinner.

Settling on a casserole, she ran through the list of ingredients. A pound of hamburger, rice, corn, fresh carrots, and onions — all these she had. But she wasn't certain she had a can of tomatoes. Putting the recipe book aside, she walked quietly to the kitchen and searched the cabinets. No tomatoes. She decided to check the basement, where she kept a variety of dried and canned foods. A glance at the clock told her it was a few minutes after four. She had better get the casserole made and into the oven if she and Sammy were going to eat by half past five.

The basement door was across from the guest room, in the hall that led from the kitchen to the living room. Again walking quietly, Mae made her way to the basement door where, with one hand on the knob she paused, thinking she had heard a noise in Sammy's room. But as she stood

16

there listening, she heard only the humming of the refrigerator and the muffled rumble of cars passing by on the street outside.

She knew exactly where on the shelves the tomatoes would be if she had any. She opened the door and flipped on the light switch. Before her stretched a wooden staircase which her father — when he had owned the house — painted green decades ago. Now the forest green paint was faded and peeling away from the endless trampling of feet. "I really should have Roy repaint these stairs sometime," she decided absently. It was an otherwise sturdy staircase — no rickety steps, no rotting wood — but it was much too steep to be maneuvered without caution.

Taking hold of the handrail, she moved gingerly to the first step and then to the second. Before going any farther she turned and shut the door behind her. Halfway down the stairs, she thought she heard the doorbell ring. It wasn't a ring so much as a loud jarring buzz that Mae had always disliked and Ellen called downright rude. *Now, who in the world?* Mae thought, but before she could so much as start back up the stairs, the bell rang again. Whoever was at the door was certainly impatient, and if he kept it up, no doubt the noise would awaken Sammy. Then she'd be back to Dr. Seuss and to Sammy's cries of, "Just one more time, Grammy."

Mae hurried up the stairs and down the hall, her slippers padding dully against the bare floor. "I'm coming. I'm coming," she mumbled.

"Please don't ring again."

She opened the door to find a ruddy-faced young man scanning papers on a clipboard. He was dressed in a blue uniform with matching padded jacket. On one breast of the jacket was an oval patch with the name "Jay" stitched into it. His regulation cap may have kept the snow off his head but did nothing to keep the wind from nipping at his ears. He wore no gloves, and he had just started to blow openmouthed on the chapped knuckles of one hand when he looked up to see Mae standing there.

"Yes?" Mae asked.

"I'm with the gas company, ma'am," he explained hastily, dropping his hand. "Here to check your furnace." His words became little clouds that hung briefly in the cold air.

"Check my furnace?" Mae frowned, puzzled.

His eyes fell to the clipboard and bounced back up. "Says here that you called with a complaint."

Mae shook her head. "I'm afraid you're mistaken. I didn't call."

The man referred again to his notes and gave an address. "That your address?" he asked.

"Yes, it is, but I'm not having any problems with my furnace."

The man fidgeted impatiently and asked, "You Mrs. Carothers? Says here a Mrs. Carothers at this address called —"

"No, I'm not Mrs. Carothers. I don't even know any Carothers on this street, but maybe whoever took the call got some numbers transposed on the address."

The young man gazed at her a moment in silence, as though he suspected she was lying about not being Mrs. Carothers. Finally, he relented, saying, "Suppose that might be possible."

Mae wanted to shut the door — she was shivering herself by now from the cold — and to get on with dinner. "I'm sorry I can't help you —"

"Well, can I use your phone? I need to talk to the office and find out where I'm supposed to be."

Mae sighed and glanced down at the man's boots. They covered his lower legs almost to the knee, and the laces were so long it would take a good five minutes for him to untie them and pry his feet out. The man picked up on what Mae was thinking.

"I guess I could take my boots off —"

"Never mind," Mae said. "Just wipe them off the best you can." She moved aside to let the man in when he had finished shuffling his feet on the mat. "The phone's there, in the living room —"

Before she could lift her hand to point toward the phone, she was interrupted by a noise down the hall — a startled cry and a crashing thump of weight against the basement stairs.

Mae gasped, then stood perfectly still, her breath frozen by the horror that filled her chest. She stared into the face of the young stranger, as though to decide by his expression whether he had also heard the crash. He stood looking past her down the hall toward the rear of the house. He had heard it too, then. Mae turned from him, and in that awful moment of turning toward the noise, she realized she had left the basement door open. She had broken her own rule: "The basement door remains closed at all times." She had left the door open in her rush to keep the doorbell from buzzing again.

"Ma'am?"

She heard the young man's puzzled question, but she was suspended in that place of disbelief, that place of knowing but of not wanting to know. She had heard the cry, she had heard the sound of someone tumbling down the stairs, and she knew that Sammy must be lying at the bottom, lying there upon the cold concrete floor of the basement. But in the instant before her mind was able to tell her feet to move, her disbelief held her rooted to where she stood, and her desire told her that if she was very quiet and did not move, did not follow through into the next logical moment, then what she had heard and what had happened would somehow be undone, would somehow be made right again.

But her reason won out as she realized that in spite of what she feared, in spite of what the next moment held, she had to move forward into it. It would not go away, and she knew even as she uttered them that her cries of "No, Sammy, no. Oh, dear God, no!" would not erase the fact that the boy had wandered from his room and tumbled down the stairs.

She rushed down the hall and stopped, terrified, in the doorway to the basement. Only for a moment did she stand there, shaking, her heart pounding wildly in her chest, her breath coming in quick gasps. She lifted one trembling hand to her mouth and whispered, "Oh, dear God, dear Lord." She started down the steps, almost stumbling down them, the steps that her father had called "a danger to life and limb" every time he descended them. Dizzy, disconnected from herself and from the present moment, she clung frantically to the handrail as she made her way down. She didn't take her eyes from Sammy, sprawled on the hard cold floor, lying there in his blue Twins shirt and his Cookie Monster socks. He lay on his stomach, his head turned to one side, one leg and one arm in front of him as though he were running.

When she reached the bottom, she knelt by the child, afraid almost to touch him, afraid to hurt him more by moving him. He lay so still she knew all the wind had been knocked out of him. *I have to get him to breathe,* she thought, *to take deep breaths, to draw air back into his lungs.* "Sammy!" she cried. "Wake up, Sammy! Open your eyes." She patted his cheek and squeezed his small hand, but his pale lashes lay still against his creamy white skin. She bent over and pressed her cheek against his, but she couldn't hear him breathe. She reached for his wrist to feel his pulse, but she couldn't find it.

The panic rose in her like nausea, while the sense of unreality weighed down on her. Mae's eyes darted over the boy and up the stairs, as though looking for a way to reverse time, to set Sammy at the head of the stairs again so that she could stop him before he fell.

She shook her head as though to clear her mind, then rushed toward the stairs, but halfway up she stopped when her eyes met the frightened gaze of the young man. He stood in the doorway, still clutching his clipboard, staring down at the scene below. Mae wanted to cry out to him, but before she could say a word, he held up one hand like a traffic cop and instructed, "Stay with the boy. I'll call for help."

He disappeared, and Mae rushed back to Sammy, taking him in her arms and cradling his head in her lap. She stroked his cheek and rocked him slightly, her body moving back and forth as though she were singing a baby to sleep. But she did not sing, she moaned, and the sound of her despair was echoed by the wail of a siren in the distance. As the sound came closer, she knew that the screaming ambulance was coming here to her house, that the driver was speeding over the city streets to end up at her door.

"Hurry," she pleaded quietly. "Oh, hurry, hurry!"

She said the word again and again, in the hopes that when the paramedics arrived she could turn the child over to them, and they would make him better. They would catch hold of the life that remained in the boy before it slipped away entirely. They would revive him, get him to breathe again.

"Oh, hurry!"

She found that by repeating the word, she didn't have to consider that Sammy's brief life might already be gone, and that if so, no one and nothing could bring it back.

Chapter 1

Mae Demaray stood at the living room window, watching. Roy was nearly fifteen minutes late already, and that wasn't like him.

In her anxiety, she scarcely noticed the full bloom of spring outside. May in Minneapolis is the annual reward for having endured another harsh winter. It is the most colorful month of the year, filled with the green of fresh grass and newly unfurled leaves, the blue of fluid lakes and open sky, the red, yellow, lavender of flowers that have blossomed in private gardens and in public parks and along the roadsides everywhere. Life in all forms has renewed itself, willing to open its eyes again to the warmth that has finally settled over the city. People shed their coats like snakes slithering out of old skins and take to the sidewalks along residential streets and to the walking paths around the lakes, breathing in the fragrances of the long awaited season. They breathe as though they have not breathed in months and feel that they themselves have somehow come to life again along with nature.

But Mae did not see the colors, nor feel within herself the renewal of life. She felt only concern, tinged with annoyance, that someone as punctual as Roy Hanna was late. He'd never before failed to catch the 8:10 a.m. bus that took him from Pillsbury to Humboldt. Invariably, if it was Tuesday morning, Roy was on her doorstep at 8:35.

"I wonder," she said aloud to herself, "whether I should try to call —"

Just as she was about to turn from the window, a stout figure dressed in red and blue caught her eye. She bent closer to the glass to get a better look. Yes, it was Roy, making his way briskly down Humboldt, a spray of lilac branches clutched in one beefy fist. If she hadn't recognized him by shape, she would have known him by the ever present cigar clenched between his teeth, the wreath of smoke circling his head and trailing off behind him. Because of Roy's habit, Mae's two young granddaughters called him the "Cigar Man."

Roy was several years older than Mae, retired now from his job as a janitor at Honeywell. He rented a room in a boardinghouse on Pillsbury Avenue, in the general area of the city where he had lived in one boardinghouse or another for most of his life. He was a round man with a wide sphere of a waist and a face as circular as a full moon. His hair, once brown and thick, was now gray and thin, but he still had enough to cover the crown of his orblike head. Even his nose was large and bulbous, his eyes round as cow eyes. There was nothing sharp or angular about Roy, and those who knew him thought it befitting his personality. He was an affable and gentle man, never giving offense, nor taking it either. Hurtful remarks rolled off of him like pebbles down a mountain of polished stone, finding no crevices in which to settle. Still, he had been the recipient of a lifetime of mean-spirited taunts made by callous or unthinking people who didn't understand that a dim mind was a mind nevertheless, filled with thoughts and emotions and ideas. He knew he wasn't bright like other people, but he had resolved early on not to let that fact or people's opinions bother him. He knew he somehow had fewer advantages than others, but that didn't curtail his enjoyment of life. Though he had spent his years doing work considered menial by most, he had done it with meticulous care and a sense of pride.

Roy brought that same dependability with him to Mae's house, where he spent every Tuesday morning doing odd jobs for her. Depending on the season and the need, he'd cut the grass, rake leaves, shovel snow, prune shrubs, pull weeds, paint shutters, sweep the garage and the sidewalk. Indoors he was handy at plumbing, carpentry, and making the usual repairs that an old house needs. Each Tuesday at noon Mae and Roy would have lunch together, then Roy would linger and smoke a leisurely cigar before catching the bus back to Pillsbury.

Even though Mae paid Roy generously for his work (in spite of his insistence that "I'd gladly work for free for my friend Miss Mae"), she never thought of him as a handyman, nor did he think of her as an employer. The arrangement between the longtime friends was simply beneficial for them both. Roy, living on a fixed retirement income, needed the extra cash. As for Mae, the upkeep of the house was too much for her alone, and she welcomed Roy's help.

But now Mae tried to keep her annoyance in check as she watched Roy coming up the walkway to her house. He bounded up the porch steps and approached the door with lavender blossoms held close to his chest, like a suitor clutching a bouquet of roses. Before his eager finger could reach the doorbell, Mae flung the front door open and stood confronting him.

"Roy, what on earth happened? I was really beginning to worry about you. You're never late," she chided, moving aside to let him pass by her.

Roy stepped into the hall, bringing in with him the odor of cheap tobacco mingled with the scent of lilacs. He pulled the cigar from between his teeth, stained brown from so many years of smoking. "I'm awfully sorry, Miss Mae," he said, blending as usual the last two words into a single name that sounded like "Mizmay." With a grin that sliced a crescent hole into his face, he explained, "I saw the lilac bushes blooming behind the house this morning, and I asked Miss

27

Pease if I could cut off a few branches and bring them to you, and you know Miss Pease, she said I could dig up the whole bush if I wanted and transplant it right in your yard for all she cared, and I said, 'Oh no, Miss Pease, just a few branches is all I want. Just a few branches for Miss Mae.' Well, by the time I found my scissors and by the time I cut off some of the branches, I had missed the 8:10 bus and had to take the next one. But it come not long after the 8:10, not long after at all."

Mae sighed and looked at Roy squarely. "But you're more than fifteen minutes late, Roy," she said.

The grin slid off of Roy's face. "I'm awfully sorry, Miss Mae," he repeated. "If it's the time, I'll make it up to you. I'll work right through lunch to make it up to you."

"Oh no, Roy," countered Mae, "it's not the time. You know I don't clock your work around here. I was just getting terribly worried, thinking something might have happened to you."

Roy stared at her with his large blue eyes, the only thing about him that bothered Mae. It was the color that disturbed her, a particular shade of violet-blue. By some odd, almost cruel coincidence, Sammy's eyes had been the same striking color. Mae sometimes found herself turning away from Roy with an indistinguishable shudder, as though Sammy were looking out at her from the face of the older man.

"Miss Mae," Roy said, grinning again, "I

28

didn't mean to make you worried, but it's awful nice of you to say you were. I mean, you're really kind, Miss Mae, to care what happens to me —"

Mae cut him off with a wave of her hand. "Never mind, Roy," she said with a short nervous laugh. "I guess I'm just an old worrywart, always more anxious than I need to be. Well, let me put the lilacs in some water."

She took the blossoms from Roy and was on her way to the kitchen when he called to her.

"Say, Miss Mae," he said. "Can I?"

She turned to look at him. She knew what he was asking. He always asked before he began his work to listen to the music box that sat amid the family photographs on the fireplace mantel. It was an antique wooden box that must have been in her family long before she was born. She didn't know who the original owner was, nor when it had been bought, but she did know that it had had a place on the mantel from the time of her earliest memory, and its melody had haunted her life from childhood. Roy said the song gave him energy to go about his morning tasks.

"Of course. You go ahead," Mae said. "I wound it for you already this morning. I'll be right back."

As she puttered about the kitchen she could see him in her mind, could envision that certain look that crept across his face as soon as the notes began to drift from the box. It was a faraway look, as though the song took him to a

29

place that only he could see, as though he was remembering something from a very long time ago.

"What does it make you think of?" Mae had asked him once.

"The lady." He spoke so softly she could barely hear.

"What lady?" she asked.

Roy seemed to be considering Mae's question as his blue eyes glazed with thought. "She was so beautiful," he finally said. He turned his gaze on her. "She looked a little like you, Miss Mae."

"Who was she, Roy?"

But then he was gone again, humming slightly and moving his head from side to side with the tune. She thought the woman must have been someone Roy had known briefly, or maybe only seen from a distance. Roy might have been somewhat infatuated with her — though hopelessly, as no beautiful woman would have loved in return this round-faced man who had the mind of a child.

After putting the lilacs in a vase of water, Mae found Roy by the fireplace, closing the lid of the music box. "Now I can work," he said with a smile. "I got my energy."

She placed the vase on the mantel beside the box. "Thoughtless of me, Roy. I haven't thanked you for the lilacs." She took a deep breath, drawing in their scent. "They're lovely."

Roy crushed out his cigar in the ashtray that Mae kept for him on the coffee table. "I'll get rid

30

of this old stogie, and then you can get an even better smell of them pretty blossoms," he said.

Occasionally Mae lectured Roy on the hazards of smoking, but secretly she didn't mind that Roy smoked in her house; she rather liked the scent of cigars. Her father had begun filling up these rooms with cigar smoke when he bought the house many decades before, and the odor of tobacco was as much a part of the house as the mortar and nails that held it together.

As she leaned toward the blossoms again, Roy remarked, "If you don't mind me saying, you're the spitting image of Miss Wollencott, the way you look sniffing them blossoms like that. I remember how she favored them."

In truth, Mae didn't physically resemble her mother at all. Amelia Wollencott's Irish ancestry had been evident in her emerald green eyes and her dark auburn hair, the latter of which would have fallen down her back in tight ringlets had she not swept it up into a knot at the back of her head. Mae, on the other hand, was a brunette with brown eyes, and her hair was as straight as the tautly pulled strings of a harp. All her life she had worn bangs across her forehead while the rest of her hair had hung loose about her shoulders or, as now, to just beneath her ears. Amelia's face had been narrow, her cheekbones high, and her skin fair and almost translucent. Mae had a rounder, fuller face, and she tanned easily every year as she worked out in the garden. And where Amelia had stood tall and slender,

31

Mae was petite and small boned. Mae noticeably resembled her mother only in some of her gestures, like the way she sat at the table after a meal with the fingertips of one hand pressed lightly to her jawline, or the way she reflexively shut her eyes while breathing in the fragrance of fresh blossoms.

Mae smiled at Roy's comment about her mother. How often fresh lilacs had adorned this very spot on the mantel when her mother was alive. "Yes, Mother did love lilacs so," Mae agreed. "She always said that the day the lilacs bloomed was the day earth was closest to heaven."

They both stood quietly for a moment, remembering Amelia Wollencott, remembering life as it had once been, thinking of life as it was now and wondering at the difference.

For Roy, thoughts of Mrs. Wollencott were all wrapped up together with thoughts of Miss Mae, as though the two women were really only extensions of the same person. They were the kindest people Roy had ever known, and they owned the largest portion of his heart. He didn't know what it was to have a mother or a sister, but he scarcely was aware that he had missed the experience — so close did he feel to the mother and daughter who had welcomed him into their lives. Mrs. Wollencott had started inviting him to their home for meals and for holidays when he was just a young boy living in the orphanage. He didn't know what had compelled her to come to the orphanage in the first place, nor to choose him to befriend out of all the children there, but he was thankful just the same. Because of Mrs. Wollencott, he had a home and a family of sorts. He had Dr. Wollencott to look up to as a father figure, he had the four boys to play with, he had Mae to be friends with, and he had Mrs. Wollencott to take the place of the mother he had never known. He couldn't have asked for a better substitute to meet his needs for nurturing. Mrs. Wollencott both figuratively and literally opened her arms to Roy, the way a mother hen gathers a chick under her wing. She always spoke gently to him, listened when he talked, and took an active interest in his life. There was no one quite like Mrs. Wollencott, except for Miss Mae.

Mrs. Wollencott had died a long time ago, and Roy still missed her, still thought of her just about every day. But at least he still had Miss Mae, thank heavens. Miss Mae was kind to him too, was his best friend. She was as devoted to Roy as Mrs. Wollencott had been. She cooked him tasty meals, made sure he wasn't alone on holidays, watched out for him in a hundred different ways. *Yes sir,* Roy often thought to himself, *Miss Mae is someone special, an angel with her feet on the ground.*

And yet, she wasn't quite the same person she had once been. She no longer possessed the joy that had been so characteristic of her. She had lost the quality of peace that had been central to her being. And saddest of all, she didn't talk about God anymore, didn't even say grace before she ate. Something terrible had happened, and it had changed Miss Mae. Roy didn't know a lot about very many things, but he knew this: Five years earlier when little Sammy fell down the basement steps and broke his neck, Miss Mae had blamed herself. And she blamed herself still. In all the time since the accident, she had never forgiven herself for what had happened.

No one else blamed her, not even the boy's parents, Ellen and Sam. Her friends didn't blame her. Certainly Roy didn't. She hadn't left the basement door open on purpose. It was an accident, just something that happened by mistake.

Roy remembered Sammy's funeral as if it were only yesterday. How he had wanted to comfort his friend as she had so often comforted him through the years. On the way to the cemetery he sat beside Mae in the back of Sam and Ellen's car, squeezing his hands together and straining to think of something to say. Mae wouldn't speak, wouldn't even look at any of them. She just sat completely motionless as though she herself had been the one who died.

A light snow fell as the police-escorted motorcade moved from the church to the cemetery, and the cars inched along the slick road as though reluctant to reach the grave. Finally, just as they passed through the wrought-iron gates,

Roy ventured a thought. "Miss Mae?" he asked quietly.

Mae turned her head toward him slowly. She seemed reluctant to pull herself up from the well of stony silence. Her eyes were blank when they met his, and she said nothing.

Unnerved, Roy nevertheless pressed on. "Remember how little Sammy used to love that peppermint-stick ice cream? I never saw anyone who loved anything more than Sammy loved that ice cream with the little bits of candy cane in it." Roy paused and sniffed. He lifted the back of his hand to his dripping nose; then, remembering, he drew his handkerchief out of his coat pocket and blew loudly. He had cried unashamedly at the church — just as he had done at every funeral he had ever attended — and even now he struggled to compose himself. "I was just thinking, Miss Mae," he continued, "that Sammy's probably up there in heaven at the banquet table enjoying a great big bowl of peppermint-stick ice cream. And he's sharing it with Miss Wollencott and the doctor and George and Willie and with Jesus too. And they're all there together eating as much of it as they want because there's no such thing as eating too much or getting a stomach-ache in heaven." He paused again a moment to consider what he had just said. Then his voice dropped to nearly a whisper as he finished by adding, "That's just what I was thinking as we were driving along here, Miss Mae, and I wanted to tell you about it."

But Mae didn't respond. Not one muscle of her face moved, not even a shadow of recognition flashed in her eyes. It was as if Roy hadn't said anything, as if he weren't even there at all.

Since then, the one regret Roy had in life was that he couldn't make things better for Miss Mae. He wished that as he worked around the house he could sweep up and carry away all the sorrow that had been surrounding his friend for the past five years. He'd take it back to his room at the boardinghouse and bear it himself if he could. He even at times imagined himself sweeping it up into a big garbage bag and carrying it home on his back, and when he reached home he prayed that Miss Mae would be happy again the next time he saw her. He had a simple prayer that he faithfully repeated, "Dear God, please let something happen that'll bring Miss Mae's joy back." But whatever that something might possibly be, it never seemed to happen. Roy always returned to Miss Mae's house to find everything the same. Yet he was determined not to stop asking, because maybe someday God would answer the prayer.

The fragrance of lilac reminded Mae of what her mother had so often said, *"Hold fast to what's good."* For a moment, she wanted to do just that. She wanted to see spring again, to walk the streets that she and her mother had walked years before, to take in the scent of mingled blossoms, enjoy the return of color to the world, and feel the warmth of the wind on her face. It was her mother who had taught her to be aware of beauty, to sift out the good from the bad in life, and to hold on to what was lovely. And it was her mother who taught her to have faith in God.

Mae turned her gaze to her favorite photograph of her mother, an old black-and-white in a silver frame on the mantel. It had been taken in 1924, and in it Amelia was surrounded by her three best friends, Helen Lewis, Edna Dey, and Clara Reynolds. All the women smiled broadly, as though the photographer had just delivered the punch line of a hilarious joke.

Amelia, twenty-six at the time, was the eldest of the group and the mother of two sons. There were two more sons yet to come before Mae, the final addition to the family, made her appearance in 1930. Helen Lewis, the youngest of the group, was also married and the mother of a son. She had wanted half a dozen children but had managed some years later to produce only one more child — a daughter. To Mae's knowledge, Helen was still alive and mentally alert, though due to crippling arthritis, she spent her days curled up in a hospital bed in a local nursing home. Edna Dey, at the time of the photo, was unwittingly years away from matrimony and "was finally taken off the shelf of spinsterhood at the age of thirty-three, the Lord's name be praised." She had managed to rear four children by having them two at a time — "Twins always did run in the family" — and had lived contentedly until her heart gave out sometime in the mid-1960s. Clara Reynolds, in 1924, was also still a spinster and a year away from marriage. When Arthur Reynolds made her his wife, he took her with him to Vermont, where they settled for good, never returning to the Midwest. Clara and Amelia had been the closest of friends, and the separation had been hard for them. But they corresponded faithfully for twenty-five years, until Amelia's death. Mae had many of those letters — her mother had kept them in hatboxes — and she enjoyed reading them from time to time. Clara still lived in Vermont, though for several years she had suffered with Alzheimer's disease. Mae continued to exchange Christmas letters with Clara's daughter Evelyn as a way of keeping alive the link between her mother and her mother's best friend.

Also on the mantel was a framed portrait of her father, a handsome but austere-looking man with a narrow face, a firm jaw, and eyes that seemed to say he had no time for nonsense. Dr. Wollencott was a man who seldom laughed, but who nevertheless was gentle and devoted to his patients. He appeared single-minded in his determination to combat disease, and he didn't take lightly the death of any one of his patients. Death was a personal affront, as though he had been to battle and lost. Mae always knew when someone had died just by the look of defeat on her father's face.

Mae loved both her parents, but her relationships with the two of them were completely different. Dr. Wollencott didn't have much time for his family, and the time he did have seemed to be devoted to the boys. As a child, Mae felt that her brothers were somehow in the inner circle of her father's love, while she could only look on from the periphery. Her father obviously regarded her as different from her brothers, and not just because she was a girl. He sometimes looked at her as though she were a stranger who had simply wandered into the house, and he seemed not to want to become acquainted with her. Her mother assured Mae that her father loved her, but Mae was never fully convinced.

The absence of attention from her father, however, was more than made up for by her mother's devotion to her. Mae had no doubt about her mother's love. The bond between them was the strongest Mae would know until she was grown and married, and still, more than thirty years after Amelia's death, Mae thought of her mother daily, felt guided by her wisdom and example, and even continued to miss her.

One of Mae's earliest memories was that of being cradled in her mother's lap and being rocked to sleep. Mae must have awakened from a bad dream, but she didn't remember the dream or even her mother coming to her in the night. She remembered only her mother's lap, the gentle motion of the chair, the dim light glowing comfortingly in the hall. And Amelia's soft voice as she sang. Even after so many years,

Mae knew the song that her mother sang that
night, knew it because she had heard it so many
times while she was growing up. She could hear
it still, rising up out the well of buried years:

Tell me why the ivy twine;
Tell me why the stars do shine;
Tell me why the sky's so blue,
And I will tell you just why I love you.

Because God made the ivy twine,
Because God made the stars to shine,
Because God made the sky so blue,
Because God made you, that's why I love you.

Mae had taken in the idea of God as easily as
she had taken milk from her bottle, and as a
child she had never doubted. Prayer was a
nightly ritual, with mother and daughter kneel-
ing beside the bed. They folded their hands together, Amelia's long fingers cupping Mae's
chubby fists. Mae loved the touch of her
mother's warm hands around her own. Then
Amelia would say, "Now shut your eyes and bow
your head," and together they would recite the
Lord's Prayer. Every night Mae saw the words
scroll through her mind like credits on a movie
screen, and she knew when the words were
done, she was safe to crawl into bed and fall
asleep without any fear of danger coming in the
night.

When she awoke, the day was an adventure of

discovery. "There's something new to learn every day," Amelia often said. "There's something special buried in these hours. Let's be sure to find it."

And so they spent their days together, extracting goodness out of the ordinary like perfume out of a rose. They made pies and cookies and breads, wearing identical homemade aprons, enjoying the scent and later the first taste of the baked goods and the sweets. They sang songs while they hung up the wash and made up stories while they made the beds. In the afternoons when the chores were done, they read poems and fairy tales together, or they drew pictures with colored chalk and embroidered samplers with colorful thread. Sometimes they listened to records on the phonograph, to Bach and Beethoven and Chopin, and whenever Amelia put on the one of Strauss, they waltzed about the living room, whirling and twirling until by the end they were exhausted and laughing breathlessly.

Every January they pored over seed catalogs and carefully chose all the seeds they wanted for spring planting, and every spring they dropped the seeds into neat rows in the garden plots out back. One plot of soil was for flowers, the other for vegetables. Amelia taught her daughter to love the scent of earth, the sweet smell of rich, life-giving soil. They tended the gardens faithfully, watering and pulling weeds, until they were finally rewarded with the colorful blossoms of the daffodils and tulips, the crocuses and delphiniums, and with plump red tomatoes, cucumbers, radishes, onions, and in some years, abundant supplies of rhubarb for pies and canning.

Of all that mother and daughter did together, the activity that Mae most enjoyed was The Walks. Nearly every afternoon, Mae heard her mother say, "Come on, Mae dear, put on your coat. We're going for our walk." Or, "Come along, Mae. Get that sunbonnet on. Best not keep the outside world waiting. She's got a lot to show us today." While they walked, they looked for summer sunlight slanting through the branches of the trees, collected colorful leaves in autumn, gazed breathlessly at the hoarfrost that clothed the winter world in icy white. In early spring they sought out the lilac bushes that grew wild throughout the neighborhood, to take in their scent and sometimes take a few branches home, clipped with permission from a neighbor's bush.

In these myriad ways, Amelia Wollencott taught her daughter to appreciate beauty. "Remember this, Mae," she lectured, "there's a great deal not to like about this world, a great deal. But if you just hold fast to the good, it'll make the journey through a whole lot easier."

How many times Mae heard her mother repeat those words, she couldn't count. Throughout her life she had tried always to cling to the good — even in the face of her mother's death, even in the face of her husband's death, even in

42

the face of all sorts of tragedies large and small. She had done her best. But finally, all the accumulated good of her life had slipped out of her hands one March afternoon like snow rushing down the side of a mountain and ending up lost in the valley below.

At the cemetery, on the day Sammy was buried, the crowd had gathered about the casket suspended above a hole chiseled out of the frozen ground. It was cold, so cold, and snow dusted the casket and whitened the red petals of the roses that lay across the lid. As the pastor recited words of eternal life, Mae remembered Sammy on the wooden horse, rocking recklessly and shouting, "Hi-ho, Silber, and away!" Away, away, away. Gone now, and lost, and never coming back.

Mae watched the casket being lowered into the ground. She watched until it disappeared into the hole that was deep but neither long nor wide, only large enough for a child. And as she watched she felt her own heart follow, sinking slowly as the wooden box dragged her heart down with it.

After a moment, she became aware of the sound of weeping all around her, of hands pressing her shoulders, of words of comfort that failed to comfort her, and finally, the crunching of boots through snow as the mourners walked to their cars and returned home to resume the routines of their lives.

Then Mae felt a hand in the crook of her arm.

Without even looking, she knew it was Ellen.

"Come on, Mother. Let's go where it's warm."

But he — he would never be where it was warm. He would lie always surrounded by frozen dirt in the winter, cool earth in the summer. She wanted to throw herself on top of him, hold him to herself, give him the warmth of her own body. And yet she herself had taken the warmth from him.

"Mother, we really have to go now."

Oh, Ellen, what have I done to you? I ache to ask you to forgive me, but one asks forgiveness for unkind words, for a promise broken, for an argument or a misunderstanding. Not for this, not for this. . . .

They walked together along the snowy ground, past the rows of granite stones, toward the car, and toward a life that couldn't possibly ever be the same again.

And for Mae, it never was. Now, while she moved bodily through her days, her mind was often elsewhere. She might be standing at the door of her closet, or pouring coffee, or polishing the furniture, but in her mind she was reliving the events of that March afternoon. She saw it played out again and again, but as it ran through her mind like a menacing newsreel, she tried to change things so that the outcome was different.

She saw herself descending the stairs, she heard the doorbell ring, she felt the movement of her legs as she pounded up the stairs again, but

44

this time she shut the door. She shut it tightly against danger. And in this revised scene, when Sammy comes out to find her, he pads down the hall in his stockinged feet and comes to where she is standing at the front door talking with the man from the gas company. Then she makes her escape from the repairman and tucks the little boy back into bed.

If only I had chosen the recipe in the morning instead of at the last minute . . . if only I had ignored the doorbell . . . if only I had shut the basement door . . . shut the door . . . shut the door. . . .

She was plagued by thoughts of what she had not done, and she moved through life with a sense of something being incomplete. She felt it drawing her, awakening her even in the middle of the night. She could not simply sit and drink her coffee, she could not simply lie in bed and sleep. Not until the task was done. Not until all was finished. *There is something I have to do. I must go and shut the door.* And at times she would actually begin to rise from the chair or from the bed and walk toward the basement door until she realized that the door was shut, that it had been shut for a very long time, and that there was never any way she could complete the action that was haunting her.

To her anguish, she could not crawl back through time, could not stretch her arm far enough back through hours and days and years to touch that afternoon and shut the door. The events were fixed, unchangeable, and all the effort her mind spent on altering the course of that day was futile. And yet she never stopped thinking of it, never stopped envisioning herself shutting the door.

It was true. She would not forgive herself. She'd been responsible for the death of a child, her own grandson. How could she forgive herself for that?

Outwardly her life did not change drastically. She continued to go to church, though she no longer prayed or read her Bible. She still sat on church committee meetings, volunteered for various church-related projects, made cakes and pies for the annual bake sale. When longtime friends called and asked her to join them for lunch or shopping, she obliged by dressing appropriately and meeting them downtown. But all that she did was done out of a sense of duty rather than desire. Her heart simply wasn't in it.

Inwardly she became like the bonsai tree that lives and matures and ages but is dwarfed because its roots have been cut off. She could not keep herself from existing, but all that makes life meaningful — joy and beauty and faith — had wafted away like the last scent of wilting roses. Only guilt was left, and regret and sorrow. She learned to live with them, to carry them around with her like so many lead weights tied to her wrists and feet.

Though much of her routine remained the same, there were two things she would not do. She no longer volunteered at the children's hospital, and she refused to baby-sit her two grand-daughters. She didn't trust herself around the little ones, couldn't bear to be with them alone. They were a reminder of the accident, of what she had done, of the act for which she would always punish herself.

Mae lifted one hand and touched the lilac petals with the tips of her fingers. Dear Roy. He tried so hard to bring bits of her old life back to her, without realizing that it could never be. Still, she couldn't help but appreciate him. Roy Hanna was a constant, his friendship an unbroken pillar in her otherwise shattered life.

She turned to him and offered him a smile. "Thank you again for bringing the lilacs, Roy," she said. "They're really lovely."

"I'll bring you some more tomorrow, Miss Mae," Roy said, "seeing as how there's plenty on the bushes over at my place and you don't have any in your own yard here."

"Well," Mae said then, turning away from the mantel abruptly, "we've both got work to do. The yard is a mess, as I'm sure you've noticed. If we don't get all those rotting leaves up right away, I'm afraid the grass will die. You know where the rake is in the garage, and I'll get you some plastic bags from the kitchen. Hopefully you can get the bulk of the yard completed before lunch."

"No problem, Miss Mae. I'll get right to it. In a couple of hours, you won't recognize the place." He headed for the back door in the kitchen. Mae followed him and grabbed the plastic bags from beneath the sink.

"Here are the garbage bags, Roy. Just pile them up beside the trash containers as you fill them."

"Sure thing, Miss Mae." He opened the back door and peered out. "Yessir, sure is nice to have spring back. And I'll get your yard all fixed up real nice. You just leave it to me."

He was halfway to the unattached garage in the alley when Mae called out to him. "Oh, Roy! Christy's birthday party," she said, speaking of her eldest granddaughter. "You remember, don't you?" She shaded her eyes from the sun and stepped out onto the back step. "It's this Saturday. Both Christy and Amy will be disappointed if you can't come. 'Make sure the Cigar Man comes to the party,' they said."

Roy turned toward her with a broad smile. Even from a distance she could see the stains on his gapped teeth. He had already lighted another cigar, which he waved in the air as though he were waving away any doubts Mae might have. "Don't you worry yourself, Miss Mae. The Cigar Man will be there. I already got my gift. Got my little Christy some ribbons for that pretty blond hair of hers."

"That's good, Roy. I'm glad you can come. Tell you what, why don't I give you a ride. I'll pick you up just before noon, all right?"

"I'm mighty thankful, Miss Mae. Saves me bus fare."

He turned and headed toward the garage again.

"Oh, and Roy? I'm making a meat loaf for lunch. I hope that's okay."

He didn't turn again but threw the words back over his shoulder. They came out in a puff of smoke. "Better than okay, Miss Mae. Meat loaf's my favorite."

Mae smiled faintly to herself. No matter what she prepared for lunch, Roy always claimed it was his favorite meal. Some things, she decided, never change.

Chapter 2

With one hand lifted to her forehead to shield her eyes from the sun, Mae stood on the back patio of her daughter's suburban house and looked out over the yard. Lawn chairs were crowned with colorful balloons; crepe-paper streamers dangled from trees. On a card table covered with a white paper tablecloth sat a birthday cake and a punch bowl filled with red punch. On another similar table was a pile of gifts wrapped in colorful paper and covered with bows and ribbons. A banner tied to the privacy fence announced in green-and-gold lettering: "Happy 5th birthday, Christy!"

Had it been five years already? When the baby was born and Ellen placed little Christy in Mae's arms, Mae had loved the child at once. Loved her wholly and intensely. For a few moments, with this newborn miracle cradled near her heart, Mae forgot completely that anything tragic had ever happened in her life, or ever could. All she felt was a wild rush of joy as she gazed at the face of her granddaughter.

"Isn't she beautiful, Mother?" Ellen had asked. Mae looked up at her daughter and at her son-in-law, Sam, and saw reflected in their own faces the first real joy they had known since —

Then she remembered. Without a word, she laid the baby back in its mother's arms where she knew it would be safe.

Roy, on the other hand, had found nothing but joy in both Christy and her sister, Amy, from the first time he laid eyes on them. Now, off toward one corner of the yard, Christy and a dozen of her friends crowded around Roy like a school of fish all going after the same piece of tossed bread. Roy sat in a folding chair with a disheveled stack of newspapers across his lap. His fingers flew, making party hats and passing them to the eager hands waiting for them.

The girls squealed and giggled, danced and hopped, and finally marched about the lawn like an undisciplined battalion of soldiers, holding their hats in place against the occasional wind. Three-year-old Amy crawled up into the Cigar Man's lap and contentedly settled herself among the remaining newspapers. Roy waved the girls on with one arm while circling Amy's waist with the other. He smiled, he laughed, he winked, he stamped his feet. He was never happier, this childlike man, than when he was among the children he loved.

And they adored him. With Christy and Amy it was always, "Where's the Cigar Man?" and "When can the Cigar Man come over again and play?" He was like a grandfather and a brother, an adult companion and a playmate all in one.

He never scolded, though he taught right from wrong. He never yelled, though he took a child's clenched hand and showed it how to touch gently. He didn't read stories from books, but he could look at a picture in a magazine and make up wonderful adventures out of his head. He couldn't drive, but he gave the bounciest, fastest piggyback rides imaginable.

Mae shook her head and smiled in amusement as she watched her granddaughters and Roy across the yard. She might — under different circumstances — have been envious of Roy's relationship with the girls, but she found instead that she was grateful to Roy for unwittingly standing in as a grandparent figure. Their paternal grandparents could afford to fly in from Connecticut only once or twice a year; their maternal grandfather, Mae's husband, had died before they were born; and as for their maternal grandmother — well, Mae knew she was not the grandmother she ought to be.

Mae loved the girls deeply, but the love was surrounded by a shell of fear, and she was unable to demonstrate fully her affection for them. Of course, there were those times when nature was able almost to unlock her hardened emotions; for instance, the times when Amy would crawl into Grammy Mae's lap, looking for some affection. Mae would instinctively hold the child in her arms, laying her cheek against the fine wisplike strands of baby hair and taking in the scent of fresh young skin. She would begin gently to rock and sing quietly, "Tell me why the ivy twine, tell me why the stars do shine. . . ." But before she could reach the second verse of the song, she would choke on the words, and tears would drop onto Amy's hair like splashes of baptismal water. *If you only knew how much I want to love you,* Mae would think. *If only I were free to love you. . . .*

Just as Mae let her hand drop from her eyes, Ellen came through the sliding glass door onto the patio, followed by Sam. As usual, Mae was struck by what a handsome couple they were. Ellen, not yet thirty, was fresh and rosy as an adolescent. Her features were fine and well proportioned like Mae's; in fact, she looked uncannily as Mae had looked some twenty years earlier. Large brown eyes, a slender nose, skin smooth as porcelain. But she had her father's wide mouth and wavy hair, which she layered to accentuate the curls. Petite like her mother, she stood a full foot shorter than her husband, who, at six feet four, tended to tower over most people. Sam Nollinger was a neatly trimmed and clean-shaven young man, with dark hair and eyes the color of early spring leaves. His nose was noticeably crooked, the result of it having been broken during a high school soccer game and never set quite right. Yet his face was attractive in what Ellen called "a rugged sort of way." The frown lines between his eyebrows and his naturally down-turned mouth made him appear serious and staid, but he was a gentle, quiet person who seemed to have endless resources of patience.

Ellen and Sam stepped out onto the porch, both carrying a gallon of vanilla ice cream. "Time to cut the cake, Mother," Ellen said brightly. "Sam's going to light the candles and then we'll sing 'Happy Birthday.' Would you be willing to dish up the ice cream?"

"Of course, darling."

The three started toward the cake table when Sam said, "Uh-oh, looks like we forgot the paper plates. Do you know where they are, Ellen?"

"In the kitchen. I think I put them in the cabinet over the sink. Mother, do you mind?"

"I'll get them. Be right there."

Mae went inside to the kitchen and found the plates where Ellen said they would be. As she was about to move away from the cabinet, she glanced out the window over the sink. The center pane of glass framed Ellen and Sam like a photograph. Sam leaned over the cake, striking a match. Ellen ladled punch into clear plastic cups. They were saying something to each other; both were laughing.

To all outward appearances, the couple had long ago come to terms with their son's death. They seemed to have experienced what Amelia Wollencott had called "our amazing ability to heal." Still, Mae wondered what lay hidden beneath the untroubled exterior. She wondered about the scars that surely remained. One didn't lose a child and simply go on as though neither the life nor the death had ever happened. In fact, she knew that Sammy remained a very real part of their lives. His picture was on the bureau in the master bedroom; another hung on the wall in the hallway downstairs. The girls knew they had a brother who had lived and died before they were born. The family visited Sammy's grave regularly, all four of them, placing flowers on the earth where he slept and touching the letters of his name carved in stone.

Mae regarded her daughter and son-in-law with a certain amount of bewilderment. They had said from the beginning they didn't blame her for Sammy's death. They said they forgave her — not for his death, but for the moment of negligence that had led to his falling down the stairs.

"Anyone could have left a basement door open, Mother," Ellen had assured her.

"Yes, but it was not just anyone who left the door open," Mae had snapped in reply. "I'm the one who did it."

"And it just as easily could have been Sam or me. Don't you see? The fact that Sammy was with you doesn't make any difference. We might have had *all* been with him, and he still could have fallen down the stairs."

Mae shook her head. "It's inexcusable," she said adamantly. "What I did is inexcusable."

"Then don't try to excuse it, Mother. Forgive yourself. Let it go. Please just let it go, or you'll never have any peace again in your life." When Mae didn't answer, Ellen continued. "Did you ever stop to consider that accidents happen every day, that people die every day? Even children. Sammy's death was not some sort of isolated event that sets us apart from all the rest of the world. We're just like everyone else, don't you see? Right this minute, out there somewhere, a little boy or a little girl is dying, and no one knows why it has to happen — least of all the parents. But you yourself always told me that no matter what happens, God loves us. Maybe you don't believe that anymore, but I do. It's the only way I can keep going."

But Mae, as though she had heard nothing Ellen had said, muttered sadly, "It doesn't make sense — Sammy's death. He was just a baby; his life had just started. He shouldn't have died in that way."

"Don't try to make sense of it, because you can't. Please, Mother," Ellen pleaded, "please let God help you forgive yourself. And please try to believe me when I tell you that Sam and I forgive you."

Ellen did forgive her mother, but that forgiveness hadn't necessarily come easily. For four days after Sammy's death, until the morning of the funeral, Ellen had stayed in bed, sick with grief. Sam called Ellen's doctor and asked for a prescription for a sedative, but the doctor refused to give it out of fear of harming the unborn baby Ellen carried. The grieving mother was on her own. Sam fumbled about the kitchen and carried food to his wife on a tray, but she did little more than nibble at it, and even then only "for the sake of the baby." Sam tried, through his own grief, to offer words of consolation, but Ellen couldn't hear them.

She knew in her head that her mother wasn't to blame for Sammy's death, but in her own mother heart, she wanted an explanation. "How many times, Mother, when I was growing up, did you tell me to keep the basement door shut? You must have said it a thousand times, and yet it was *you yourself* . . . oh, Mother, how could you be so stupidly careless?"

The darkened room where Ellen lay aching for her son became a theater for memories, haunting her like the ghosts of Christmas in the Dickens story. There was Sammy, his blond hair a mat of curlicues, his violet-blue eyes wide with wonder. *"Luff you, Mommy!"* he was saying. *"Luff you! Luff you!"*

"And I love you, Sammy. I'll love you till Hungary eats Turkey on China!"

But he was too young yet to play the game, too young to understand the game that Ellen, as a child, had so often played with her mother.

"I love you, Mommy!"

"And I love you, sweetie. I'll love you till Hungary eats Turkey on China!"

"And I'll love you till the moon is sliced up and served as cheese sandwiches!"

"And I'll love you till the ducks by the lake fly upside down!"

"And I'll love you till the snow falls up instead of down!"

"And I'll love you till . . ." Her mother would pause, squinting her eyes as she thought ". . . till all the water in the seas dries up!"

"And I'll love you, Mommy, till . . ." Ellen would hop on one foot as though to set her thoughts in motion ". . . till all the mountains turn inside out and become valleys!"

"I'll love you, Mother," Ellen said to the empty room, "I'll love you till you kill my son, and then I won't love you anymore."

No, that was a lie! Her mother, Mae Demaray, could never intentionally hurt anyone. Never. She was simply incapable of hurting anyone, and of that Ellen had no doubt. And Ellen could never hate her mother. As much as she wanted an explanation for her son's death, she wanted more to throw her arms around the older woman and comfort her. "It's all right, Mother; really, it is. I love you and nothing can change that, not even Sammy's death."

Ellen lifted her hand to her cheek and remembered how it felt when Sammy pressed his chubby cheek against her own when he kissed her. His kisses had always been quick and cursory. Once he reached two years old, he hadn't cared much for cuddling. He had been like his uncle Mike, Ellen's brother, in that regard. Always too distracted by other things to spend much time hugging Mother. So different from Ellen when she was growing up.

58

Ellen, as a child, had found great comfort in pressing her cheek against her mother's, so soft and always smelling sweetly of powder. Her mother had never pulled away or claimed to be too busy to spend a few affectionate moments with her daughter. Her arms were always open, her lap always free, her voice always soothing, no matter what might be cooking on the stove or how much cleaning there was to be done before Daddy came home for dinner.

For as far back as Ellen could remember, her mother had been the embodiment of gentleness, the type of woman the American artist Mary Cassatt might have painted to represent motherhood. Mae Demaray was devoted to her family, and her family knew it. Her whole day revolved around the wants and needs of her husband and children. Ellen recalled that her mother's more liberated friends encouraged her to think of herself once in a while, but Mae always claimed that she *wanted* to take on the roles that the followers of the new feminism were trying to escape: housekeeper, laundress, chauffeur, nurse, chief cook and bottle washer.

"Mommy, are we keeping you from having a career?" young Ellen had asked.

"Darling, you are *my career,"* her mother had answered.

When Ellen thought back to those years, she couldn't count the number of friends who had commented, *"I wish my mom were more like yours. Mine's always yelling and complaining all the time.*" Most of her friends, it seemed, didn't have good relationships with their mothers, especially after they reached adolescence. But even after Ellen moved out of the house and into the dormitory at the university, she took the bus home two or three times a week just to visit. She didn't share the desire that so many other girls had of escaping their mothers more or less permanently. Ellen considered her mother her best friend and primary confidante. It was a family trait — strong mother-daughter relationships — and Ellen had always felt that the very first blessing in her life had been the gift of Mae Demaray for a mother.

She believed that still, even in the depths of her grief. She was a grown woman, a married woman with a caring husband to support her. Yet it was her mother she yearned for, the way a dying soldier calls out for the one who loved and nurtured him. She longed for her mother to comfort her, and she longed to comfort her mother in return. She wanted her mother to walk with her through this loss as she had walked with her through every other loss in her life. She decided the only way they could move forward with their lives now was if they held each other up along the way.

Finally, spent from grief and feeling more drained by Sammy's death than she had been from her struggle to give him life, Ellen said aloud to the image of Mae in her mind, "For the carelessness that caused his death, Mother, I forgive you."

Mae couldn't accept it, though — the forgiveness of her daughter and son-in-law. There were no cracks in the wall of guilt through which she could take it in. She told herself that the words were merely the stuff of propriety; the conscience of good people like Ellen and Sam prodded them to extend forgiveness, and so they did. But it was all as hollow as church-bulletin prayers whispered by agnostics who — for one reason or another — found themselves attending a Sunday morning service. Their lips moved to form the words, but it was only empty ritual. No corresponding feelings or beliefs existed to give meaning to the prayers.

From where she stood at the window by the kitchen sink, Mae saw Ellen look toward the house. The candles on the cake were all lighted, and the children had gathered around to sing "Happy Birthday" to Christy. They were waiting only for her to arrive with the paper plates.

She would go out now and join the children in their song. She could join them in their song, but not in their innocence. How she wished that she were one of them! A child again, with all of life ahead, stretched out like a path without footprints, untouched by mistakes and accidents and haunting memories.

Once, she had been just as these little girls were. And in her childish innocence, she never could have imagined that her life would turn out the way it had.

Chapter 3

As a child, Mae — perhaps like most protected children — believed a sort of magical hedge surrounded her that would keep out all the sadness of the world. Though she had been born during the first year of the Great Depression, in the Wollencott household there was always enough food in the larder, plenty of clothes hanging in the closets, sufficient coal to feed the furnace in the basement. Though the children would have liked to have had more of what they wanted, they certainly had everything they needed.

Mae was, of course, vaguely aware that terrible things did happen to other people. She sometimes overheard her parents talking about Dr. Wollencott's patients, men and women who were struggling with illness, with the death of loved ones, with something called unemployment. Many of his patients couldn't keep up with their medical payments because of the depression, whatever that was. And more and more, scraggly men dressed in smelly old clothes came around to the back door of the house looking for food. Mae watched curiously as her mother prepared a cold sandwich or a plate of leftovers for the visitors, and while she felt sorry for the men, she was at the same time glad they belonged to a whole different world than her own. The world outside the hedge.

It was Roy more than anyone who made Mae aware of tragedy. She learned his story from her mother in more than just overheard bits and snatches, and she thought it was just about the saddest story she'd ever heard. Still, like the dirty men in the smelly old clothes, the sadness itself belonged to someone else and never ventured any further into Mae's life than the back door.

Mae couldn't remember the first time she met Roy Hanna. She'd grown up with four older brothers, and just as they had been there from the start, it seemed to Mae that Roy had too. The Wollencott house was so full of males that Mae, when she was very young, assumed the round-faced boy was just another brother. But later she realized that even though he appeared at the dinner table about once a week and was generally around for holidays, and even though he sometimes did chores around the house like the other boys, Roy was seldom with the family for more than a few hours at a time. A day at most. Many days he wasn't around at all. And he didn't sleep in either of the two rooms where the other boys slept but always disappeared before bedtime. It dawned on her little by little that Roy was in fact different from her brothers, but who exactly he was and why he continually showed up in their home was a mystery she at first had no inclination to ponder. She simply accepted Roy's sporadic appearances as a matter of course.

Once when Mae was five years old, Roy was again at the dinner table sharing the family's evening meal. At the sound of a fork scraping rapidly across a plate, Mae looked up from her pork chop to find Roy furiously shoveling mashed potatoes into his mouth. Mae's eyes weren't the only ones turned toward the source of the commotion; all eyes around the table were on Roy.

"Good heavens, son," said Frank Wollencott, wiping his mouth with a cloth napkin. "Don't they feed you at the orphanage?"

Roy's fork paused in the air, midway between his plate and his mouth. He swallowed the mound of potatoes that had just passed his lips and turned a great smile toward the doctor. Bits of potato filled the gaps between his teeth. "Oh yes, sir, Mr. Doctor," he answered. "They feed us over there."

The doctor delicately sliced another bit of pork off the chop on his plate. "You act as though you haven't seen food in a week," he commented mildly.

Roy shook his head vigorously. "No, sir. I seen food. But I know if I don't hurry up and get this all swallered down, I ain't gonna get seconds."

Amelia reached out and put her hand on

Roy's, the one holding the fork. "Now, Roy, you just take your time and enjoy your food. The way you eat you hardly have time to taste it before it hits your stomach. We have plenty. You know you can always have seconds when you're with us. You've never gone away hungry before, have you?"

Roy's violet-blue eyes widened, becoming, if possible, even more round. "Oh no, ma'am. I've sure never gone away from here hungry!"

"And you won't, either, I'm certain," Amelia said, smiling and patting the boy's hand. "Now help yourself to more potatoes and try to breathe while you're eating."

Roy looked startled and replied, "Oh, I'm breathing, Miss Wollencott. I'm breathing, all right. If I stopped breathing, I'd be dead. No, Miss Wollencott, I wouldn't do that."

Amelia appeared to suppress a laugh. "I just mean, Roy, that you should try to eat a little more slowly."

"Oh yes, ma'am," Roy said. "I'll try real hard, though this old fork don't wanna slow down."

"Well, do your best, son," advised Dr. Wollencott. "It's better for your digestion to eat slowly."

"Yes, sir, Mr. Doctor, I think I can get this fork to go a teeny bit slower."

As the family turned back to their plates, Peter, the eldest at thirteen, remarked to no one in particular, "I remember seeing animals on Uncle Dan's farm eat that way."

Dr. Wollencott rapped his fork against his plate. "Here, here," he said, glancing critically at his son, "we don't need any comments like that."

The four brothers, trying unsuccessfully to stifle their laughter behind soiled napkins, gave up all at once and burst out into loud snickers. Roy, wanting always to be like the other boys, laughed eagerly along with them. Even Mae found herself giggling into the palm of her hand until the doctor's steely gaze managed to silence them all.

The next afternoon when Mae and her mother were out for a walk, Mae asked, "Mama, what's that place where Roy comes from?"

Her mother gave her hand a squeeze and said, "Look, Mae, over there. See it? Coming through the red maple."

Mae looked to where her mother was pointing with her free hand and saw the sun's rays slanting through the red leaves. "Oh yes, Mama! It's so pretty!"

They walked on in silence until Mae realized that her mother hadn't answered the question. "But, Mama," she repeated, "what about where Roy comes from? What did Daddy call it last night?"

Her mother was quiet for a moment, as though trying to recall the conversation. Finally she said, "Do you mean the orphanage?"

"That's it!" cried Mae. "What's an orfanny, Mama?"

"An orphanage, dear," her mother said, enunciating the word, "is where children live who don't have a mother and a father to take care of them."

"Doesn't Roy have a mama and a papa?"

"No," Amelia sighed. "The poor child has no parents."

Mae looked up at her mother with questioning eyes. Suddenly there was a story behind this boy who was repeatedly showing up on their doorstep, and Mae wanted to know what it was. "What happened to Roy's mama and papa?" she asked.

Her mother shook her head briefly, then plucked a leaf from a low branch of a linden tree as they passed. "I'm afraid they're no longer living, darling," she said.

"But how did they die?" A hint of terror tinged the little girl's voice.

Her mother pursed her lips as though reluctant to answer. Finally she said, "There was an accident — an automobile accident, I believe."

"But how did it happen, Mama?"

"I don't know, darling. I'm afraid I don't know all the details."

"You mean Roy's mama and papa went up to heaven together, at the same time?"

"Yes, from what I understand they went to heaven at the same time."

"Well, why didn't Roy go with them?"

"I don't think Roy was in the car at the time of the accident."

Mae let out a heavy sigh. "That was lucky for Roy, wasn't it?"

"Yes." Amelia nodded. "And a blessing for us too, I'm sure."

"Did you know them — Roy's mama and papa?"

"No, Mae. I never met them. But I'm sure they were very good people."

"Do you think Roy misses them?"

Her mother cocked her head and let her eyes drift across the cloudless sky. "It seems to me he doesn't remember them. At least he never speaks of them — not that I've heard, anyway."

The two walked on quietly while Mae considered what it would be like not to have a mother or a father. She clung to her mother's hand even more tightly, as though to assure herself that she was there.

"Mama?"

"Yes, darling?"

"Daddy calls Roy 'son' sometimes."

"Yes. It's a term of endearment."

"What's that mean?"

"Lots of men call boys 'son,' even if the boy is not really their son. It's just, I don't know, a nice thing to do. It makes the man and the boy feel like there's some sort of connection between them."

"Even if there's not really?"

"Yes. They're not father and son, but your daddy is fond of Roy, and Roy certainly seems to like Daddy, so they're connected in that way."

Mae imagined invisible ropes binding her father to Roy. There must be ropes like that between her father and her brothers too, but even stronger ropes because they were a family. And ropes, too, between herself and her mother, and between herself and her father. It was nice to think that they were, as her mother said, "connected."

"Daddy likes Roy, then?"

"Of course he does. We all do. Don't you?"

"Yeah," Mae shrugged. "I like him all right. As good as my brothers anyway, I guess." She stopped and thought about how Roy looked at the dinner table, shoveling mashed potatoes into his mouth. While her brothers were pests, at least they had some table manners. "But why, Mama?" Mae continued. "Why do we have to have him over for dinner all the time?"

"Because it's good to show kindness to people less fortunate than ourselves."

Mae frowned as she thought about Roy. Finally she asked, "Is Roy sad, Mama?"

Her mother rolled the stem of the linden leaf between her thumb and forefinger as she answered. "No, darling, I don't think he's sad — though he certainly hasn't had an easy life for one so young."

"You mean because his mama and papa died and now he doesn't have a house to live in like we do?"

"Yes, among other things."

After another moment, Mae asked, "Mama,

what's wrong with Roy?"

"Nothing's wrong with Roy," she answered absently, but then added, "Well, what do you mean?"

"He can't read good like Peter and Willie, and he says stupid things. Roy's stupid, isn't he?"

"Well, Mae, he's not very bright. But we must never, never call him stupid, especially to his face. He's just not as clever as other people."

"But why, Mama?"

"I don't know."

"Was he borned that way?"

"Yes, I'm afraid so."

"Then God made him stupid."

"Well . . . yes, God made Roy as he is. But it wasn't a mistake. I'm sure God had a good reason."

"But why, Mama?"

Amelia chuckled quietly. "Some of God's purposes are a mystery to me, I'm afraid."

Mae wanted to know God's reason for making Roy stupid, but if her mother didn't know the reason, Mae was sure no one did. It was one of those unknowable things that, as Mae was discovering, people had to put up with. She did intend, however, to add it to her list of things to ask God when she got to heaven, a list that seemed to grow longer every day.

That resolved, she asked her mother, "So is that why we have to be nice to Roy, because he lives in the orfanny and he's stupid?"

"No, darling, we are kind to him because

70

everyone deserves kindness. And Roy doesn't really have anyone in the world except us. Think of how he'd feel if we weren't nice to him."

"But maybe someday some mama and papa will go to the orfanny and take him home. Then he'll have a family."

"Oh, I don't think so, darling."

"But why not, Mama?"

"Because he's already ten years old. Most parents who adopt children prefer to get them as babies. Also, there's a depression on. People can hardly afford to feed their own, much less adopt another mouth to feed."

Suddenly Mae, feeling generous, exclaimed, "I know, Mama! Why don't we 'dopt Roy? We can let him live with us, and he can pretend you're his real mama and papa's his real papa, and he'll never be sad again, if we just 'dopt him!"

"*A*-dopt, dear. Adopt. It begins with an *a*."

"Well, why don't we do that since you and Daddy already like him so much?"

Her mother gave a quick laugh that, to Mae, didn't sound quite real. "We already have five children," she said. "Four of them boys! No, the best we can do is invite Roy to visit us, but I think that's enough. He seems to be satisfied with that, anyway. Oh dear, look at the time!" Her mother peered at the watch hanging on a delicate chain around her neck. "We'd best get home and get dinner in the oven, or Daddy and the boys will be growling for their food."

The next time Roy came to dinner, Mae studied him from across the table. She watched his head bobbing over his plate, his jaw working as he chewed, his lips curling up in laughter anytime someone even hinted at a joke. He still appeared silly and uncouth, but learning about Roy's parents had cast a whole new light on this frequent visitor. Something terrible had happened to him when he was very young, just about the worst thing that could happen to anyone — he had lost his mother and father. Poor Roy must not have a hedge around him the way she did to keep all the bad things out. As she considered his loss, Mae felt a rush of tenderness toward Roy, a mixture of pity and compassion. She was deeply sorry that he didn't have a mother to love him, didn't have a father to feed and clothe him, didn't have brothers or sisters to play with him. Her family was the closest Roy had to a family of his own, but Mae thought that it wasn't nearly close enough to count. She was aware that her brothers tolerated Roy's visits only reluctantly.

"Now you be sure to include Roy in your games, boys," Dr. Wollencott often told his sons.

"Aw, Dad, do we gotta?"

"Yes, you have to, and I don't want to hear any whining from any of you. If I find out that you're mistreating that boy, there'll be the piper to pay."

They answered in a chorus of great reluctance: "Yes, sir."

But Mae knew that her brothers appointed Roy the seeker in the game of hide-and-seek, and while he counted to twenty — slowly, and often forgetting a number or two — they sneaked off to play elsewhere while Roy was left to search unsuccessfully about the yard for them. Amelia would find him sitting on the front steps an hour later, scratching his head and wondering how all the boys managed to disappear into thin air.

Mae knew that on occasion she was no better than her brothers. There had been times when they had laughed at Roy and she had joined in, never thinking of how cruel the laughter was. And there had been plenty of times when she wished Roy hadn't come to visit. She thought of the rainy afternoons when her mother, admonishing her in whispers to "be nice," handed her crayons and drawing paper and sentenced her to the kitchen table with Roy. She liked to draw and to color, but not with Roy. He always insisted on working on the same piece of paper with her, and he invariably ruined whatever scene Mae was creating by coloring the dogs pink and giving the flowers wings instead of leaves. Mae, exasperated, couldn't understand how someone who was practically a grown-up — after all, he was five years older than she — didn't know what color things are supposed to be and what things really looked like. More often than not she crumpled up their mutual creation in disgust and told Roy she wished she were playing dolls instead with her next-door neighbor Sally Ann.

Now she was sorry she had ever been impatient with him and promised herself that, like her mother, she would always try to be Roy's friend, no matter what.

Chapter 4

Mae and Ellen sat at the small gateleg table in Mae's kitchen eating homemade lentil soup and cheese and tomato sandwiches. Ellen dropped by at least a couple of times a week either for lunch or simply for a cup of coffee and a chat. She was the mother of two young daughters, a part-time graphics designer for a small publishing company, and a volunteer hospice worker, but she still penciled time into her calendar for her mother.

"A new antique shop just opened up over on Hennepin," Ellen said between bites of her sandwich. "Want to do a little shopping with me on Saturday?"

Mae frowned as she stuck a stray slice of tomato back into the folds of her sandwich. "Yes. Well, maybe. I'll have to see."

The ambivalent answer was what Ellen had come to expect. Her mother didn't seem to want to get out of the house much anymore, and if she did accompany Ellen somewhere, it was without enthusiasm, as though she were somehow obligated to go. There had once been a time when mother and daughter spent almost every Saturday indulging their penchant for shopping. They were well acquainted with most of the antique shops and secondhand bookstores in Minneapolis and the nearby town of Stillwater. Ellen recalled how Mae had loved to speculate as to the original owner of an antique item — a vase, a sewing box, a bit of lace. And she had loved to surround herself with musty old hard-cover books. She'd had piles of them around her chair in the living room with bits of scrap paper marking her progress through them. Clothing they preferred to buy new, so in the spring and fall the two women made the rounds of the malls to catch the sales. Such shopping trips had been a mutually enjoyed tradition. Now Ellen could enjoy only the memories of browsing, of stopping for lunch at a coffee shop or cafe somewhere, of coming home with armloads of parcels and packages.

What Ellen couldn't remember now was the last time her mother had bought herself a new dress, or an old book, or a pretty but completely frivolous item at an antique shop. Mae simply didn't seem to take pleasure in anything anymore.

Far more than the shopping, Ellen missed her mother. She missed the mother Mae had been before the accident, now five years behind them. The accident had severed her mother's life in two, had left it cut off and dangling like a worm sliced through by a gardener's spade. Mae Demaray before the accident was cheerful, outgoing, compassionate. Mae Demaray after the accident was somber and withdrawn. Not even Ellen could coax her back to life, though she continued tirelessly to try.

"Sam promised to take the girls fishing on Saturday — you know, as a kind of father-daughter thing," she went on. "So I'll have the day free. I'd really like it if you'd go antiquing with me. I've heard this shop is really something. It takes up nearly half a block and supposedly has antiques from around the world."

Mae casually shook pepper into her lentil soup. "Well, all right, then," she conceded. "It might be worth seeing. By the way, how are the girls?"

"They're fine," Ellen answered, quietly annoyed that her mother was changing the subject. Ellen liked to make definite plans, but Mae was adept at sweeping such outings aside. Sighing, Ellen went on. "Amy seems to have a bit of a cold. Just a runny nose. I let her go to day care anyway, she enjoys so much being around the other kids."

"Hope she doesn't pass her cold on to anyone."

Ellen shrugged. "I doubt it. It might even be allergies — I'm not sure. I suppose the day will come when we'll have to have her tested. No doubt she takes after her father. Sam can't even hear about a cat without sneezing."

Mae took a bite of her sandwich and chewed thoughtfully, then swallowed and asked,

"How'd Christy enjoy her birthday party?"

Ellen, with her mouth full, made an affirmative noise and nodded. "Loved it," she said. "Claims she can't wait till next year, as though we need to rush the years along." Ellen laughed briefly, then took a long drink of water. Setting the glass back down, she said, "Isn't it amazing how slowly time goes for kids? Too bad that changes when we grow older. By the way, thanks for helping out. Christy claims you're a better ice cream scooper than I am because you give more."

Mae smiled. "Tell her I said thanks. I was glad to help, of course."

Ellen glanced at the calendar taped to Mae's refrigerator. "Speaking of time flying, I can't believe it's almost June. Did I tell you I volunteered to teach at Vacation Bible School this summer? I've been meaning to ask you if you'd help me prepare some of the lessons. Remember those stories you used to tell when Mike and I were kids in VBS — you know, about the family of thimbles that lived in the tailor's sewing box? Do you remember those stories?"

Mae shook her head and sighed. "Oh, honey, that was so long ago —"

"Do you think you might have a copy of them somewhere? We always enjoyed them so much as kids and —"

Mae was still shaking her head. "I doubt I ever wrote them down. It seems I just made up those stories as I went along."

Ellen thought for a moment. "Well, maybe between the two of us we can recreate them. I remember the one about Thelma Thimble being lost by the tailor's grandson, and how the tailor put all his work aside to look for her. . . ."

Ellen's voice trailed off as she watched her mother rise from the table and carry her dirty dishes to the sink. Mae then reached into the cupboard for coffee cups and saucers, and though she settled two sets on the counter, it was as though Ellen wasn't there at all. Mae filled the cups with coffee and carried them to the table, placing one in front of Ellen and one in front of herself. Then she looked up, smiled faintly, and said, "How is everything with Sam's business?"

She'd done it again. She'd changed the subject, this time right in the middle of Ellen's sentence. Obviously her mother had no intention of helping her with the Bible lessons. Ellen would have felt rebuffed had she not been used to her mother's way of steering around subjects she didn't like.

All right, Mother, Ellen thought, *never mind about Thelma Thimble. We'll do it your way.* Aloud, she said, "Sam says it's going really well. He's always busy and loving it as much as ever." About a year earlier Sam and a couple of his college buddies had pooled their resources and started their own business in personal computer sales.

"I guess they're pretty popular, those computers," Mae commented.

Ellen nodded as she stirred sugar into her coffee. "They're starting to be. Most people who have them say they don't know how they got along without them. It's like converting to pocket calculators after years of using a slide rule, only bigger."

"I still don't understand what people need them for."

"Oh," Ellen said, shrugging, "lots of things. Especially if they run their own business. Some people just like to keep track of their household expenses on them. Writers use computers all the time, of course. The possibilities are endless."

Mae shook her head. "We got along just fine without them in my day."

"Yes, but with a lot less convenience. Imagine a writer pecking away at a typewriter. They're dinosaurs now!"

"Well, a typewriter was good enough for Hemingway and Thomas Wolfe and Pearl Buck."

"Oh, Mother." Ellen laughed. "Typewriters were good enough because that was all they had. Times change. Everything changes."

Mae took a sip of coffee, then settled the cup back into the saucer with a clink. She stared off toward the window as though remembering something. Finally she said, "Yes, you're right. Everything does change." She turned to look at her daughter, who was gazing at her uneasily. "More coffee, darling?"

"No, thanks. I'm still working on this cup."

Ellen glanced at her watch. "One-thirty, already. I bet the mail's come. I'll check and see."

Ellen was relieved to leave the kitchen and walk the length of the front hall to where the mail was dropped through a slot in the door. She gathered together the envelopes and circulars and returned to her seat at the kitchen table to thumb through them. "Not much," she announced. "A couple of bills. Some advertisements. Oh, here's a letter postmarked St. Petersburg. No return address, but it must be from Sophie."

Mae was pouring her second cup of coffee. "I haven't heard from Sophie in a while," she said. "Open it, would you, and read it aloud. I've always found it a chore to decipher her handwriting."

Ellen sliced open the envelope with her thumb, then unfolded the two thin sheets of paper inside and began to read:

Dear Mae,

I know I've owed you a letter for weeks and weeks, but I can only offer the feeble excuse that I have simply been too busy to write.

" 'Too busy' is underlined once," Ellen said.

Whoever would have thought that retirement would be like this? Not at all what I pictured with some trepidation years ago — that I'd be a tiny white-haired creature confined to a wheelchair and too stiffened with arthritis to so much as knit. I'm having the time of my life!

" 'Time of my life' is underlined twice," Ellen interjected again.

Here I am sixty-six years old, and I feel more like sixteen. I really ought to be ashamed of myself, but I haven't had this much fun since before Albert died. Eleven years is a long time to be alone, but I seem to be making up for all that now. I only wish I had retired and moved to Florida earlier than last year.

It really is wonderful here in the warm south, Mae, and the fact that there's no winter to speak of is only the beginning. Imagine, no ice or snow to contend with. I don't miss winter at all! My days are full to the brim with friends and social activities. Bridge every Tuesday and Thursday, square dancing on Wednesday afternoons, golf on Sundays, picnics, trips to the shore, excursions to museums and art exhibits — all sponsored by the Senior Citizens Center down the road here. And you wouldn't believe the people I've met. Others who, like me, are finding freedom and excitement in retirement, not boredom. I've made some wonderful friends — I know you'd like them.

And, Mae, the most wonderful thing of all

is that I have a gentleman friend! Can you imagine? Romance at my age. I blush at the thought of it! I never thought there'd be anyone after Albert, but along came Howard, and he just swept me off these old bunion-studded feet of mine like a prince right out of a fairy tale. We met last month at the Wednesday square dance lesson, and we've been partners ever since. We're practically inseparable. That's why I say I feel sixteen again. It's all as exciting as the first time Albert kissed me behind the garage in the alley.

Ellen laughed briefly with her hand over her mouth, while Mae raised her eyebrows over the rim of her cup.

Howard's been a widower for about five years, and he says he's about ready to settle down again. So who knows, there may be wedding bells in my future.

I know I say this every time I write, but I just have to say it again. Mae dear, you really must think about selling that house of yours and coming down here to live. That old house is far too big for one person, and I hate the thought of you rattling around in it all by yourself. And the upkeep — well, it just must be the proverbial albatross around your neck! Cast it off, Mae dear! and come on down to Florida and join us in our freedom. Leave the

Minnesota snows behind and come and enjoy the sunshine. I haven't missed Minnesota for a minute, and as I say, I wish only that I had retired and come to Florida earlier. There's everything imaginable for you to do. It's not as if we're a bunch of old fogies sitting around playing Bingo all the time, though I will admit they do offer the game once a week at the Senior Center. There are plenty of friends to be made around here and a good stock of eligible bachelors. Not young, mind you, but still with lots of miles left in them. Seriously, Mae, I would so love your company, and I know it would only be good for both of us if you were here. Write and tell me you'll think about it, won't you? And in the meantime, why don't you come for a visit? I'm sure then that I could persuade you to move down for good.

Well, I must go now. Howard and I are going shell seeking. Lovely to walk along the sandy shore in your bare feet with your pant legs rolled up and scour for shells. I must remember to take my sun hat this time. Last time I came away with a nose the color of raspberry wine! I suppose we'll spend the afternoon at the shore, and then Howard will probably suggest dinner somewhere. He does love fine dining and spares no expense. Last time it was lobster and stuffed crab. Tonight, who knows — perhaps filet mignon? Doesn't it all sound divine!

" 'Divine' is underlined once," said Ellen.

My love to you, dear, and do take care of
yourself.
Affectionately,
Sophie

Ellen laughed and, carefully folding the letter,
put it back in the envelope. "Sophie's a character, isn't she?"

"Always has been for as long as I've known
her," Mae said, rising to carry her half-empty
cup to the sink.

"Nice that she takes the time to write."

"Mmmm, I suppose," Mae said, "though I'm
really not sure why she does."

"Why shouldn't she? You were friends, after
all."

Mae nodded. "Once. A long time ago when
both our husbands were alive. We were a foursome then, but mostly because it was our husbands who were friends first. After the men were
gone, well, Sophie and I didn't seem to have so
much in common. And, of course, she was quite
a bit older than I. And then I scarcely ever saw
her after . . . after a while."

Ellen knew her mother had nearly said "after
the accident" but had stopped herself.

"When she moved away to Florida I really
never expected to hear from her again. You
know how friendships just kind of peter out."

"Some do, I suppose. But it hardly sounds as

though Sophie thinks of your friendship in the past tense. She sounds very determined to have you move to Florida."

"Yes. Silly, isn't it?" Mae turned off the coffeepot and sat down at the table across from Ellen. "Imagine me selling this house and moving down to that retirement community. Why, I'm only fifty-two. The last I knew, that was still considered middle-aged, not elderly."

"Well, Mother, you don't have to be elderly to move to Florida, you know. And to be honest, it doesn't sound like a silly idea to me. I know we've talked about it a number of times before, and you've always been determined not to move away from here, but I'm with Sophie on this one. I think you ought to consider it."

Mae studied the back of her hands, as though inspecting for age spots. "I can't think of a single good reason to move to Florida," she finally replied.

"Well, like Sophie says, the weather is certainly better and —"

"I've never complained about the weather here."

"But the winters are so hard, with all the shoveling."

"I have Roy to help with that."

"Roy's not young anymore, Mother. He won't be able to do chores like that forever."

"Then I'll hire someone else. I hardly think snow shoveling gives me sufficient reason to sell my home."

Ellen tried to chuckle. "It's not just the winters, of course, it's —"

"It's what, Ellen? What exactly are you getting at?"

Ellen paused a moment before answering, hoping to keep Mae from becoming defensive. "There's nothing wrong with making a fresh start, Mother. Sometimes it's a good idea."

"I don't believe I need to make a fresh start."

"Well, but in Florida, you'd have the opportunity to make so many more friends. You'd be meeting new people all the time."

"I have friends here. Why should I leave them behind in search of new ones?"

Ellen sighed. Mae did have friendships, but only because the women were faithful enough to continue calling her. As Ellen knew from her own experience, Mae rarely initiated an outing, rarely was the one to pick up the phone to invite someone to join her for the afternoon.

Ellen was dancing around the issue, but she could hardly blurt out the real reason she wanted Mae to move. She couldn't say she thought her mother should leave the house on Humboldt because this was where the accident had happened, and as long as she was here, in this place, she would never allow herself to live again.

How could she respond to her mother's arguments for staying? How could she convince her to consider moving without blatantly speaking of the reason? Fighting a sense of defeat, Ellen said weakly, "It just sounds like Sophie's having a lot of fun. I'd like to see you having fun like that."

Mae shook her head. "There are more important things in life than having fun."

"I don't mean just having a good time, though. I mean — well, being joyful. You don't really seem to enjoy anything anymore." Ellen sensed she was making a mess of things, but she pressed on. "And you know, Sophie's right about this being too large a house for one person. I hate thinking of you alone here. To tell you the truth, I'd like to see you get married again."

Mae looked at Ellen incredulously, then let go a brief laugh. "Marry again?" she said. "Oh, Ellen darling, how can you entertain an idea like that even for a moment? Talk about ridiculous! I have no more hope or desire for marriage than I have for walking on the moon. I'm far too old for that kind of nonsense now."

"Too old! Mother, you just pointed out yourself that you're only in your middle years. And besides, do you know how many people in their fifties, sixties, even seventies get married? You're fourteen years younger than Sophie, and it sounds like she'll be at the altar soon. If you were ninety, okay, I might agree. But fifty-two? And on top of that, look at you. You hardly look a day over forty."

"Pshaw," Mae sputtered with a wave of her hand.

"It's true, Mother. You're a beautiful woman

and still youthful. No, don't you roll your eyes at me!" Ellen chided. "There'd be dozens of men after you if you gave them half a chance. Your only male companion around here is Roy, and that's hardly challenging for a woman with a keen mind and a lot of life yet ahead of her."

Mae got up from the table and, grabbing the sponge from beside the faucet, began wiping the counter. She stopped suddenly and looked out the window above the sink. "Roy's a loyal friend," she said. "More than that, I've known him so long he's like family."

"I know that, Mother. We all love him. I'm not saying we don't."

"Who would he have left if I were to move to Florida? What would he do? I don't think I could leave him alone like that."

Ellen thought a moment. "Take him with you," she said. At Mae's raised eyebrows, she argued, "Why not? Moving to a place like Florida would be an adventure for him. He might really like it there."

"Impossible," Mae retorted, going back to her scrubbing. Her arm moved in wide circles over the Formica counter top.

"It's not impossible. It's just your own stubbornness telling you that it is. Sam and I can sit down with you and work out all the details — everything from selling the house to finding a moving company to getting you settled in down there."

Mae paused and turned slowly to look at her

daughter. "I'd like to know, Ellen, why you're so determined that I should move to Florida. It almost sounds as though you want to get rid of me." She spoke evenly, but the words were tinged with anger.

Ellen had been afraid it might come to this. She sighed and folded her hands on the table.

"Mother," she said mildly, "I don't want to get rid of you. You know I don't. If I had my way, you'd give up this old house and come live with Sam and me and the girls. But I know you'll never do that." She tried to hold Mae's eyes, but Mae looked down at the toes of her shoes. Ellen dared to touch on the subject, but only lightly. "It's just that everything's different from what it used to be, you know? And it really hurts me to see how things have changed. There used to be people coming in and out of this house all the time — remember how Mike used to say he might as well replace the front door with a revolving door because your friends were constantly coming and going? Well, maybe you don't miss those days, but I do. I miss them for you." Ellen paused a moment to see if there would be a reaction from Mae, but there was none. "I love you," she said firmly. "That's why I want you to think about moving. I want you to be in a place where you can meet lots of people and enjoy life." Her heart pounded against her ribs, but she forced herself to say what was on her mind. "Mother, I want you to leave the past behind."

Mae turned away sharply and slapped the sponge back down on the rim of the sink. Ellen wondered whether she had said too much, ventured too far into that place where her mother sat nursing her pain. After a moment, Ellen pleaded quietly, "Won't you think about it, Mother? Won't you write Sophie and tell her you'll think about it?"

Mae shook her head. "There's nothing to think about. I can't leave my home." She moved to the refrigerator and dried her hands on the towel that hung on the door handle.

"Oh, Mother —"

"Come on, let's go into the living room. There's a magazine article I've been wanting to show you."

"But, Mother . . ." Ellen's eyes followed her mother as she stepped into the hall and disappeared. Ellen sighed again and shook her head. To the empty kitchen she whispered, "You're just too stubborn for your own good."

If she weren't so unyielding, Ellen thought, if she would only let go of her anger at herself for the accident, life would be better for all of them. Forgiving didn't always come easily, Ellen knew. Even now, she herself sometimes struggled to control her own anger over the loss of her son. Moments still came when she wanted to demand, "Tell me why you didn't watch Sammy more carefully, Mother. How could you have let this happen?" But she never spoke the words because her mother's fractured soul couldn't bear the weight of them. They would break her completely. For Ellen, it was a silent struggle to forgive again and again, whenever memories stirred the grief that time had really only begun to lessen.

But that was the difference between her and her mother. Ellen worked at forgiving, while Mae clung to her anger with a white-knuckled grasp. From the beginning Ellen had worked to pry her mother's fingers from the quiet but all-consuming rage — with no success. She remembered the time she'd convinced her mother to visit a grief counselor, only to have Mae walk out of the man's office after a mere twenty minutes. What a fiasco that had been.

Now Ellen wanted to call her mother back into the kitchen and say, "Just a minute; I wasn't finished." But she knew it was no use trying to talk with her mother about Florida or about starting a new life. Mae would no more hear the words than did the refrigerator, the dishwasher, or the rusting pipes that gurgled placidly beneath the sink.

Chapter 5

Mae and Ellen never talked about the episode with the grief counselor three years earlier, but if they had, they might have realized it held a different significance for both of them. For Ellen, it was one more bit of evidence to suggest that her mother was simply refusing to forgive herself. For Mae, it only underscored her belief that there was no use in even trying.

Mae remembered Ellen mentioning the counselor for the first time about a year after Sammy's death. She also remembered that it had been the eve of her forty-eighth birthday. Ellen had handed over the bit of advice, Mae thought, as though it was supposed to be a part of her birthday gift. *"Happy birthday, and by the way, if you ever really expect to be happy, I think you need to see a shrink."*

Of course Ellen hadn't put it that way at all, but to Mae, she might as well have. As soon as Ellen mentioned the doctor, Mae took offense.

"But, Mother," Ellen protested mildly, "I'm only suggesting something Sam and I are doing ourselves. We've been seeing Dr. Garrett since

Sammy's death, and we've found it to be a great help." She went on to explain that Dr. John Garrett was a compassionate man, patiently talking with them and drawing out their pain so that they could work through their grief.

Mae couldn't help but cringe. She hated the expression, "Work through your grief." It sounded as though a person could get rid of pain the same way one might work through an impersonal mathematical problem by using a set of axioms and theorems. In the instance of grief, where were the axioms? What were the theorems? How could she take out pencil and paper and work through it all — adding, subtracting, multiplying — to achieve a satisfactory answer in the end? How, exactly, was it done?

"I just don't think it'll do much good for me to talk with anyone" was Mae's response to Ellen.

"Well, you don't know until you try," Ellen countered.

"It would only be a waste of time and money."

"Won't you even think about it?"

"There's nothing to think about. I don't want to go."

"You're so stubborn. Do you know that?" Ellen retorted, more hurt than angry. "Maybe you want to go on as you are, but I don't want you to. I want you to forgive yourself and to have some joy in your life. I want you to be able to do things again, like go back to the children's hospital and be Mother Mae to those little ones who need you —"

Mae cut Ellen off with a sharp glance. "I can't go back," she snapped. "That was all part of another life. That person doesn't exist anymore."

"Nonsense, Mother," Ellen said. "You're the same person you always were — or you could be if you'd just allow yourself to get beyond the accident. But you've made up your mind, haven't you, that you're going to go on punishing yourself for the rest of your life. Well, have you ever stopped to consider how much it hurts *me* to have you blaming yourself for Sammy's death?"

Mae turned from her daughter to hide the tears, pretending to straighten the curtains on the living room window. She was stung by the thought of hurting Ellen more than she already had. Mae didn't want her daughter to be in pain, but she didn't think she could possibly let go of her own. Quietly she said, "But how can I ever forget . . ."

When she didn't go on, Ellen said, "I don't expect you ever to forget. None of us can forget Sammy. But you can *forgive* yourself, with God's help."

But Mae wasn't convinced. "Things can never be the same, Ellen. I can't go back to the life I was living before. There's no use even in trying."

The next morning, the morning of her birthday, Mae gazed for a long while at her reflection in the bathroom mirror. She did not know what she had expected to see, but not this. Not someone who still looked pleasantly youthful and attractive when inside she felt not forty-eight, not fifty-eight, not even sixty or seventy or eighty, but beyond age altogether. A long time ago — perhaps it had been when the first gray hair, the first wrinkle, appeared — she had wondered what it would be like to die. Now she knew. She knew because inside she was dead. The physical dying would be nothing more than a closing of the eyes. A simple closing of the eyes, and that was all.

She shook her head as she thought of Ellen's pleading with her to go see the doctor. *What foolishness*, she thought. *There's no use trying to piece back together someone who's already dead.*

In spite of Mae's obstinacy, Ellen had persisted. After many months of pleading, Ellen finally persuaded her mother to meet with Dr. Garrett. "But just once," Mae said. "I'll go just once so you'll stop asking me to go. But it won't do any good."

A week later Ellen and Mae entered the empty waiting room of Dr. Garrett's office. Mae was relieved to see that no one else was there. She didn't want anyone, not even a stranger, to wonder why she had come to see a psychologist. She felt almost certain that if someone studied her long enough, he would be able to see the guilt rising from her the way steam rises from a boiling pot.

A young receptionist beyond a sliding window greeted Mae and Ellen with a cheerful "Good morning," but Mae said nothing in return. She let Ellen do the talking. The receptionist passed a clipboard of insurance and history forms through the window, and Mae took it with a sigh. Frowning, she turned away and sank heavily into one of the vinyl chairs.

Ellen sat down beside her. "Do you need any help with the forms, Mother?"

"No," Mae said curtly, without looking up. "I can manage." Her scribbling was accompanied by repeated sighs, until she finally stood and thrust the clipboard under the receptionist's nose without a word. The bewildered young woman accepted the clipboard with a hesitant smile.

When Mae returned to her seat, Ellen whispered, "Honestly, Mother, what's wrong with you? It isn't like you to be so impolite."

"Well, I don't like it," Mae grumbled, wringing the strap of her purse with tense fingers.

"You don't like what?"

"The whole thing." Mae waved her hand toward the center of the room. "This — being here. I don't like the idea of talking about it with someone I don't know and have never even met."

Ellen was the one to sigh now. "Dr. Garrett is a good man and an excellent therapist. Give him a chance, Mother, please."

Both women fell silent. Ellen reached into her purse for a paperback she'd brought along to read. Mae picked up an outdated magazine and flipped through it without seeing a single photo or reading a single word.

A moment later the door to the back offices opened, and a man stepped out with his hand extended. "Mrs. Demaray?"

Mae looked up and hesitantly shook the man's hand. "Yes?"

"I'm Dr. Garrett. I'm very pleased to meet you. Hello, Ellen" — he swung his right hand toward Ellen — "so nice to see you again."

"Hello, Dr. Garrett."

"Will you be joining us this morning?"

"No, I told Mother she could speak with you alone."

"Of course. Please make yourself comfortable, then."

Ellen held up the book. "I brought my own entertainment."

Dr. Garrett smiled, then turned his gaze toward Mae. "Will you follow me, Mrs. Demaray? Right this way, please."

Mae rose and reluctantly followed the man's back as he led her down a narrow carpeted hallway and into a cramped but neatly kept office. "Please have a seat." Dr. Garrett, with a wave of his hand, indicated where she was to sit. He then took a notebook and some papers off his desk and sat down in a black leather chair across from her.

"Coffee?" he offered.

"No." Mae shook her head slightly. "No, thank you."

"Give me just a moment, then, to look over

your personal history, and we'll get started."

Mae gazed at the doctor as though trying to decide by his appearance what kind of person he might be. She didn't know exactly what she had expected Dr. Garrett to look like; something like Freud, perhaps. Scholarly. Formal. Dark-framed glasses with oval lenses. A gray pointed beard. But Dr. Garrett was a pleasant-looking young man who might have passed as a counselor at a children's summer camp. He was tall and hefty and looked like the type who enjoyed the outdoors. She could imagine him teaching kids how to swim or sail or play volleyball. She wondered whether he had children of his own, but a glance at his left hand revealed no wedding ring, and there were no family photos in the office. Interesting, Mae thought, that such an attractive young man wouldn't be married. Then she decided he was probably too busy trying to salvage other people's lives to have much time for his own.

Mae let her eyes wander from the doctor to his office. From the numerous framed photographs on the wall, she was satisfied she had been correct to think he enjoyed the outdoors. He was probably an amateur photographer as well. She recognized scenes of the North Shore — the coast of Lake Superior — covered with a blanket of winter snow, a copse of birch trees against a pale blue sky, a rainbow stretching across the lake after a summer storm. They were really quite pretty, the photos, and for a moment Mae almost forgot where she was.

Her eyes came finally to rest on a scene of a herd of sheep grazing in a meadow. It looked like pictures she had seen of England — the grass was so strikingly green, much greener than the grass of Minnesota — and she wondered whether the doctor might have traveled there. She had always wanted to visit England herself but had never made the trip. She probably never would now.

She heard Dr. Garrett flip a page on the clipboard, but she didn't drop her eyes from the photo of the sheep. A thought captured her and kept her there. *"He makes me lie down in green pastures. . . . He restores my soul."*

Alfie had died of his cancer a few days after Sammy's accident. The children's hospital had called, had asked her to come be with his family. A friend who was with Mae at the time got on the phone and explained about the death of Mae's grandson. The staff at the hospital sent flowers and condolences, called many times to check up on her, and asked her to come back when she was ready. But she had never gone back, and the calls became less frequent until they finally stopped altogether.

It wasn't the children's hospital Mae thought of as she studied the photograph. It was Alfie. He had been so proud when he recited for Mae the Twenty-third Psalm. Nearly two years had passed, but she could still see his face and hear his voice.

"I had to ask my mom about the 'He restores my soul' part," Alfie had said. *"I didn't really understand it, but I guess I do now."*

"And what did your mother say?"

"She said it means I might not get fixed up on the outside, but God will make sure I'm always all right on the inside."

Alfie hadn't got fixed up on the outside, but as his mother wrote in a note to Mae, "He has gone to play with the stars. He's in heaven, and he's finally well."

Mae breathed deeply as she remembered. *"We sometimes can't change what happens on the outside, but our true self — what's inside of us — is always safe with God."* That's what she had told Alfie the last time she saw him. Back then Mae had believed that no matter what happens, no matter how terrible it might be, He always restores our soul. How foreign that belief seemed to her now.

"Well, Mrs. Demaray," Dr. Garrett said kindly, interrupting her thoughts, "how can I help you?"

Before she could realize what she was saying, Mae told the doctor, "I'd like to go home, Dr. Garrett."

The young man sitting across from her raised his brows. "I beg your pardon, Mrs. Demaray?"

Mae dropped her eyes from the photograph and met his gaze. She saw his puzzlement and realized how ridiculous she must have sounded. He couldn't have known what she meant, couldn't have known she wasn't speaking of the house on Humboldt. She wanted to climb back in time, to go back to the days before the accident, to reclaim all that she'd once had.

But that was impossible.

"Actually, Dr. Garrett," she replied sadly, "I don't think you can help me at all."

Dr. Garrett thrust his chin out slightly and crossed one leg over the other. "If you truly believe that, Mrs. Demaray, then perhaps I can't. But I would be terribly sorry to think so." The two looked at each other until Dr. Garrett broke the silence by saying, "Well, maybe you can tell me what brought you to see me."

Mae frowned and sat up straighter in the chair. "I thought you knew. After all, you've been talking with my daughter and son-in-law for some time now."

"Ellen and Sam, yes." Dr. Garrett rubbed his chin absently with the same hand that held his pen. Mae wondered whether he would end up with lines of ink on his clean-shaven face.

"Then you know why I'm here," she said.

"We've talked at great length about their son's death."

"Then you also know that I'm responsible."

"I know it was an accident," Dr. Garrett countered.

His gaze was piercing, but Mae allowed no emotion to register on her face.

He leaned forward in his seat. "Mrs. Demaray," he said pointedly, "do you believe that your grandson's death was an accident?"

Mae turned her gaze from him and stared hard at the photograph of the sheep in the meadow. *"He restores my soul,"* the psalmist had written. But surely there was no hope —

When Mae didn't answer his question, Dr. Garrett sighed and sat back again. "Mrs. Demaray, guilt can be a very debilitating, a very crippling thing. You're steeped in it. The accident was almost two years ago now. It's normal to grieve for two years. It's normal to experience feelings of grief for even longer than that. I'm not saying that you shouldn't grieve. In fact, to grieve is healthy. It's a necessary part of the healing process.

"But guilt is not healthy. We have a job to do here, you and I, and that is to rid you of these feelings of guilt. We must root them out because they're planted where they don't belong. A confessed murderer, Mrs. Demaray, is guilty. A person who plots and strategizes to kill another is guilty. Even someone who commits manslaughter, someone who doesn't plan a murder ahead of time and yet in the heat of the moment takes a life — he is guilty.

"But someone like you, Mrs. Demaray, who accidentally but innocently leaves a door open — you are not guilty. Guilty perhaps of a momentary negligence, but that is hardly equivalent to murder. You didn't will for your grandson to die. You didn't intend for it to happen. Even a murderer can forgive himself — how much more should you.

"That's our goal, Mrs. Demaray. However you define the act of what you've done, whether negligence or murder, you must forgive yourself. Only when you forgive yourself will you be able to move forward into a productive life."

He fell silent, folded his hands in his lap, and waited. In the silence that followed, Mae felt herself wanting to grasp hold of his words "not guilty" and hold them to herself until she believed them. She wanted to lie down in green pastures, to walk beside the still waters that she saw in the photographs on the wall, so that somewhere, somehow, her soul could be restored.

But Sammy is dead, she told herself. *How can I go on living?*

At last she said quietly and evenly, "Dr. Garrett, what you have said and all that you could possibly say cannot and will not change what has happened. Nothing *I* do or say will change what has happened. The past is unchangeable. I'm guilty of leaving the door open. I wish it weren't so. Believe me, I wish it weren't so. . . ." Her words trailed off as she rose from the chair and headed toward the door.

"But, Mrs. Demaray . . ." Dr. Garrett began, but before he could say more, she had disappeared, leaving him with a few scribbled notes and the terrible sense that somebody who deeply wanted help had just left without it.

Chapter 6

As was not unusual in the Midwest, the spring of 1982 was rife with unexpected storms, as though Mother Nature found an abrupt shift in the weather an amusing pastime. So while the sky had been calm and cloudless when Mae went to bed, she wasn't surprised to be awakened sometime in the night by an angry storm. It started with distant thunder that quickly crept closer and grew louder until it seemed to be trampling right on top of the Humboldt house with huge invisible feet. It was the thunder that awakened Mae, but it was the lightning that rattled her every time a flash ripped through the darkness around her. She felt as though a huge finger of electricity was rudely poking its way into her room, prodding her and keeping her from sleep. Then the thunder came and pressed down upon her with the weight of sound. Her body was heavy with it, and the house shivered against the vibrations from the clouds. She lay awake for a long while, watching and listening. The lightning came again and again, flashing, flickering, lighting up the room, then abruptly withdrawing and leaving her in the dark. The thunder followed with its initial piercing clap, and then it sank and rumbled and ended with a final drawn-out boom. And yet between the fierce interruptions of lightning and thunder, a steady rain fell almost music-like onto leaves and soggy lawns and wet streets outside.

Sometime after three o'clock the storm subsided, crawling away like a defeated army, the far-off thunder its last stubborn round of artillery. Mae finally drifted into a restless sleep.

Dawn was nothing more than an almost imperceptible lightening of the glass of the unshaded window. When Mae became aware of her last dream images giving way to the more solid shapes of the lamp, the clock, and the half-read book on the bedside table, she knew that in spite of her weariness she would not be able to sleep any longer. Outside, a soft rain continued to fall. She could hear the raindrops rustling the leaves of the trees. One undaunted bird sang just beyond the window. Mae did not share his optimism. She disliked days like this — dark and wet and dreary.

Reluctantly she pushed back the covers, sat up, and eased her legs over the side of the bed. She searched with her feet for her slippers, then burrowed her toes into the soft caverns of terry cloth. She threw her robe around her shoulders and, with a groan, lifted herself off the bed and wandered down the hall toward the bathroom.

It seemed a very long stretch of time before night would fall again. Mae yawned and rubbed her eyes with a thumb and index finger and wondered how she should fill the hours ahead of her. In her grogginess, she strained to remember what day it was.

Tuesday. Oh yes. Roy was coming, as usual, which gave her another reason to bemoan the weather. She had intended to have Roy cut the grass, as the lawn desperately needed to be trimmed. Now she would either have to wait another week or have Roy make an extra trip out. If the rain kept up all day, it could be a while before the grass was dry enough for Roy to run the mower over it. Maybe she could ask him to come Thursday or Friday. She knew he wouldn't mind. She could just hear him now: "I'd be happy to come anytime, Miss Mae. You just give old Roy a holler, and I'll be there."

As for today, maybe she could call the boardinghouse and tell him not to come. She couldn't think of anything she needed him to do indoors. It was still too early to call the boardinghouse, but after breakfast she could catch Roy before he left for the 8:10 bus.

In an hour, though, when she got around to picking up the phone, she thought a moment, then returned the receiver to its cradle. She suddenly decided that she and her old friend could pass a pleasant morning by indulging in a little reminiscing.

She felt her heaviness begin to lift when Roy showed up, wet and dripping, at her front door. He wore a yellow raincoat with the collar turned up, but he had no hat and his hair was matted to his head in wet strands. His face was slick with rainwater, and a drop clung tenaciously to the tip of his round nose. Between his teeth he clenched the stub of a soggy cigar that was beyond hope of ever being lighted again.

"Goodness, Roy," Mae said as she opened the door, "I'll never understand why you don't carry an umbrella."

"I like the rain, Miss Mae," Roy answered. "It feels good to walk in it."

"That may be, but you're likely to catch pneumonia one of these days, and that'll be the end of your walks in the rain. Well, never mind. Leave your boots on the porch and hand me your raincoat. I'll hang it in the laundry room to dry. Now come on in and get warm."

"Thanks, Miss Mae," Roy said as he tugged at his boots. "I'm not very cold. It's a nice spring day, really. Just a little wet, but that makes the flowers grow all the bigger."

"Yes, and the grass too, unfortunately." Mae took the raincoat that Roy held out to her, then stepped back to let him pass into the hall. "Lock the door behind you, will you?" she said as she hurried toward the laundry room with the dripping coat. "I'll be right back."

When Mae disappeared, Roy crept across the living room floor in his stockinged feet and stood by the mantel. There he lifted the lid of the music box and stuffed his hands into his jeans pockets while he listened. Mae returned to find him in his old familiar stance — dreamy, preoccupied, his mind wandering to where Mae couldn't follow.

When the song had finished and he shut the lid again, Roy turned to face Mae and said, "It's nice to listen to the music box on a day like this. Like you're all cozy inside the house while all the rain is dripping outside." He smiled and tossed his soggy cigar into the ashtray. "Guess I won't get no more puffs out of that one," he said, "but I was almost done with it anyway. Well, Miss Mae, what do you got for me to do today?"

Mae shrugged and said, "I was going to have you cut the grass, but the rain changed my plans."

"Sure thing, Miss Mae," Roy said with a laugh. "No use trying to cut the grass in the rain. Want me to do something inside, then? Want me to lift furniture so we can vacuum the house real good upstairs and down?"

"No, I don't think so, Roy. Actually, I thought we'd do something different today, and maybe you can come back later in the week and cut the grass. Would you mind?"

Roy smiled broadly. " 'Course not," he said. "Soon as the sun dries up the lawn I'll be out there with the mower. Anytime, Miss Mae. You just call Miss Pease and leave a message for me, and I'll be on my way over."

"Thanks, Roy. Maybe Thursday, if you don't have other plans."

Roy shrugged. "No plans that I know of, Miss Mae."

"That should work, then. As for today, have you ever seen my collection of family photos?"

Roy looked pensive, his eyes traveling to the ceiling. Finally he said, "You mean what you got over there on the mantel, Miss Mae?"

"Well, that's part of them, but I have many more than just those few. I keep them in boxes upstairs. There are lots of photos of Mother and Dad that were taken before you and I were born, and pictures of other people in my family too. Would you like to see them?"

"I sure would, Miss Mae," Roy said agreeably.

"Well, why don't you have a seat at the dining room table, and I'll go get them." She headed toward the stairs, then hesitated. "And, Roy, have I shown you the letters?"

Roy knit his brows, then shook his head. "I don't think I remember any letters, Miss Mae."

"May I read you a few? I have letters written by my parents and grandparents, and of course Mother kept all the letters the boys sent home during the war. I also have a huge collection of letters from my mother's best friend, Clara Reynolds. She moved to Vermont after she got married, and my mother never saw her again, but they corresponded for many years. You might not find them as interesting as I do, but maybe I could read you just a few."

"I'd be proud to hear them, Miss Mae."

Mae smiled and headed eagerly for the stairs. "Just have a seat, Roy," she said over her shoulder, "and I'll be right down."

"Can I help you carry that stuff down here?" Roy hollered after her.

Mae paused on the bottom step, from which she could see Roy still standing by the mantel in the living room. "Oh no," she said. "The boxes are small and I'll just bring down a couple." She lifted her foot to the next step, then paused again. "About lunch — I've got some chicken in the refrigerator. I'll fry that up, and we can have some baked potatoes too. How does that sound?"

"Mighty good, Miss Mae," Roy said as he rocked on the balls of his feet. "Chicken's my favorite!"

It was a day that Roy later remembered as one in which the past and the present were all mixed up together. He and Mae sat leaning over the edge of the large walnut table in the dining room, scanning dozens of old photographs lying side by side on the table's polished surface. Roy, picking up each photo carefully and holding it briefly in front of his nose, recognized some of the faces captured by the camera; others he had never seen before. Scattered among Mae's immediate family were grandparents, aunts and uncles, cousins, distant relatives, and family friends.

Roy lingered longest over the photos of Mae and her parents and brothers. There they were, in dozens of small black-and-white squares, looking just as he had known them years ago.

Mrs. Wollencott standing in her garden, smiling brightly. The doctor, relaxing in the overstuffed chair, looking absently away from the camera. The boys, tousle-haired and sweaty, throwing a football around the lawn. There was Willie as he looked a year before going off to war. There was Jimmy holding a frog up next to his face, his mouth pulled back in a grin that matched the frog's grimace. There was Mae, a toddler yet, watering a patch of crocuses with a watering can that was nearly as big as she.

A good feeling settled over Roy as the early days of his life came back to him. The evenings spent around the Wollencotts' dinner table, where there was plenty of food and people who cared about him, were among his first and happiest memories. He had been told that he was five years old, almost six, when he met the Wollencotts, but that seemed to him the beginning of his life. He had little recollection of what came before, only snatches here and there of an early childhood that no one ever spoke of, and of which he had no record. His long-ago social worker, Miss Sills, once told him that he had arrived at the orphanage at the age of five, but of his life before that she could tell him nothing.

Sometimes in his dreams and on certain occasions in his waking moments, Roy heard the echo of a familiar voice he couldn't quite place. It was a woman's voice — not that of Amelia Wollencott, nor of one of his teachers at school or the Sisters at the orphanage. He saw, too, in his mind a woman's face, and though he couldn't see her clearly and certainly couldn't remember her name, he knew he had loved her in those five lost years.

"That's Mother and Dad on their wedding day," Mae said, breaking into Roy's thoughts. "They were married in 1920. Hard to believe, isn't it?"

Roy pinched one corner of the photo and held it up to the light to study. Finally he said, "Miss Wollencott sure was beautiful. And just look at that dress. That's some mighty fancy needlework. I sure wish I coulda seen Miss Wollencott on her wedding day."

"Well, that would have been a little difficult, since you weren't born yet."

Roy laughed. "Yeah, I can see where that might have made for a problem." He set the photo down and picked up another. "Who's this little baby, Miss Mae? Looks a whole lot like Christy when she was a baby."

Mae looked at the photo in Roy's hand. "Yes, I guess it does look like Christy, doesn't it? But that's me. Let me see, what's it say on the back?" She took the photo from Roy and turned it over. In her mother's handwriting were the words, "Mary Amelia Wollencott, six months."

Mae continued. "That was one of the first photos taken of me, I guess. According to Mother, I was six months old at the time."

"Your real name's Mary, Miss Mae?" Roy asked.

"Yes," Mae said, nodding. "But everyone has always called me Mae."

Roy picked up the picture carefully, as he had the wedding photo. He smiled and gave a long, teasing whistle. "Would ya look at that?" He chuckled.

"What is it?" Mae asked, leaning closer to Roy.

"Look at the head you got on ya. Round as a pumpkin. Round as mine!"

Mae laughed with him.

"Yes, I guess I was a bit roly-poly, wasn't I? Just baby fat."

"I betcha I looked something like that when I was a baby. 'Course you thinned out real nice, Miss Mae, while the rest of me went on to be just as round as my head!" Roy patted his stomach to underscore his point. Then he asked, "Don't you have any earlier pictures of yourself? Say, when you were only a week old or something?"

"I've never seen any. No, I think this one is the earliest."

"But lookey here," Roy said, holding up a couple more photos. "Here's Kenny at six weeks old, and here's Jimmy at five days old! That's what it says on the back. I wonder why Miss Wollencott waited six months before she got your picture."

Mae shrugged and shook her head. "I don't know, Roy. I guess that happens sometimes with the last child. You're not as enthusiastic about picture taking and keeping baby books and whatnot, since you've already done it all before. And Mother was busy. . . ."

"Seems strange, though, you being the only girl and all. You'd think Miss Wollencott would want to take your picture soon as she first saw your pretty face."

Mae laughed lightly, but Roy noticed the troubled frown that creased her brow. She seemed to be wrestling with a thought, but whatever it was, she dismissed it and said, "Well, anyway, here's a photo you've never seen. My grandparents. Grandpa and Grandma Wollencott. I never knew my grandmother on my father's side, but I have lots of fond memories of Grandpa. You remember him, don't you?"

Roy grinned again and lifted his gaze to the window, as though the old man were standing just outside. "I sure do," he said. " 'You call me Gramps, son,' he used to tell me, and every time I saw him, he'd reach into his shirt pocket and pull out a pack of chewing gum and give me a piece. Sometimes two or three pieces, so I'd have a whole big wad of it in my mouth at once."

Mae, still looking at the photo, made a sound of wistful agreement. "Hmmm. Yes, I remember. He said he couldn't stand the stuff himself, but he carried the gum around in his pocket to give to us grandkids because he knew we liked it."

"He lived far away from here, I think," said Roy.

"Over in Sioux Falls with his other son and daughter-in-law."

"Sioux Falls ain't in Minnesota, Miss Mae?"

"No, South Dakota. Not far over the state line."

"Wish I coulda gone sometime. I'm fifty-seven and I never been out of Minnesota at all!"

Mae waved her hand and put the photo of her grandparents back on the table. "Well, Roy," she said, "traveling's not what it's played up to be. Whenever I traveled, I always ached for home again. Nothing's better than home."

Roy briefly touched several of the faces preserved by the photos in front of him. "No, I guess you got a point there, Miss Mae," he said. "I can't think of anything better than home."

Mae glanced at her watch, then pushed her chair back from the table. "It's after ten already," she said as she stood. "I'll go pour us some coffee, and then we can read some of the letters. I think you might enjoy them."

"That's fine, Miss Mae. A cup of coffee sure would taste good right about now." Roy watched Mae's back as she disappeared into the kitchen. A moment later she returned carrying two large mugs on a tray.

Roy took the mug that Mae offered and sipped noisily. "Mighty good," he said. "A cigar's just the thing to make it perfect." He took one out of his shirt pocket and lighted it.

"Don't forget your ashtray. It's in the living room," Mae warned.

"I'll go get it." He lumbered out of the room like a ponderous bear, leaving a thin trail of smoke behind him. When he returned with the ashtray, he found that Mae had put away the photos and was pulling letters out of a box. He sat down again at the table beside her.

"I have lots and lots of letters," she said, "but I'll just read a few."

Mae unfolded one of the letters and began to read. Roy took long lingering puffs of his cigar and intermittently slurped his coffee while trying to concentrate. Mae's voice was crisp and sonorous and tended, like music, to cause Roy's mind to wander. The few times Mae had taken him to hear the Minnesota Orchestra, he had come away with no recollection at all of what had been performed, so preoccupied had his mind been with his own daydreams. He'd always been that way. He never really heard music because he was too busy listening to the thoughts that the music stirred up. And likewise, when anyone read to him, almost at once his mind began to travel into side streets and byways that often had nothing at all to do with what was being read.

"And this one," Mae was saying, "was written almost a hundred years ago by my great-great-uncle to his sister, my great-great-aunt Bessie. It's dated August 9, 1887, and was written from Buffalo, New York. It's just about the oldest family letter I have. 'My dearest sister Bessie,' he begins, 'I take my pen in hand to greet you this morning with the news of our family. . . .' "

Roy puffed and chewed on the end of his cigar, squinted his eyes, and squeezed the coffee mug, but try as he might, he could not follow the formal rambling of this great-great-uncle, a man whom he had never known and could not now imagine. He could only picture a gnarled and trembling hand clutching a ball-point pen. He then began to wonder where Buffalo was and whether the people living there saw buffalo roaming outside their windows every day. He had heard about the buffalo of the Old West and was acquainted with the story of a man named Buffalo Bill, but he had never known before that there was a place in New York called Buffalo. He wondered what the people there did in case of stampedes and whether there were any cowboys and Indians left to hunt the animals. If so, he thought he might like to go there someday. He'd never actually seen a buffalo.

By the time he was able to turn his thoughts back to the letter, Mae had reached the closing words. All Roy heard were the man's wishes for good health for his sister and her children and his promise to write again soon.

Mae smiled and folded the letter reverently. "When I die," she said, "of course all these family letters will go to Ellen, and she in turn will pass them on to her girls. We want to keep things like this in the family. It'd be a shame for them to get lost or just thrown out with the trash."

Roy nodded, hoping she wouldn't ask what he

had thought of the letter. "That's sure, Miss Mae," he said. "Ellen and Christy and little Amy will take good care of all the nice family things you got. I'm sure of that."

Mae pulled another letter out of its envelope and opened it. "Now, this one was written by my mother to my father back in 1918, before they were married. Mother's family used to have a summer house in Duluth, so that's where she was writing from. She says, 'Dear Mr. Wollencott, Our train arrived safely in Duluth last night at six o'clock. It is always a delightful trip to head north from Minneapolis. . . .' "

Again Roy chewed his cigar and frowned and tried to listen, but he was lost to the memory of Amelia as he had known her, the sweet Miss Wollencott of his childhood. Images of her tumbled one after another through his mind. Momentary fragments of time came to the surface of his thoughts like goldfish appearing briefly on the surface of a lake. He heard nothing of the letter beyond the first couple of lines, but when Mae finished he was glad that she had read it. It had triggered memories and feelings that had lain dormant for a long time.

"It was a nice letter, wasn't it, Roy?" Mae asked.

"Very nice, Miss Mae," he replied, smiling. "I hope you'll read it to me again sometime."

"Of course I will," she said. She was already unfolding another letter. "This one," she explained, "was written by my mother's dearest friend, Clara Reynolds. She's in that photo with

Mother on the mantel. You know the one."

Roy nodded.

"Mother must have kept hundreds of letters that Clara sent her over the years," Mae continued. "I have three hatboxes upstairs filled with letters just from Clara. I've often wondered whether Clara was as diligent to keep the letters Mother sent to her. I'm glad to have these letters, but how much more I'd cherish the ones Mother wrote. I've thought on occasion that I should write to Clara's daughter — Clara herself has Alzheimer's disease and can't remember a thing — but I thought I could write to Evelyn to see whether she has any of Mother's letters she could send me. I haven't done it yet — guess I feel a little funny. I met Evelyn only once, when she and Clara came for Mother's funeral. We've exchanged Christmas cards, but that's about it.

"At any rate, Mother and Clara corresponded for twenty-five years, if you can imagine that. I have letters from Clara dated every year from 1925 to 1950. Quite a stretch, isn't it? Every year, that is, except for 1930, which seems funny, since that was the year I was born. You'd think she would have written to Clara about finally having a girl."

Roy scratched at his chin with his thick fingers. "Guess Miss Wollencott didn't take any pictures or write any letters for a while, since she was so busy with the boys and a new little baby."

Mae nodded her agreement, but again her puzzled frown appeared. It bothered Roy that something should be bothering his friend. "Or maybe there's pictures of you as a little bitty baby somewhere, but you just don't know where they are," he offered by way of encouragement. "Seems likely Miss Wollencott mighta kept those photos in some special place, along with the letters about your being born."

"I suppose that's possible," Mae said hesitantly. She was quiet for a moment but then seemed to brush aside her thoughts as she offered Roy a smile. "Well, anyway," she went on, "how about one more letter, and then I'll start lunch."

When all the reminiscing was done, Roy was a little sorry to see the morning end. He would have been happy to look at more photos and listen to more letters, even though he hadn't really been listening at all. To him it didn't matter. What mattered was the remembering, the recalling of Miss Wollencott and the doctor and the boys and Mae as they had been, and even of his own life as it had been years ago.

They had had the best of lives, he thought. There may be other lives that were just as good, but surely none were better. Roy felt nostalgia for those early days, those years that appeared even sweeter in retrospect, especially now that everything was so different for Miss Mae. She had been happy, too, back then, but she wasn't happy anymore.

How Roy wished she would forgive herself for what happened to Sammy! But he knew that would be especially hard for Mae. The morning had jarred in his mind a long-buried memory, pushing it up to the surface where Roy could view it again.

"I'm afraid Mae has a very hard time when it comes to forgiveness," Mrs. Wollencott had told him many years ago when the incident occurred. They were standing outside Mae's locked door, trying to coax her out. Roy couldn't remember what had happened, but he knew he wanted to tell Mae he was sorry, wanted to hear her say it was all right and that they could be friends again. But he and Mrs. Wollencott, who knocked repeatedly, were finally met with angry words. Mae wouldn't come out, and she wouldn't play with Roy anymore. *"I'm so sorry, Roy,"* Mrs. Wollencott had said kindly. *"She's only five years old, I know, but she's as stubborn as an old woman. Don't worry, though. Eventually she'll forgive and forget. You'll be friends again; you'll see."*

Mae never did say she forgave him, but she must have forgotten just as Mrs. Wollencott had predicted, because they did go on being friends. Roy remembered, though, how awful he'd felt as he stood outside Mae's door, waiting and hoping to hear her words of reassurance. *Miss Mae must feel just that awful now,* Roy thought, *'cause she won't forgive herself, and she sure won't ever let herself forget about leaving that basement door open.*

When he sat down to a plate of fried chicken and a huge baked potato, he pushed this one unhappy memory aside and said, "It's been a real good morning, Miss Mae."

Mae dabbed at her potato with a pat of butter. "I guess it has been at that," she said, "in spite of the rain."

"I'm not sorry it rained, since it meant I got to see all your fine family things. Thanks for sharing them with me, Miss Mae."

"I'm glad you enjoyed them, Roy. I've spent a lot of hours digging through those boxes. Those photos and letters are very precious to me."

"I sure can understand that, Miss Mae. You got a fine family. It's good to keep all those things like you do. I would, too, if I had a family. I'da taken a bunch of pictures and woulda kept every single letter that was writ."

"Well," said Mae, slicing her chicken, "we can do this again another time. You know, I just realized, we have photos of you, too, from the holidays you spent with us and whatnot. I should have brought them out today but — well, next time we'll look through that box. Would you like that?"

Roy smiled. "I'd like that just fine, Miss Mae. Looking at the pictures — well, it kinda takes me back to a real happy time. We've had a real good life together, haven't we, Miss Mae?"

Mae chewed quietly for a moment, then she smiled placidly and said, "Yes, Roy, there was a time when we were happy."

The rain continued to patter against the kitchen window while Mae and Roy went on to eat their lunch in comfortable silence.

Chapter 7

She wasn't quite sure how or why it had all come about, but Mae and Roy had indeed lived out their lives together — making the journey on the same bus, so to speak, if not sitting side by side in the same seat. It was with Roy, and sometimes through him, that Mae had learned life's hard lessons.

When they were both young children, Mae knew nothing of Roy's life away from the Wollencott home. It was left to her imagination to decide what the orphanage was like, as she didn't think to ask Roy about it, and he never offered any clues himself. She believed it to be a terrible place, like in Dickens' *Oliver Twist*, where the children went dirty and hungry and unloved. She never considered that Roy showed up at the Wollencott home clean, plump, and happy.

When Mae entered first grade at the local public school, she was surprised to find Roy there. She had assumed he was too stupid to attend classes like other children. Her mother explained Roy's presence at the school by saying,

"Well, Mae, he's not very bright, but he still deserves the chance to learn. The Sisters at the orphanage told me they decided to put him in public school so that when he's a little older he can go into the vocational training program. You know how he likes to build things and tinker with things. Just the other day Sister Catherine told me they think Roy will be able to support himself and live on his own someday. That's what they're hoping for, anyway."

Mae saw Roy at school nearly every day but generally only from a distance. She attended her own classes while Roy eventually did go into the vocational training program. She gave about as much thought to Roy as she did to her own brothers, which was very little.

But gradually, as she grew older, she came to realize that things weren't so easy for Roy. She watched in alarm as other students taunted him and made him the target of practical jokes. Whenever Roy appeared in the hall or in the lunchroom, someone was sure to begin the chant, "Roy, Roy, the stupid boy," or "Hanna, Hanna, his brain's a banana." Frequently, expletives and hateful slurs were added to the taunts.

When Mae was eleven years old, she decided to challenge some of the young tyrants who constantly harassed Roy. One afternoon just after school let out, she heard the familiar chant, "Hanna, Hanna . . ." and she spotted Roy on the school steps, looking calmly at the half dozen

125

students surrounding him. Mae had intended to walk home with Sally Ann, but she told her friend to go on without her. Then she turned and marched back up the sidewalk that led to the school's front steps. As she climbed up to the circle of hecklers, she hugged her school books to her chest to hide her beating heart, took a deep breath, and forced out the words that she had long been stifling. "Shut up!" she cried. "Just shut up, all of you! I'm sick and tired of listening to you say these stupid things over and over again. You all think you're so big and tough by picking on someone who's not as smart as you are. Well, you're not! You're stupid! You're the stupid ones, not Roy. Why don't you just leave him alone?"

Her face burned and she was breathing hard by the time she finished. The others, surprised by her outburst, stared at her. Finally, one of the seventh-grade boys said quietly, as though in disbelief, "Well, look at her sticking up for the idiot."

"Yup," said another boy, a sixth-grader. "Can you believe it? Looks like these two are sweet on each other."

Mae looked desperately at Roy, who grinned sheepishly at her and shrugged. "We are not," she defended herself to the group, "and you know it too."

"Yes, you are," the boy pressed. "Everyone knows how Roy's always showing up at your house, eating dinner with you, and all."

"So what if he does?"

"Means he's sweet on ya. Means he aims to marry ya."

"That's just silly, Bill Evers, and you know it!" Mae yelled. "It means no such thing. Roy's just a friend of the family, that's all."

"Why ya sticking up for him, then?"

"Why can't you just leave him alone?" Mae retorted angrily. "Why do you have to make fun of him every day?"

Another boy, Bill's friend, piped in, "Ah, poor Roy, the stupid boy. Can't he take a little kidding?"

One of the girls turned to Mae with a sneer. "Better watch out, Mae. Soon you'll be pushing around a little idiot in a baby carriage."

Mae's anger burned, and she was tempted to snap back at the girl. But she knew the conversation would keep going around in circles, getting nowhere, and the only way to end it was to leave. She tugged at Roy's sleeve and said, "Come on, I'll walk you to your bus."

Together Mae and Roy broke through the group of students who continued to throw stinging comments at their backs. When they had almost reached the bus, Roy said, "Gee, Miss Mae, awful nice of you to stick up for me the way ya did." Even then, for reasons known only to him, Roy had started calling his friend Miss Mae.

"Forget it, Roy," Mae said. "They're just mean people, that bunch. I hope you don't let them bother you."

"Naw, Miss Mae," Roy said, shaking his head emphatically. "They don't bother me."

"Well, I don't know about you, but I really am sick and tired of hearing them make fun of you all the time."

Roy shrugged. "I guess they don't mean no harm."

"They're cruel, is what they are. They're just a bunch of big babies themselves, picking on someone like . . ." Mae paused and looked at Roy. He stood by the door of the bus, smiling. Mae shielded her eyes from the sun to better see his face. She finally understood that, between the two of them, she was the only one who was angry. "They really don't bother you, Roy?"

Roy shrugged again and shifted his books from one arm to the other. "Naw. Mr. Thomas — he's the woodshop teacher, you know — Mr. Thomas and me's good friends. He says I cut a piece of wood straighter than just about anybody he knows. He says when the kids make fun of me, it's just because they're jealous on account of they can't cut wood as good as me."

Mae felt her anger slowly fade, being replaced by a thankfulness for this Mr. Thomas, a large, roughhewn man she had seen from a distance but had never met. He had given Roy a good thought to hold on to.

"You *are* a good carpenter, Roy," Mae agreed. Then she added, though she knew it wasn't true, "I guess it does make the other kids jealous."

Roy smiled and shrugged. "I'm not trying to

make anyone jealous, Miss Mae. I just want to do a good job because, you know, Jesus was a carpenter. I want to make Him proud, seeing as how me and Him are kinda in the same profession."

Mae laughed lightly at the thought. "Well, I'm sure He's very proud of you," she said. "Don't worry about that."

"Mr. Thomas says so, too, when I tell him why I want to do good at carpenter work. He says Jesus would be glad to hire me on in His carpenter shop over in Nazareth if it was still open. Only it closed up a long time ago. Anyway, Mr. Thomas — he's my good friend."

"I'm glad Mr. Thomas is your friend, Roy."

Roy nodded. "He's a nice man."

Mae remembered her childhood promise. "I'm your friend too, Roy," she said. "Don't forget that."

Roy smiled eagerly. "Oh no, Miss Mae, I couldn't forget that! You've been my best friend ever since I was a kid, you and Miss Wollencott."

After that incident and to her dismay, Mae's promise of friendship was put to the test. News of her attempt at sticking up for Roy bloomed on the school grapevine, and she was kidded endlessly. To make matters worse, Roy now followed Mae and her friends around the school halls more than ever before.

"Roy, you don't have to help me, really," Mae would plead whenever he tried to take her books.

"Naw, Miss Mae, I want to. I'm your friend, ain't I? And you're my best friend. I'm proud to carry your books, Miss Mae."

"But you really don't have to, Roy. Look, I'm late for class. I gotta go." Clutching her books and hurrying off, she felt her face burn as Roy called after her, "See you tonight, Miss Mae! Miss Wollencott invited me for supper."

Mae's friends suggested she tell Roy to just buzz off, but she could only sigh at their advice. "I don't really want to get *rid* of him. I mean, I don't *hate* him or anything. I just —" But she didn't really know what she wanted. She did know her friends were getting tired of Roy's following her around like a late afternoon shadow. All their efforts at popularity were being undermined by the constant appearance of the school idiot in their midst. Mae understood her friends' frustration; she felt somewhat the same way.

Yet she also nursed that old sense of pity and compassion for Roy. She didn't want to snub him, to be as unkind to him as the other kids at school. She found it an odd mixture of feelings, the annoyance and the compassion that mingled inside of her. She wanted to be kind to Roy yet at the same time protect her own reputation. To her adolescent mind, the problem loomed large and seemed to have no solution. It was a delicate balance between looking after self and looking after Roy, and the scales seemed always tipped too far in one direction or the other. She wished Roy would go to a different school, or leave school altogether, so she could be free of this wearisome balancing act.

In December of that year, she got her wish. One day the country was at peace, and the next, it plunged headfirst into war when Japan attacked the U.S. Pacific Fleet at Pearl Harbor. The need for soldiers drained the nation of its manpower, leaving wide open a host of jobs on the home front. Roy left school to become a janitor at Honeywell, and three months later, at the age of seventeen, he left the orphanage with twenty dollars in his pocket and the desire in his heart to have a place of his own.

"I got a room!" he announced happily to Mae one evening when he was visiting the Wollencotts. "Got a room in a boardinghouse over on Emerson. Miss Sills — she's my social worker — she went with me and helped me arrange it all. She told Miss Yost, the lady that owns the house, that I'm honest and clean and responsible. That's what she said. And Miss Yost said I could have the room long as I pay my rent on time. I promised I would, and I will too. So now I'm a workingman, Miss Mae."

"That's swell," Mae responded, offering Roy a smile of congratulations. Inwardly, she was relieved he had left school. It would be much easier to be his friend if he wasn't around anymore.

He may have left school, but Roy was still around, still showing up at the house on

Humboldt at Mrs. Wollencott's invitation. In that regard, life remained the same. In many other ways, though, life changed, even for Mae, as the country shifted from a peaceful civilian economy to an active war machine. Factories stopped making cars and started manufacturing planes and munitions. Foods, gas, leather, and other products were rationed. Newspapers shrank in size as paper became scarce. Streetlamps were shaded and blackout curtains went up, while air raid sirens wailed periodically to announce mock attacks by the Germans and Japanese. Young men exchanged their "civvies" for uniforms and suddenly vanished by the hundreds. In the front windows of houses everywhere, blue stars were hung to indicate that one of their own had gone off to war.

By the autumn of 1943, three blue stars hung in the front window of the Wollencott home. One of Mae's brothers had been drafted; two more voluntarily enlisted. The eldest, Peter, had shipped out in the summer of 1942 and was stationed in North Africa. Will and Jim had both left in early 1943, Will to join the air force, flying raids over Europe, while Jim was on a navy ship somewhere in the South Pacific.

Mae, thirteen years old, wanted to do her part to help America win the war. After school, she and her friends rolled bandages and put together care packages at the Red Cross. They took part in newspaper, rubber, and scrap metal drives. When the wounded started returning home, they went to the hospitals to visit the young men and help them write letters.

Sometimes her mother asked Mae to invite Roy along on their various outings and drives. "He needs to feel like he's a part of the war effort, helping out in some way."

"But, Mom," Mae complained, "it's embarrassing to be with him sometimes. People think I *like* him."

"But you *do* like him, don't you?"

"Well, yeah, but not in *that* way. You know what I mean."

"Mae, you're talking nonsense. No one's going to suspect you of being a couple. You have to stop thinking about yourself so much and consider how Roy feels."

Mae was slightly stung by her mother's comment. She didn't think about herself too much, in her opinion. After all, she spent hours and hours helping out the soldiers both at home and abroad. She could be using that time for herself, indulging in her own interests and hobbies, but she didn't. And here she was being chided for not thinking about Roy.

Roy, Roy, Roy. Always Roy. The boy from the orphanage — now the man at the boardinghouse — was all too often the albatross around Mae's neck, and just because her mother had decided years ago to be nice to him.

On a Sunday evening in mid-December 1943, with Christmas only a week away, Mae and Roy sat by the radio in the living room listening to Christmas carols. Dr. Wollencott was at the hospital, where he spent more time than ever; the youngest boy, Kenny, was visiting a school chum; Amelia was in the kitchen cleaning up after the modest dinner she had shared with Mae and Roy. The latter had offered to wash the dishes, but Amelia insisted that she preferred to do it. "I have to stay busy or I start to worry," she said as she shooed Roy off to the living room with Mae.

The two young people sat there subdued, refusing to be cheered by the holiday tunes coming over the radio. Roy pulled absently on a cigarette; in spite of rationing, he had started smoking shortly after moving into the boardinghouse. Mae flipped through a movie magazine, wishing she had the face and hair of any one of the stars. She wished, too, that Roy would go home. She'd rather be talking on the phone with Sally Ann. Even sitting alone would be better than spending the time with someone who, for Mae, often became a tiresome guest. Maybe, if she ignored him long enough, he'd grow bored and leave.

She glanced over at him and noticed with annoyance that he looked relaxed and comfortable in the overstuffed chair. His feet were propped up on the footstool, his head rested on the back of the chair, and he didn't appear to have any intention of leaving anytime soon. Instead, he seemed lost in thought.

Mae went back to her magazine and flipped

through the pages noisily. Roy lifted his head and looked over at her slowly, as though pulling himself up out of a deep sleep. After a moment, he said, "Miss Mae, you know what I wish?"

Mae sighed audibly. "No, Roy, I guess I don't," she replied without looking up.

Roy didn't seem to notice the impatience in her voice. "I wish I was smart enough to go to one of those places where the fighting is," he said.

Puzzled by such a comment, Mae lifted her eyes to meet Roy's gaze. He was looking at her intently. "Why on earth would you want to go to where the fighting is?" she asked.

Roy pushed aside the footstool with his feet and leaned forward in the chair. "The way I figure it, if I went over there, maybe one of your brothers could come home. Maybe I could take the place of one of them, you know? Because they got a mother and a father and brothers, and they got you, Miss Mae. And it don't seem right that the three of them should be there when they got a family back here that loves them." Squinting his eyes, he continued. "But see, I don't have a mother and a father and brothers. If I died, there wouldn't be anyone missing me. But you take Peter or Willie or Jimmy — now, if one of them died, there'd be a whole bunch of people missing them. That's no good, Miss Mae. It'd be better if I was the one to go."

When he finished speaking, Mae looked for a long time at the young man seated across from her in the overstuffed chair. She studied the round face, the bulbous nose, the violet-blue eyes of this so familiar person who somehow managed to evoke such a tangle of emotions inside her: pity, annoyance, impatience, compassion. Of one thing she was certain: she didn't pity him now. She saw no reason to pity him. He didn't feel sorry for himself, didn't take thought at all of himself save what he could do for someone else.

Mae had never considered what it would be like to say good-bye to Roy at the train station, to see him off to war, because she knew he had no more chance of being eligible to serve than she did. But now when he talked about going in the place of one of her brothers, the thought of Roy as a soldier disturbed her deeply. She pictured him in uniform, pictured him with a helmet on his head, planted atop his hair like a turtle perched on a globe. She pictured him standing at attention, his rifle at his side, his khakis neatly pressed, his shoes polished to a shine. She saw him at the front, fumbling with his gun, too kindhearted to shoot even the enemy, taking the bullet into his own chest before shooting a bullet into the chest of any other man. He would never survive a war, never. He was simply too gentle to survive.

"Oh, Roy," she said quietly, closing the magazine to let Roy know he had her attention at last. "That isn't true at all. Why, if you were to go to war and be killed, Mom and Dad and my brothers — they'd all miss you. And so would I, Roy. I'd miss you too."

Roy sat silently with his head cocked, his eyebrows knit as though the thought of being missed were almost incomprehensible. He looked at Mae. "Would you, Miss Mae?" he asked shyly. "Would you really miss me?"

"Yes, Roy," she assured him. "I'd miss you very much."

Roy nodded slightly and clasped his hands together. "Thank you, Miss Mae."

The voices of the Andrews Sisters singing "I'll Be Home for Christmas" filled the living room. In the kitchen, Amelia hummed along with the radio. Outside, a light snow fell, laying a fresh covering of white over the world.

"Miss Mae?"

"Yes, Roy."

"If you was to go to the war and die, I'd miss you very much too."

One corner of Mae's mouth turned back in a brief smile. "Thank you, Roy," she said.

They were quiet then, saying nothing more until Amelia came from the kitchen and warned that it was getting late and Roy would miss his bus if he didn't get going. She told Roy they were looking forward to having him spend Christmas Day with them, and Roy said he was mighty happy to be asked and that he'd be there bright and early Christmas morning. He put on his coat and hat, said good-night, and headed out the door into the cold winter night. The light of a

137

full moon shimmered on the falling snow. Roy turned up the collar of his worn coat and, without turning around, lifted up one hand in a motionless wave, as though he could feel Mae's eyes upon his back. She watched him disappear down the walk and into the dark street, and she was glad, very glad, that he was coming back for Christmas.

Mae was aware that the first rule of war is that young men die. Still, she didn't believe the rule applied to her brothers. Because they were her family, nothing bad could happen to them. Somehow the hedge of protection that surrounded her extended to them as well.

While she thought about them a great deal as she went about her daily routine, she didn't worry about her brothers. But at night, it was different. In the dark hours of sleep, all of them — Peter, Will, Jim — became the wounded soldier she had seen in *Life* magazine, or the dead soldier she had heard talked about down at the drugstore soda fountain.

In her dreams, she saw one of her brothers struck down in battle, saw his body shudder at the impact of bullet to brain, saw his rifle fly away from his open hands, saw him — arms out, as though signaling surrender — falling forward, landing with a thud on the ground. He lay crumpled in a circle of moist red dirt. When Mae awoke, staring wide-eyed into the darkness, the final dream image hung in her mind like the last bit of light on the horizon at sunset. She didn't know which of her brothers it was; she knew only that she had seen him die a hundred times in a hundred ways, night after night after night.

Will was the one in Mae's dreams, the brother who didn't come back from the war. Not even his body was returned home, as it couldn't be found. On March 6, 1944, six hundred sixty bombers were sent to raid Berlin for the first time, and sixty-nine of them were lost. Will's plane was one of those shot down. It didn't spiral to earth with a tail of black smoke but rather exploded and fell to the ground in fiery pieces. All ten men aboard were presumed dead.

For Mae, that same explosion blew a gaping hole into the hedge that she had imagined around her, ushering in the first real loss she had known.

Will's funeral was held on a snowy evening at the church. But instead of a casket, there was only, on the communion table, a framed portrait of Will in his air force uniform, staring out at the mourners through eyes that dared them to weep.

"Not at *my* funeral," he would have said. "I won't have a bunch of wailing women and weeping men spoiling my moment."

Will would have been pleased to know he'd died in the service of his country. There was something heroic about such a death. Far better than a lingering illness or a traffic accident, far better even than succumbing to natural causes as an old man. This way, a measure of pride softened the grief; mothers, fathers, wives could say, "He died *for* something. There was a purpose."

That was what Mae's father told his family the evening before the funeral. *"Will's a hero,"* Dr. Wollencott had said. *"We can be proud."*

Mae's father knew a lot about death, so he must have known what he was talking about. But Mae couldn't quite muster up the pride he had said she should feel. Maybe she would feel it later, but not now. Her brother Will was dead, and inside Mae found no room for anything other than sadness.

She sat stiffly in the first pew of the sanctuary, her mother and father on one side of her, Roy and Kenny on the other. Mae was not surprised to see that her father stared dry-eyed up at the pastor, as though listening to a routine Sunday sermon, while she and her mother wiped away at a continual stream of tears. Somehow men were able to do that — keep their emotions in check even in the worst of times. She wondered whether it came with practice, or if men just didn't have the same kind of emotions women had. Yet she'd noticed Kenny discreetly brushing his cheeks with the palm of one hand. And then of course there was Roy, head bent, shoulders heaving, sobbing as though his whole world had come to an end. Did Roy count as a man, or was he different because he wasn't smart? Mae wasn't sure, but she realized she appreciated his tears. Will was dead, and hero though he may be, he ought to be mourned.

After the service, when everyone was directed to the church basement for refreshments and coffee, Roy turned to Mae and said, "I'da gone if I coulda, Miss Mae." His lips quivered as he drew in a deep breath. "Honest, Miss Mae, I'da gone in Willie's place if I coulda."

Mae looked into his eyes, the whites now red from crying. "I know you would have, Roy," she said quietly. She drew in her bottom lip to check the tears and turned to her mother, who had just made her way to them.

"Now don't you worry about Willie, Roy," Amelia said. She smiled in spite of her tears and dabbed at her nose again with her handkerchief. "He's in heaven with Jesus now, and it's a beautiful place. There's no fighting there, only peace."

Roy nodded. "I know, Miss Wollencott. I guess Jesus musta gone to Germany and took Willie to heaven to live with him."

"Yes, Roy," she said. "And now Willie's waiting for us there."

"You think he'll remember me when I get up there, Miss Wollencott?" Roy asked anxiously. "You think Willie will remember me?" He looked at her with eyes that were filled with sorrow and uncertainty.

"Oh yes, he'll remember you," she assured him. "Of course he will."

"Then I'll tell him I woulda gone if I coulda. Woulda gone in his place if I coulda."

Fresh tears came to Amelia's eyes as she

141

pulled Roy to her, resting his head on her shoulder. "He already knows, Roy," she whispered. "I believe he already knows."

Mae looked on as her mother comforted Roy. It comforted her as well, the thought that Will was in heaven. But she struggled against the realization that her brother's death had brought: she was just like everyone else after all. She had thought it was her privilege to look out on the world from a safe place, but now she discovered she was not set apart. Tragedy could reach her too, and she would have to decide how to act and what she would believe about life in the face of it. She would go on clinging to faith and goodness as her mother had taught her, but added to that now was a terrible sense of dread, a wondering when grief might come her way again.

She did not have long to wait. On a chilly April afternoon three years after the war, Mae stood beside a hospital bed, trying to find in her mother's face the beloved woman she had always known. But there was little of the mother she knew in the drawn, blanched features that lay against a background of white linen. The left side of Amelia's face looked as though an invisible hand were pressing against it, flattening the flesh from temple to chin. Her left eye drooped, and the corner of her mouth was pulled down in a frown.

Mae lifted her gaze from her mother and looked around the room at each of her brothers.

She wished that one of them would ask their father the question that surely must be on all of their minds. She didn't want to be the one to have to ask. She felt light-headed and weak as fear moved through her like an army of crawling ants. Even her fingers and toes tingled with it. She shivered as she took her mother's hand. It was cold and limp, like something already dead.

Mae turned toward her father and studied his expression, but there was nothing in it to tell her what to think or to hope for.

When she couldn't bear the not knowing any longer, she forced herself to speak. "Dad?" The word came out in a choked whisper. She drew in a deep breath, locked her knees, and asked, "Is Mother going to be all right?"

There, it was said. The dreaded question hovered over the bed, poisoning the air with its implications like miasma floating over a marsh.

Dr. Wollencott looked at Mae with his professional eyes. He tried to smile, but the attempt withered and resulted only in a tremor running through his cheeks. "It's too early to tell," he replied. "Many people who suffer strokes enjoy a complete recovery. We can hope that your mother will be so fortunate."

"But what do *you* think, Dad?" Mae persisted. "Do you think she'll be all right, just the same as before?"

The doctor hesitated before answering. Then he said quietly, "It wasn't a mild stroke that your mother suffered. We can hope, but right now the odds are not in our favor." He looked at his sons and at Mae, then continued in a voice barely audible. "We have to be prepared for the worst."

The worst? Did that mean, then, that her mother might die? They had only too recently lost Will, so recently that the wound in the family's heart was still tender. Surely they had had their share of suffering for a while. It wouldn't be fair if they were to lose yet another loved one.

You have to let her live, God, Mae thought. *You just have to let her live, or else —*

Or else what? Mae found no words to finish the sentence. By now she knew that terrible things happen to people, even to her, and that sometimes there wasn't anything at all a person could do to change the unfolding of the years.

But Amelia did live, and after a month in the hospital, she was taken home again. She couldn't walk, and she couldn't speak, and her left hand remained a useless claw that dangled at her side. But when her husband carried her into the house on Humboldt, the right side of her mouth turned up in a wide smile and her right eye sparkled and unmistakable sounds of joy gurgled in her throat. She knew that she was home, that her husband and children were around her, and most of all that she was still alive.

That night Mae went to her mother's bedroom where she found her awake and staring intently at the ceiling. At the sight of Mae, she offered her a half smile and patted the bed weakly with her right hand, motioning for Mae to sit.

Mae sat down and said, "I just came in to say good night. Can you reach the bell if you need anything?"

Amelia moved her good arm toward the bedside table to indicate that she could.

"Good," said Mae. "Dad just called from the hospital to say he'll be home soon. He said he hopes to find you asleep by the time he gets here. But can I get you anything? Do you need anything before I turn out the light?"

Amelia moved her head slightly to indicate that she needed nothing.

"I'm so glad you're home, Mom," Mae continued, smiling. "And you're going to be back to your old self in no time. You'll see. We're all going to help you. Peter's working on a chart right now, a massage and exercise chart, he says. We're all going to take turns massaging your muscles just like the doctor showed us, and when you get a little better we'll help you walk. Of course, we can't take the place of your physical therapist, but we can help. It'll be nice when you're well again, won't it, Mom?"

Her mother nodded happily. Her *joie de vivre*, the defining characteristic of her life, remained unaltered.

Many months later, Amelia was able to get out of bed. She learned to walk with the use of a cane. Her face relaxed and her tongued thawed so that she could speak again, though many of her words continued to be slurred. The movement in her left arm and hand was never fully restored, but she was thankful it wasn't her right side that was affected. She could still write letters to her best friend, Clara Reynolds. She could still sew and bake and turn the pages of a book.

All through the months of her recovery, Amelia insisted on Roy's coming to the house as usual. At first he was startled to see her — the fallen face, the curled hand, the foot that refused to move. He didn't know how to react, and he stuttered when he tried to talk, his face burning red. But Mae put him at ease by explaining to him that "Miss Wollencott" was the same on the inside as she had always been, even though she was a bit different on the outside. She was improving every day and with a little help from everyone, including regular visits from Roy, she was sure to be as good as new in no time.

Mae's optimistic estimate of "no time" stretched into two years, but the day came when Amelia was very nearly the person she had been before the stroke. With only traces of the paralysis left, she could walk and sing and run the household again, and she was enjoying her first two grandchildren — Peter's daughter and Jim's son.

With the help of Mae's friend Sally Ann, Amelia threw a surprise party for Mae on her twentieth birthday. On that day in late April the house was filled with young men and women who eyed each other furtively and dreamed of future possibilities. Mae's attention was turned to one young man in particular, George Demaray, an assistant manager at Donaldson's Golden Rule. Mae had been working as a salesgirl at Donaldson's since her high school graduation, having no desire to go on to college. What she wanted was marriage and motherhood, and she was fairly certain that in George Demaray she had found the man who would fulfill her dreams.

They were back in the peaceful stream of living. And that is why everyone was initially more shocked than grieved when Amelia suffered another stroke and died in the early autumn of 1950. Dr. Wollencott, Mae, her brothers, Roy — they couldn't believe that she had appeared fine one day and had collapsed the next. They were hit broadside with the numbness of surprise before the pain of grief broke through and settled in.

During the funeral service at the grave site, Roy stood hunched over as though in physical pain, shaking with sobs. Mae let go of George's hand, gave him a knowing look that told him Roy needed her, and took a step closer to her old friend. She put her arm around his shoulder, but Roy didn't lift his head to acknowledge her. Mae herself felt as though all the joy had fallen out of life, leaving only the bare framework of waking and working, eating and sleeping. Her happiness had never been quite complete until she shared it with her mother; the ache of sorrow had never been soothed until she had received her mother's comfort. Now everything would be left half done, everything would be incomplete because her mother would not be there to tidy up the endings.

When the casket was lowered into the ground and the mourners began to move away, Mae tried to comfort Roy as she remembered her mother comforting him when Will died. "Mom's in heaven now, Roy," she said. "She's in heaven with Willie. Remember she told you she'd see Will again? Now she has. Now they're together."

Roy blew his nose hard and wiped at his cheeks with the soiled handkerchief. His lower lip trembled as he spoke. "We'll see them there, Miss Mae? Up in heaven?"

It took all of Mae's strength to answer him. "Yes, Roy." She nodded her head and drew in a deep breath. "We'll see them there."

"And we'll all be together again, just like we always got together for dinner at your house?"

"Yes, I think so. Something like that."

Roy stuffed his handkerchief into his pants pocket and put on the too-small fedora that sat awkwardly atop his round head. "I'm glad for that, Miss Mae," he said. "Glad we'll be seeing Willie and Miss Wollencott up in heaven."

Mae took Roy's arm and followed her father and brothers and George out of the cemetery.

She considered how the childlike Roy believed in heaven without question, believed that they would all gather in this invisible place as easily as they had gathered around the dinner table in the house on Humboldt. She believed, too, but not without doubts, not without a struggle. She had seen the lifeless body of her mother. How could it be that Amelia Wollencott was alive somewhere in an eternal place, a place where Mae would one day be reunited with her? It all seemed so unreal, beautiful but farfetched, like the fairy tales she and her mother had read to each other when Mae was a child.

Yet, even so, it was a matter of choice, of faith, and she would choose to believe in this place she couldn't see. *"Hold fast to what's good,"* her mother had taught her. And, Mae considered, that meant even now, today. She would determine to hold fast to the faith that her mother had passed on to her. On that blue-sky afternoon as she left the cemetery and her mother behind, Mae could feel the unshaken core of it hanging in her heart — belief in God, belief in heaven, belief in hope.

With her mother's death, Mae thought she had seen the very worst that life could give, and she had survived. Nothing could possibly happen now that would take away from her all that she believed.

Chapter 8

On a warm Saturday in late June 1982, Mae and Ellen sat together on a slightly moth-eaten blanket by the shore of Lake of the Isles. The blanket was littered with empty soda cans, crumpled napkins, the remains of half-eaten sandwiches and partially nibbled fruit on paper plates, a plastic ice chest, and abandoned sweaters. A short distance away, Sam, Roy, and the girls tossed a Frisbee to each other. Roy was trying to show Amy how to toss it so it would catch the wind just right, but she couldn't get the hang of it. Instead of sailing horizontally, the Frisbee headed skyward vertically, then dropped straight down to the ground.

"Poor Amy," Ellen said, laughing. "I think she's a little young yet for Frisbee."

"You have to give her credit for trying," Mae commented. She began gathering up the trash on the blanket and stuffing it into a paper bag.

"Roy's so patient with her," Ellen said.

"Sam too," Mae pointed out. "You have a good man for a husband."

Ellen smiled contentedly and looked at her husband. "Yes, I do. I consider myself very fortunate. He's a loving husband and a good father to the girls."

Mae followed her daughter's gaze until her eyes rested on Sam, now tossing the Frisbee to Christy. He *was* a good man — like her George. Mae had always been glad that Ellen married Sam, that Ellen enjoyed as happy and stable a marriage as she had had with George. Sam was a good provider. He was a faithful husband and devoted father — endlessly doting over his girls.

Mae wondered, though, whether Sam hadn't wanted one of the girls to be a boy. When Christy was born, it had been a relief to Mae that the child was a girl. She had feared that the baby would grow to look like Sammy, and that she would be endlessly reminded of the one who had been lost. But the child was a girl, and Ellen and Sam were thrilled with their daughter. Christy was all they talked about, and they snapped more pictures than friends and even relatives cared to see. Sam started coming home from work early just to spend time with Christy, and even when she was an infant, he would strap her in a carrier on his back and take her out for what he called "father-daughter shindigs."

When Ellen became pregnant again, Mae hoped, and yet didn't hope, that the child would be a boy. For her own peace of mind, she wanted another girl. Ellen said she'd be equally happy with either one. But Mae thought Sam might want to complete their family with a boy. After all, men especially were eager to produce sons. A

151

son was someone who looked up to his father and tried to emulate him — all men craved that kind of admiration. With a son, a man had a child through whom his own dreams and goals could be perpetuated. The age-old pride with which so many men had added "and Sons" to the name of the family business still existed. Fathers and sons. Buddies. Pals. Someone to toss a ball to; someone to take to sporting events; someone to teach to be a man; someone to mold into one's own image. Men did seem to appreciate daughters, but Mae had always noticed that there was an extra tinge of pride in a man's voice when, in introducing his offspring, he said to someone, "And this is my son. . . ." At least that's how it had been with her own father.

But Sam had never voiced the desire for a son, nor did he say he preferred a girl, for that matter. Whenever anyone asked the expectant couple that ever expected question, "What do you want, a boy or a girl?" both Ellen and Sam answered with the standard expected response, "We don't care, as long as it's healthy."

When the child was born a girl, Mae harbored within herself a sense of gratitude, but she was also fearful that Ellen and Sam might be disappointed. She wondered whether this second child might be loved less because she couldn't take the place of Sammy.

Mae wanted to ask Ellen if she and Sam were disappointed, but she never dared. Over the years Mae could only observe, and she had to admit that she never so much as glimpsed a trace of disappointment. In fact, she had observed just the opposite. Ellen and Sam were proud of their daughters. As parents they were loving and patient without being indulgent. They were strict disciplinarians — meaning "no" when they said "no" and not allowing tears or tantrums to change their minds. They didn't hesitate to dole out punishment when it was called for. And they certainly doled out a lot of love. On the whole, the foursome appeared to be a happy and well-adjusted family, as loving and close-knit as any family Mae had ever known.

Still, early on, Mae had thought Sam and Ellen might have one more child in the hopes that it would be a boy. But just before Amy's second birthday, Ellen mentioned to Mae in passing that she and Sam were content with the size of their family and didn't intend to have more children.

"You're happy with just the two, then?" Mae asked.

"Of course," Ellen answered. "Weren't you happy with your two?"

"Well, yes, of course. Very happy." But that had been different. There had never been one that was lost.

Mae was thankful that her daughter seemed happy, that Ellen and Sam had a fine family and a loving home. But sometimes, as now, when she watched Sam with his girls, she couldn't help feeling remorse for what he would never have.

"Uh-oh," Ellen said, her head turned away from Mae as she peered out over the lake. "It looks like Sam's tossed the Frisbee into the lake." Sam was standing on the water's edge, reaching for the floating disk with a long stick.

"Keep an eye on the girls," Mae warned. "Don't let them get near the water." Then to the girls who were galloping after their father, she yelled, "Christy, Amy, stay away from the edge of the lake! Get back from there." She waved an arm to motion the girls back toward the blanket. The girls looked at their grandmother and hesitated a moment before taking a few disobedient steps toward their father.

"Don't you worry, Miss Mae," Roy hollered as he trotted up behind the girls and grabbed each one by the hand. "I got ahold of them. They'll be safe with me."

"Bring them away from the edge of the water, will you, Roy?" Mae instructed. "Why don't you all come back and have something more to drink? It's time to take a little rest anyway."

"Aw, Grammy," Christy protested as she let Roy lead her away from the water. "We don't want to rest. We want to keep throwing the Frisbee. Can't we, Mom? Can't we keep on playing with the Frisbee?"

"It's all right with me," Ellen said, "as long as your father can get it out of the lake."

Just then Sam tossed the stick aside and made a final grab at the Frisbee, getting his Nikes wet but coming away triumphant. He shook the water off the plastic disk and held it up. "All right, whose turn is it?" he hollered, running back toward the girls to start up the game again.

"Throw it to the Cigar Man, Daddy," Amy said, jumping up and down and trampling the grass with her blue tennis shoes. Her father complied and threw the Frisbee to Roy, who in turn sent it sailing to Christy.

After giving the players an encouraging cheer, Ellen turned to her mother and said gently, "You don't need to worry so much about the girls, Mother. They've both had swimming lessons and have done very well. In fact, they're both regular fish in the water. They're not afraid of it."

"Be that as it may," Mae said, "you can't be too careful."

Ellen pulled the tab off a can of soda, but instead of drinking, she chewed at her lip in annoyance. Even though it was never mentioned, it was always there. The accident. The uninvited guest at every event of their lives. It was there because her mother dragged it along with her wherever she went, refusing to give it up. After so many years, Ellen had begun to abandon the idea that she and her mother would ever again have the relationship they once had. Assurances of forgiveness on Ellen's part, offered again and again, went unaccepted. But Ellen still believed that her mother could find some semblance of normalcy, maybe even a certain measure of happiness, if only she would get away from the scene of Sammy's death. That was the one hope Ellen had left for her mother.

Before Sophie Mills moved to Florida, Ellen had spoken with her about encouraging her mother to sell the house and move along with her. Sophie agreed that what she needed was a change of scenery, a more active social life, a new set of friends.

"Oh, but I don't know, dear," Sophie had said. "I love your mother, and once, I considered her among my best friends, but I've scarcely seen her since — well, you know." She looked hesitantly at Ellen, who only nodded. Sophie continued. "Not that I didn't try to keep our friendship going, of course. Why, as soon as I heard of the accident, the first thing I did was rush right over and take Mae in my arms, but she was stiff as a board. Wouldn't even cry. It was as though she had become completely empty, like a shell or a robot or something. I thought she would eventually get back to being Mae, but she never did. I kept calling her and inviting her to get together, but she'd never call me. And when I *was* with her, well, I got the feeling that she didn't want me around. And that hurt, you know? It soon became depressing. After being with Mae I'd go home and think, 'Well, Sophie, you were in a perfectly good mood before you saw Mae, and now you're more surly than a constipated spinster' — pardon the expression, dear. But, Ellen, I finally just gave up. Since that's how it is between us, I can't imagine my just coming out of the blue and asking her to move to Florida with me. No, I think she would find it awfully strange if I did."

"Yes, I guess you've got a point," Ellen agreed.

Nonetheless, the two women decided that Mae wouldn't think it strange for an old friend to want to correspond, so Sophie gladly agreed to send an occasional letter up from the land of the sun, extolling its virtues. Maybe the letters would tempt Mae to take advantage of such a retirement haven herself.

But so far, Mae hadn't been tempted.

"Mother," Ellen said, taking a sip of the soda and stretching her legs out on the blanket. "Sam and I have been thinking about Christmas."

Mae let go a brief laugh. "Christmas! Here it is only June. It seems like just last week that we vacuumed up all those pine needles on your living room rug."

"Seems a little early, I know," Ellen agreed, "but this year we want to take a trip during the holidays."

"A trip? To where?"

"The girls have been talking about Disney World ever since our neighbors went with their kids last year. At first Sam and I blew off the idea — too much money and all that. But lately we've been thinking it would be a lot of fun and a great place to take the girls on their first trip. Sam says he thinks we can swing it financially, especially if we start now to put some money aside."

"Sounds like a wonderful idea, darling. I think the girls would love it. Disney World — now, is that the one in California or Florida?"

"Florida," Ellen replied. "Orlando. Just imagine — I bet the girls will get a kick out of seventy-degree temperatures in December."

"No doubt about that. Well, if you're wondering what I think, I say you should go. Splurge a little — why not? You and Sam deserve it, and it'll be something special for the girls. No doubt I'll be hearing about it for months afterward."

"Well, actually, that's what I wanted to talk with you about."

"What's that?"

"We'd like for you to come with us."

"Me?" Mae asked in surprise. She waved one hand in the air. "Oh, heavens, I'm too old for that type of thing. I'd just slow you down and ruin the fun. No, you young people go on and have a good time. If you're worried about leaving me to spend Christmas alone, you needn't be. Roy and I can always have a little celebration together."

"I'm sure the two of you would be perfectly happy together, but we'd really like to have you come along with us," Ellen insisted.

Mae looked sideways at her daughter and knit her brows. " 'We' as in you and Sam, or just you?"

"Of course Sam too, Mother. And — well, we were talking about keeping it a surprise, but I've already spoken with Mike, and he says he'd love to meet us there and spend a few days in Orlando with us."

"Really?" Mae's face lit up with joy at the thought. "You mean, he's willing to fly out from California?"

"Of course. It's been — what? — a year or more since we've seen him? He says a little family reunion might be fun."

Mae shook her head in disbelief. "Well, in that case, of course I'll want to go. Now why on earth would you want to keep that a secret?"

Ellen shrugged. "I don't know, Mother. It was Mike's idea. I guess he wanted to see the look of surprise on your face when he showed up in the hotel lobby."

"Look of surprise?" Mae echoed. "I suppose I would have fainted dead away!" She shook her head thoughtfully. "Funny how different the two of you are. Mike the Maverick, your father used to call him. Always so independent, going his own way, seemingly never attached to anyone — not even his own mother!"

"Oh, he loves you, Mother. Mike's just not very good at expressing those types of things. But he's quite excited about the trip, really."

"Well, a family reunion would be wonderful. But what about Roy? I hate to leave him here to spend Christmas alone."

"Why should we leave him here?" Ellen said. "He can come along too."

"Oh, now, you know we can't do that," Mae protested. "Just who is going to pay his way?

Certainly Roy can't afford such a trip."

"Between you and me and Sam, we ought to be able to scrounge up enough cash to cover Roy. We'll only ask that he pay for his own cigars."

Mae chuckled at Ellen's comment. "You know," she said, "he told me just the other day he's never been out of Minnesota. It would be quite an adventure for him, wouldn't it — going all the way to Florida. He's never seen the ocean — he's never even seen so much as a real palm tree before."

"There you have it then, Mother," Ellen said. "How can you possibly deny Roy the chance to see a real live palm tree?"

"All right, but before we say anything to him, let's do some figuring and make sure we can afford to take him. We'd be looking at a plane ticket, a hotel room, meals for a week. Anything else?"

"A rental car."

"Oh yes, I'd guess we'd need a car to get back and forth from the hotel to Disney World."

"It'd be helpful, I think! But also, we'd like to take a little side trip while we're there."

"Oh? Where were you thinking of going?"

Ellen stalled by taking a long sip of her soda. Finally she said, "St. Petersburg." When her announcement was met with silence, she added, "It'll give you a chance to see the city."

Mae turned her face fully toward her daughter and said not unkindly but rather with amusement, "You never give up, do you?"

The slightest hint of a smile crossed Ellen's face. "Sometimes I can be as stubborn as you, Mother."

Mae looked away and began to twist the wedding band that she'd continued to wear since George's death. After a moment, she said, "I ought to be angry with you."

Ellen swatted at a gnat that hovered annoyingly close to her face. "Well," she said, "are you?"

Mae's shoulders sagged. She stopped twisting the ring and clasped her hands together. "No, not angry. I appreciate what you're trying to do. But taking a trip to St. Petersburg is just plain foolish."

"Why?"

"Because I have no intention of moving. If I want Florida, I can stick a couple of plastic flamingos in the front yard and turn up the heat to seventy-five," she said with a laugh. "No need to transplant myself hundreds of miles away. I've lived my whole life in the house on Humboldt, and I plan to die there as well."

"Oh, Mother, there's no harm in just going to see the place."

"But I just explained, Ellen — there's no reason to."

"If you don't like it, no one's going to force you to move. But you can at least see Sophie, meet her friends, give the place a chance, for heaven's sake."

"Do you have any idea how far St. Petersburg is from Orlando?"

"Oh, it's not far at all. Just a little more than a hundred miles, I guess." Ellen and Sam had already calculated the distance on a map.

"Still, that seems like a long way to go just to see a place no one really wants to see."

"Oh, Mother," Ellen said again. She tried to stifle the irritation that was rising in her. "It could be a fun trip, even if you decide you don't like St. Petersburg and never want to return to Florida again."

Mae was pensive a moment before asking, "Is Mike in on this little scheme?"

"No one's scheming anything, Mother. I spoke with Mike about the possibility of your moving to Florida when I called him, but I don't think he has much of an opinion one way or the other. Except, of course, he doesn't think anyone in their right mind would choose to live in Minnesota when there are warm places in the world like southern California and the Gulf Coast."

Mae let go a little chuckle that sounded like a sniff. "Well," she said, "maybe if I lived in Florida, Mike would be more inclined to visit his mother once in a while."

The two women sat without speaking for a time, letting their eyes follow the people who moved along the walking path and listening absently to the babble of voices, the honking of geese, the occasional snatches of music from a passing car radio that blended together into the one simple sound of summer.

"Mother?" Ellen said.

"Yes," Mae answered without turning toward her daughter.

"If you lived in Florida, you might also be visited by a few gentleman callers," Ellen said. "I'd like that for you."

"Nonsense," Mae said abruptly, but it was followed by a brief laugh. "I'm no Sophie Mills."

"No," Ellen agreed. "You're far more attractive than Sophie, and you deserve to be just as happy as she is."

Mae said nothing but patted her daughter's hand spread out against the blanket. In a moment the Frisbee players returned, sweaters were claimed, the blanket was shaken out, and the little group headed home.

Chapter 9

There had once been a time — two or more years after George's death — when Mae thought she might like to marry again. George would never be completely out of her heart, but she was lonely and still young, and she wanted to share her life with a companion. She hoped to know again the kind of joy she had had with George.

When Mae married George Demaray in 1952, Dr. Wollencott gave them the house on Humboldt as a wedding gift. George had enthusiastically pumped the doctor's hand and said, "Thanks, Doc — er, Dad. It's a great gift, really great. We'll be proud to make this house our home and raise our children here." Then George added, "We'll want you to go on living here, of course, just the same as always."

Dr. Wollencott had never had any intention of leaving the house, and so the three of them took up their life together.

As far as Mae was concerned, it was the happiest of lives. Not only were George and she husband and wife, they were best friends. They talked about everything, sharing their joy, unburdening their sadness. They liked no one's company better than each other's. George often came home with roses or with small gifts he had picked up at the store — jewelry, scarves, perfumes. Mae baked his favorite desserts, wrote an occasional poem for him, and even found great satisfaction in keeping his shirts and handkerchiefs clean. Like every couple they had their disagreements, but their arguments were generally brief explosions that were quickly subdued with apologies and kisses.

After the children were born, George helped Mae as much as he could, warming bottles and even washing diapers, which endeared him to Mae all the more. She delighted in being a mother and often marveled at the little lives she and George had created together. *Imagine it,* she thought, *a little part of George and a little part of me all wrapped up in this lovely little person.* When Ellen and Mike became older and could walk and talk, the real joys of motherhood began for Mae. Now she could begin to teach her children how to live lives filled with beauty and wonder.

She walked with them to the lake and showed them the tulips and daffodils in bloom. She told them to listen to the whistling of the ducks' wings and watched them respond with childish amazement. She read to them and listened with pride to their own first attempts at reading. She baked sweets with them, sang with them, made snowmen on the front lawn with them. She answered their questions and calmed their fears and cradled them in her lap just as her own mother had done with her.

And like her mother, Mae knelt with them each in turn and cupped her hands around their folded fingers every night and recited the Lord's Prayer. She smiled at their mistakes: "Hello Ed be thy name," and "Forgive us our debts as we forgive our debbies." She wondered whether they saw the words scrolled in their minds as she had when she was a child, and more important, whether they felt as secure and unafraid as she had when crawling between the covers after the "Amen" was said.

Mae worried about her children, but not excessively. She laid down the rules about where they could play and with whom and for how long, and whenever they were out of her sight she said an extra prayer for their protection. But otherwise she was relaxed in her role as guardian, believing that if she were careful and watchful, her children would be fine.

The year Mike started first grade and Ellen entered third, Mae was left with a number of empty hours on her hands. Some of her more liberated friends encouraged her to take college courses or to get a part-time job. "It's time for us women to get out of the house and start making a mark in the world," one of them said. "We're more than just cleaning ladies and baby-sitters, though heaven knows my own husband doesn't think so. I had to threaten divorce before he'd let me take classes in interior decorating. 'I have talent and a brain,' I told him, 'and I intend to use both whether you like it or not.' "

But Mae couldn't understand her friends' enthusiasm for career chasing. During the four years she had worked as a salesgirl for Donaldson's, she'd had more than enough of time clocks and disgruntled customers. She was content to leave wage earning to men. Let the men go out and run businesses and build bridges and construct skyscrapers. These things were necessary, of course, but Mae — though she never voiced her opinion to anyone — believed the most important role in the world was that of wife and mother. What task could be more valuable than creating and maintaining a secure home? What job more significant than that of influencing the next generation to be responsible adults and valuable citizens?

Even with the children in school and extra time on her hands, she still had no desire for either a formal education or for a job in what she considered a far-too-competitive world. But she did want to be doing something, helping others in some tangible way. She was a caregiver. She had always been the type to lend a hand somewhere, going all the way back to the war when she rolled bandages for the Red Cross and visited wounded soldiers in the hospital.

When she read an article in the local newspaper about the children's hospital, Mae knew what she wanted to do.

"Do you suppose, George," she asked, "that

they need volunteers at the children's hospital?"

"Well, I can't say for sure, but I would imagine so," George answered. He sat beside her on the couch reading the sports section. "All hospitals use volunteers for one thing or another, don't they?"

Mae sat quietly for a moment. Then she folded up the paper and asked, "How would you feel if I offered to help out there? Just a few hours a week, of course. But, you know, now that the children are in school, I'm a little more free to get involved in things outside the home."

George didn't even have to think about it. "It sounds like a splendid idea," he said. "I'm sure they'd be thrilled to have someone like you around."

Mae smiled placidly at her husband. "Someone like me? You always think too highly of me, George."

"Not at all," George replied. "I simply believe in calling a spade a spade. You're the closest thing to a saint that I know."

"Pshaw!" Mae said, laughing. "It seems to me you might be a bit biased in your opinion, dear, but nevertheless, I thank you for the compliment. It's nice to know my husband admires me."

"Always have and always will," George replied, planting a kiss on his young wife's forehead.

"Well, I think I'll see whether there's anything to be done at the children's hospital, then."

George nodded and went back to the list of

scores he'd been wading through. After a moment, he looked up suddenly and frowned. "Of course," he said cautiously, "you know it might be — well, somewhat difficult."

Mae cocked her head. "What do you mean?"

"You have such a soft heart, Mae, especially where children are concerned. I don't want to dampen your enthusiasm, but you're going to go in there and see children who are sick and hurt and maybe even dying —"

"I know, but —"

"And you're not going to be able to do anything about it. What I mean is, you won't be able to make them well or take away their pain."

Mae thought for a moment. "I know you're right, George, but maybe I'll be able to give them a little bit of comfort or joy — or maybe even a few minutes of laughter."

George studied his wife's face, serene but determined. Finally he replied, "If anyone can, you can, dearest. If you want to do this, I'm behind you one hundred percent. Just don't let your heart be broken."

In spite of George's gentle warning, Mae's heart was broken time and again as she entered the hospital and held the little patients in her arms, their frail bodies wracked with illness. But from her broken heart flowed a special compassion that washed over the children like a balm. She sang to them, told them stories, whispered words of assurance, and prayed over them as they fell asleep in her lap. She became Mother

Mae to hundreds of children over the many years that she visited the hospital.

"Mother Mae, sing me a song."

"Mother Mae, read me a story."

"Mother Mae, let's draw a picture together."

"They always look forward to your coming," the head nurse once confided to Mae. "They always feel safe with you."

Throughout all the years of Mae's marriage, Roy Hanna remained a permanent fixture in her life. George had asked Mae early on exactly who Roy was and why he seemed always to be around. "Is he part of the family or what?"

"Sort of, but not exactly," Mae answered.

George looked at her quizzically. "I don't get it. Fill me in."

"Well, he's an old family friend who has just always kind of been there," she explained vaguely. "I realize you didn't know my mother very well, but you only had to meet her once to know what a kindhearted person she was."

George nodded in agreement. He had become acquainted with Amelia only a short time before her death. But even in those few months, he'd been impressed by her warmth and her unselfish concern for everyone around her.

Mae continued. "I don't know exactly how Mother found Roy — I never bothered to ask — but at some point she must have gotten it into her head that she wanted to do something special for a child who was not so privileged as her own children. I suspect she just went to the orphanage one day and asked whether there was a child our family could befriend. I'm sure the people at the orphanage suspected that Roy would never be adopted and could use just such a family. Mother must have done it before I was born. Roy's been around as long as I can remember. I wasn't always sure I liked him very much." Mae paused to laugh, remembering some of her childhood run-ins with Roy. "He often annoyed me when we were children, but he's very dear to me now. He never was adopted, you know. He's always been alone, first in the orphanage, and ever since he was old enough to be on his own, he's lived in boardinghouses. Not much of a life for most people, though I think Roy's happy in his own way." Mae looked at George, suddenly worried. "You don't mind, do you, George, that he often comes to the house? Does he bother you?"

George looked at Mae with raised eyebrows and a smile. "Of course not, darling!" he said. "He seems like a nice enough fellow. I think it's good of you to be his friend. Not everyone would want to be."

And so just as he had for years, Roy continued to show up once or twice a week at the Humboldt house, now at Mae's invitation rather than her mother's. In time — as Ellen and Mike grew older, as George got to know him better, and after Dr. Wollencott retired and needed a companion — everyone in the household looked forward to Roy's visits.

The children were especially fond of their Uncle Roy and greeted him rambunctiously whenever he visited. They knew Roy had plenty of time for them and wouldn't tell them to run off and play as other adults sometimes did. Roy always tried to join them in whatever they were doing. He wasn't good at cards or board games, and whenever the children got a new book, they had to read the story to Roy rather than the other way around. But Mike said Uncle Roy threw a mean baseball and knew how to build the best and speediest go-carts, and Ellen successfully lassoed her Uncle Roy into playing dolls when her own playmates weren't around. "Daddy and Grandpa won't play dolls with me," Ellen told her mother. "They say men don't play with dolls, but Roy does, and he's real good at it too. Our dolls have such wonderful adventures!"

When Dr. Wollencott finally retired after suffering a heart attack, he began to enjoy for the first time in his life a genuine friendship with Roy. Sometimes the two men took walks together — slow, short walks — so the doctor could get exercise. More than once Dr. Wollencott came home leaning on Roy's arm. Other times, when they were relaxing after dinner, the doctor would point to a newspaper article and engage in a long — and to Roy, incomprehensible — monologue about one current event or another. Caught up in the heat of his own tirades and forgetful of his companion's intellectual shortcomings, Dr. Wollencott invariably ended with, "Don't you think so, Roy? Don't you agree?"

And Roy, dumbfounded but devoted, would utter, "Yes, sir, Dr. Wollencott, if that's what you think, then I agree."

After George bought the family's first television set in 1957, Dr. Wollencott and Roy spent hours together staring at the screen. *The Ed Sullivan Show*, *I Love Lucy*, *Dragnet*, *Perry Mason*, even *The Howdy Doody Show* — they loved them all. Roy never ceased to be amazed by what he called "the contraption," though he gradually understood that the people they saw on that little box were either on film or in a studio somewhere. They were not little people living within the confines of the box itself.

George, too, came to think of Roy as a friend. He invited Roy on summer evenings to sit on the front porch with him and to talk about their interests, their experiences, their work. George always listened intently while Roy talked about disinfectants, floor scrubbers, and paper shredders. And then George in turn spoke simply about his own work down at the store — the new merchandise, the employees, holiday sales. After a while Mae invariably appeared at the screen door and scolded the men for smoking too much while they passed the time together. But George argued, "Got to, dear. It keeps the mosquitoes away. Isn't that right, Roy?"

And Roy, swatting at the air to add emphasis

to the argument, said, "That's right, George. Or else we just might be eaten alive."

Roy was also somewhat of a helper for George, who detested yard work and chores like cleaning out the garage. Together they shoveled snow, trimmed the hedges, chopped wood, painted the garage, changed the oil in the car. But, at George's initiative, they interrupted their work with long breaks and story-swapping sessions. In the autumn Mae sometimes found her husband and her old friend out in the yard on a Saturday afternoon, leaning on their rakes and enjoying a smoke together — George with his pack of cigarettes and Roy puffing away on his ever present cigar.

"Why don't you boys make yourselves comfortable on the porch," Mae chided, "and we can just hope that the wind blows the leaves into neat piles on the lawn."

Roy's friendship with Dr. Wollencott and George Demaray was the first genuine male camaraderie that Roy had. He outlived both men by many years, and when they died, he took it hard. Dr. Wollencott suffered a slow death from heart disease and finally passed away one night in his sleep. Some years later George slumped over in the porch swing on a warm spring afternoon and never got up again, the victim of a heart attack.

At first one funeral and then the other, Roy, in the midst of choking sobs, asked of Mae the question that she had come to anticipate. "We'll see him in heaven, right, Miss Mae? We'll see him up there in heaven when we get there?"

And Mae, in spite of her deep grief — especially at the loss of her beloved George — answered patiently, "Yes, Roy. In heaven."

"Because Miss Wollencott told me that anyone who believes in Jesus goes to live with Him up there when they die, so every one of them — Willie and Miss Wollencott and the doctor and George — they're all up there with Jesus now."

Mae sighed over the ever lengthening list but only replied quietly, "Yes, Roy. They're all with Jesus now."

When George died, Mae considered the months and years and perhaps even decades yawning before her, and it all appeared as empty as a long stretch of beach at low tide. But she was familiar with grief by now, with the initial weight of it as well as with the eventual lifting of that weight with time. People were created with an amazing ability to heal, just as her mother had been known to say. Pain lessens, hearts mend, and though at times scars remain, still the open wound closes over with new flesh. Mae would recover from George's death too; she knew that. She just had to give herself time to allow the unexplainable process of healing to take place.

The months were a journey out of darkness, and when Mae had moved from black to gray, when the unbearable grief had lessened to a more manageable pain, Mae began to think of remarriage. It was still a far-off possibility, and she was considering no one in particular, but the thought was there. She would let two, maybe three years go by, and then she would consider spending time with a few of the single men at church who had already sought out her company.

But then, before she became fully adjusted to widowhood, the unthinkable happened. She left the basement door open, and her grandson was killed when he fell down the stairs.

On the way to Sammy's funeral, Roy had tried to comfort Mae with his story about the peppermint-stick ice cream. Sammy was up there in heaven, he'd said, eating peppermint-stick ice cream with Miss Wollencott and the doctor and George and Willie.

Mae listened to the story, but she wasn't comforted. She did not want to be. Not this time. Death had come repeatedly and taken those she loved, but this time was different. She hadn't started the war that had claimed her brother Willie's life. She hadn't caused the stroke that had killed her mother, nor had she been responsible for the weak heart that had stopped beating in her father's chest. And she certainly hadn't brought about the heart attack that had stolen George away from her. She wasn't guilty when it came to these, and so, even in her grief, she was able to cling to a certain hope that her heart would mend. But not this time. Her own carelessness had led to the death of a child, and this time Mae Demaray believed it was her just punishment to remain broken and excluded from the normal circle of loving.

Chapter 10

On the Tuesday morning following the picnic at Lake of the Isles, Mae awoke to find her emotions riding a seesaw. The wooden plank eased upward as she thought of telling Roy about the trip to Florida. Her mind drifted back to the night before, to the hand-clapping, toe-bouncing, squealing excitement of her granddaughters when they were told they'd be going to Disney World with Grandma and the Cigar Man, and that Uncle Mike would be meeting them there. Mae knew that Roy would be equally excited when he learned about the trip, and she looked forward to his delight.

And yet the seesaw plummeted and hit the ground with a thud as she considered the task she and Roy had to do that morning. The previous evening had ended on a withering note when her daughter asked a favor of her. The two women were sitting at Ellen's kitchen table drinking herbal tea and talking about the trip when Ellen abruptly changed the subject.

"Oh, listen, before I forget, Mother, our church is planning a flea market." Ellen had grown up in her parents' church but had switched to her husband's church — one of the oldest in the city — at the time of her marriage. Now the pastor and staff of the aging house of worship were trying to raise money to renovate the sanctuary and paint the Sunday school rooms. "We need items to sell," Ellen explained. "Everyone's being asked to donate things to raise money. I've gathered a few items together, but I was wondering whether you might go through your basement and see what's down there that we could have."

"Well, what kind of things are you looking for?" Mae asked tentatively.

"Odds and ends. Anything, really. I know from all my childhood explorations that you have a basement full of junk that could be cleaned up and sold," Ellen said, smiling. "Seems I remember seeing a bunch of kitchen utensils down there and furniture and toys and whatnot. And I *know* you've got about a hundred copies of *National Geographic* stashed away from decades ago. I used to read them by the hour when I was a kid."

"Nobody's going to buy my old junk," Mae protested.

"You'd be surprised what people buy. Like you always used to say, 'One man's trash is another man's treasure.' Whatever we don't sell we plan to donate to the Goodwill, so you won't have to take it back again. It'll give you the chance to clean out the basement and help the church at the same time."

Mae didn't know how to answer her daughter. Didn't Ellen remember . . . didn't Ellen know how Mae felt about the basement . . . how could she just ask her mother to . . .

Mae shook her head. "Darling, I couldn't. . . ." Her voice trailed off as her gaze shifted to a place beyond the present.

"Couldn't what, Mother?"

She had not been down the basement steps — had not even opened the basement door — for more than five years. The only people who had been down there in all that time were the two men who delivered and installed the new water heater a couple of years ago. Even then, Mae had merely pointed them in the direction of the basement, then had waited nervously in the kitchen until the job was done.

Avoiding Ellen's question, Mae said, "I really don't think I have anything worth selling."

"Well, you won't know until you look. Please, Mother, these building renovations are expensive, and the church needs all the help it can get. Ask Roy to give you a hand — he's always eager to help. Just pick out a few items, that's all we need."

Mae felt flustered, and the words she wanted to say stuck in her throat. How could Ellen ask such a favor, putting her in such a position? She sensed a certain resentment swirling in her chest. "Ellen, surely you know how I feel. . . ." But again her voice tapered off into silence.

"About the basement, Mother?" Ellen asked. Mae nodded.

Ellen continued. "I know, but if you move to Florida, you'll have to clean it out anyway. You might as well get a head start."

"I won't be moving to Florida," Mae answered stiffly.

"We don't know that. Why don't you wait until after the trip to decide whether or not you'll be moving?"

Mae pursed her lips. She was suddenly feeling manipulated by her daughter and didn't like it. "I'm willing to write a check to the church to help with renovations, but I won't go down into that basement," she stated firmly.

Ellen got up from the table and walked across the kitchen to the stove. Picking up the kettle of tea, she asked, "Another cup, Mother?"

Mae shook her head and held her hand over the teacup in front of her. "Thank you, no, dear. I've had plenty."

Ellen poured herself another cup, then sat down again. "If you feel that strongly about it," she said quietly, "I'll come over and look through the basement myself. Of course I won't make you go down there."

Mae frowned while she studied the backs of her hands. She knew she was being irrational — refusing to go into her own basement, refusing to give away her old junk to a church flea market. Her mind stumbled about, seeking a solution, settling finally on Roy as Ellen had suggested.

She sighed resignedly and said, "Never mind. I will ask Roy to help. In fact, I can have him haul the stuff up to the guest room, and I can sort through it there. I'm sure there must be something among all that junk you can use for the flea market."

By half past eight on that Tuesday morning, Mae was on her third cup of coffee while she waited for Roy to arrive. She had just glanced at her watch for the umpteenth time when the phone rang. She answered it to find Ellen on the other end, talking hurriedly.

"Mother, I've just been called in to work. We've got a pressing deadline and the full-time designer is sick," she explained. "The girls are going to day care, but I'm still left with a problem."

"Anything I can do to help?" Mae asked.

"Yes, if you don't mind doing some baking. I've got a meeting tonight with some other volunteers at the hospice center, and I'm supposed to be bringing refreshments. You know how impossible it is for people to discuss things without taking in calories at the same time." Ellen laughed, then continued. "I was going to bake some banana bread this morning, but now I'm not going to be able to get to it. Would you mind, Mother?"

"Of course not. You need just the one loaf?"

"That should be plenty. Thanks, you're a lifesaver. I'll stop by around six to pick it up."

After hanging up, Mae began to search the

kitchen cupboards. No nutmeats, and not enough baking powder either. Nor did she have any bananas. She'd have to run out to the grocery store, but she decided it was just as well. While she was out she could run a few errands she'd been putting off — she could go to the drugstore for a couple of items, stop by the gas station and have the attendant check the air in the Buick's tires, then go to the bank to deposit some money into her savings account before going on to the grocery store. If she timed it right, she could spend the morning away from the house, return for lunch with Roy, then bake the bread in the early afternoon.

As she sat down to scribble out a grocery list, Roy's voice reached her from the front hall. "Miss Mae? Got my boots on. Can I come in?"

"I'm in the kitchen, Roy," she hollered back. "Yes, come in. Don't mind the boots." The house was bound to get dirty anyway with Roy bringing all the dust of the basement up to the first floor.

Mae heard Roy's quiet footsteps along the hardwood floor in the hall. He always tried to walk lightly in the house because he thought that would cause less dirt to fall off of his shoes.

He appeared in the kitchen doorway wearing a blue cotton shirt with a pack of cigars in the pocket, faded jeans that were nearly worn through at the knees, and a pair of heavy, steel-toed working boots. On the top of his round head sat an ill-fitting baseball cap bearing the emblem of the Minnesota Twins. Roy removed the cap when he saw Mae. The hair beneath was matted with sweat and twisted into disheveled layers. His skin was tanned from the hours he spent working in the yard, and the two large hands holding the cap were rough and callused. Beneath his fingernails was wedged the crusted remnants of oil and grease from the cars of the other boardinghouse tenants. They were always calling on him to do small maintenance jobs so they could save a few dollars. Mae thought that with a couple of tattoos on his forearms, Roy would resemble the stereotypical rough and worldly truck driver who hauled a rig from coast to coast for a living. At a glance, Roy sometimes didn't look like the gentle, ingenuous man that he was.

"Sure feels good in here, Miss Mae," he said. "It's already hot outside. It's supposed to get up past ninety today, and we might be setting a record for the twenty-ninth of June. That's what they said on the radio." Roy had bought a radio in 1963 and had been so proud of it he'd never exchanged it for a newer model.

"Yes, I know. I shut the windows and turned on the air conditioning an hour ago. No use waiting till the house is sweltering," Mae said.

"That was a good idea," Roy agreed with a nod. "Had my fan going in my room this morning. Seems like just yesterday the floor was like ice when I got up in the morning. You know how Miss Pease is real stingy with the heat and won't let us use any space heaters in our rooms."

"I remember you mentioning that last winter. I don't know why you never took my advice about sleeping with socks on."

"Well, Miss Mae, like I said, I figure the sheets stay cleaner longer if you don't rub your dirty socks all over them while you sleep."

"Well, Roy, you know you can put on clean socks when . . . well, never mind about that now. We've both got a lot to do today so we might as well get started."

"Noticed your grass when I was coming up the walk, and it looks like it could use a trim. Wore my hat, just in case, to keep the sun out of my eyes. It's a good hat but a little snug, and look" — Roy pointed to the plastic adjustable strap on the back — "I got it on the last notch too. There's not much that fits this old head of mine. You'd think a head this size would be able to hold a whole lot in it, but it seems most of the things I learn just keep falling out. But anyway, I filled up the lawn mower with gas last time I used it so it's all ready to go, if that's what you want me to do."

Mae shook her head. She had continued to work on her grocery list while listening to Roy. "No, we'll worry about the yard later," she said. "I don't think it looks too bad for now. There's something else we need to do today."

She explained to Roy the task of hauling things up from the basement to the guest room. "While you begin doing that, I've got to run out to the grocery store. I'm going to make some banana bread for Ellen this afternoon and I don't seem to have half the things I need. While I'm at the store, I figure I might as well do a little shopping for myself. Is there anything in particular you'd like me to pick up for lunch?" Roy looked pensive a moment, as though mentally walking through the aisles of food at the store. Mae continued. "I was thinking that a chilled seafood salad from the deli might be good on a day like this. Does that sound all right to you?"

Roy looked delighted. "That'd be mighty good. Makes my mouth water just to think about seafood."

"Fine. Then seafood salad it'll be. I've got a couple of other errands to run also, but I'll try not to be gone too long. The coffee's still hot. Help yourself if you want some. Oh, and there's fresh lemonade in the fridge. You might want that instead on a warm day like this."

Mae, trailed by Roy, walked to the hall closet to get her purse. When she opened the closet door, she saw the light bulbs that she kept stored on the shelf. "That reminds me," she said. "I haven't been down in the basement in ages." She glanced sideways at Roy, hoping he wouldn't calculate just how long it had been or just when the last time was that she had hurried down those stairs. "I suspect the light bulbs are long dead. If that's the case, use the flashlight going down — you know where it is, on top of the refrigerator — and take a couple of these bulbs down with you. One light is right at the bottom of the stairs, and there's another toward the center of the room. Now be careful, please, going down in the dark. Those stairs are steep."

"Sure thing, Miss Mae," Roy said. "You don't have to worry about me."

Mae dug around in her purse and pulled out her car keys. "Like I said, I'll try not to be gone too long. Is there anything you need before I go?"

"Naw, you go on. I'm all set," Roy said confidently. "I'll have a bunch of stuff for you up in the guest room by the time you get back. We'll have that old basement cleaned out in no time."

Mae headed toward the kitchen again. She had her hand on the knob of the back door when she stopped a moment. "Oh, and Roy?"

"Yes, Miss Mae?"

"There's a rocking horse in the basement. Leave it there. I don't want you bringing it up to the guest room."

Roy shrugged slightly and reached into his shirt pocket for a cigar. "Sure, Miss Mae. I won't touch the rocking horse."

Mae walked out the back door, glad to be escaping the house while Roy began the task of clearing the basement.

Roy watched Mae walk across the backyard. A moment later the familiar white Buick backed out of the garage, stopped briefly while Mae pushed the remote to lower the door, then disappeared down the alley. Roy turned then and walked quietly toward the basement. When he opened the door it squeaked loudly on its hinges. Roy took the unlit cigar from between his lips and let out a soft whistle. "That's one noisy door," he said aloud. "Better remember to put some oil on those hinges."

He flicked on the light switch. As Mae had predicted, nothing happened. "Yup. Burnt out," Roy said. He reached into his shirt pocket again and fished out a pack of matches. He stood a moment at the threshold of the basement and lighted his cigar, taking puffs that made him look like a guppy grabbing at fish food in an aquarium.

"Better find that flashlight." He found it on top of the refrigerator where Mae said it would be. He then returned to the hall closet and grabbed a pack of bulbs. "Sixties ought to do just fine," he told himself. Back at the basement doorway he turned on the flashlight and shined it down the staircase. He'd been down those stairs many times in his life, most often as a child, eager to explore all the treasures hidden under the house. Later he had stacked firewood down there with George, and then there was that time when he and George had helped install the new furnace sometime back in the early seventies. What a job that had been. But he hadn't recalled that the stairs were so steep. It must have been years since Miss Mae asked him to carry something down to the basement.

Then he remembered. The accident. Little Sammy. Miss Mae said no one was ever to go down those basement steps again. She had asked Roy to put a padlock on the door, but Roy had pointed out that if the key were lost, it'd be hard to get into the basement if something happened to the furnace or the water heater. Mae relented and the door remained closed but not locked.

Roy's lower lip stuck out as he surveyed the stairs, remembering. "Poor Miss Mae," he mumbled. "I feel real sorry for her. She didn't mean it . . . didn't mean what happened." Though he'd already said his usual prayer for his friend that morning, he prayed it again. "Dear God, please let something happen that'll bring Miss Mae's joy back."

He sighed while his lips, in a wavelike movement, dragged the cigar from one side of his mouth to the other. He tucked the pack of light bulbs under his right arm, held the flashlight in his right hand, and groped for the railing with his left hand. Holding on tightly, he started down into the dark. The stairs creaked angrily and seemed to sag beneath his weight. He stepped slowly, trying to be careful as Miss Mae had warned. Finally he reached the bottom. He shined the flashlight on the dead bulb hanging from the ceiling, then reached up and unscrewed it. The bulb squeaked and grated against the grooves of the socket and dropped dust into Roy's upturned face, throwing him into a fit of sneezing. When he recovered, he set the old bulb on a shelf and screwed a fresh bulb into the socket. He squinted against the light when it came on. "Good enough," he said. "Now where's that other one?"

He found it toward the middle of the room. This time he shut his eyes and turned his face away as he unscrewed the bulb. When the new bulb was in and working, Roy turned off the flashlight and laid it on an old wooden workbench that was up against one wall. Then he scanned the room to see what was there.

It was a small room, running less than half the length of the house. It appeared smaller still by all that had been crowded into it over the years. The walls — what could be seen of them — were bare stone. The ceiling was a mass of plumbing pipes and electrical wires running in all directions. The entire room was filthy, covered with dust and cobwebs and smelling heavily of must. Roy dug a handkerchief out of his pants pocket and wiped at his eyes and nose. Then he continued his survey, wondering where to begin, what to carry upstairs first.

Built against two walls of the basement were shelves crowded with more than Roy could possibly take in at a glance. He moved closer to the wall near the staircase to survey the jumble of junk. Huddled together on one of the shelves was an assortment of old paint cans, bottles of paint thinner, and aerosol cans of spray paint. The shelf above it was loaded down with jars and cans of food on which the dust was so thick Roy couldn't tell what was in them. Crammed into the remaining shelf space were piles of magazines.

The shelves along the other wall were crowded in part with cardboard boxes of mysterious content — some were labeled "Christmas Supplies" and "Old Clothes," but most gave no clue as to what was inside. The shelves also held an odd collection of garden tools and flowerpots, children's toys, an old phonograph, some camping gear, including sleeping bags and a tightly folded canvas tent.

The items spilled out from the shelves like ivy run amuck and sat in heaps on the basement floor. In one dark corner, among the largely unidentifiable mass, was a baby carriage with rusty wheels, a lamp without a shade, a wagon with its back two wheels missing, and the rocking horse that Miss Mae had mentioned.

The rocking horse was the only thing she had said not to carry up to the guest room, but Roy couldn't imagine that she wanted everything else hauled up. This wasn't a task for one morning. There was enough here to keep him busy for a week. He thought it would be a whole lot easier if Miss Mae just came down and sorted through things in the basement. He usually didn't question her, but this time he scratched his head in confusion. "Don't mind helping Miss Mae," he muttered, "but sure seems like a lot of extra work to haul all this stuff from one room to another, 'specially when I gotta take it up that steep staircase. But Miss Mae wants me to do it and she knows best, so I better just get started."

He walked over to the shelves nearest the stairs, squatted down, and pulled out one of the magazines. Its cover was shaded with dust. Roy took his cigar out of his mouth, placed it on the shelf with the burning tip hanging over the edge, and blew on the magazine. A cloud of powdery dirt flew off in all directions. Roy sneezed loudly again several times, then pulled out his handkerchief and blew his nose noisily. He tucked the handkerchief into his back pocket. The magazine was still dusty, so he rubbed at the cover with his closed fist. Then he sounded out the name. "Na-shun-al Ge-o-graf-ic." Miss Mae had told him that Ellen wanted these for the flea market. Good. He could begin by carrying these upstairs.

He grabbed a stack of the magazines and turned on the heels of his feet. As he turned he noticed the firewood that was neatly stacked beneath the stairs. It was the last cord of wood he and George had ever chopped together. About half the pile had been burned in the fireplace the last winter before George died. Roy thought of how George loved to build a roaring fire on blustery evenings when the snow was falling thick as lamb's wool outside. George and Roy used to sit by the flames for hours, smoking and swapping stories and talking about all the insignificant events of their lives.

Thoughts of the fireplace reminded Roy of the

music box on the mantel, and he realized he hadn't listened to it that morning. To skip it just didn't seem right. He believed his work would go better if he listened to the music box, and he certainly could use the help today. He'd just carry up this one stack of magazines, listen to the box, and then come back down for more.

Upstairs in the guest room, Roy laid the magazines in a neat pile on the floor. He then sauntered into the living room where, after wiping his hands on his pants to get the dust off, he gingerly lifted the lid of the music box. The notes began to play, but slowly, heavily, as though the box were a weary musician longing for sleep. Roy closed the lid, turned the box over, and wound the key as Miss Wollencott had shown him years ago, being careful not to wind it too tightly.

He replaced the box on the mantel, lifted the lid, and smiled. Now the notes came out briskly, as though the musician had gotten his second wind and was ready to play again. Roy shut his eyes and listened, taking in each sweet, clear note as it escaped from the box. Behind his closed lids he could see the face, not clearly, not distinctly, but rather like an image seen through tinted glass. It was a gentle face, and kind, and seemed to be smiling down on him with a look of compassion mingled with pride.

The song finished but after a brief pause began again. Roy always tried to shut the lid during the pause. He didn't like to cut off the song before it was finished, nor to open the lid and have the song begin somewhere in the middle. He decided to let the music run its course again. It would only take a minute, and he had plenty of time before Miss Mae got home.

Roy couldn't remember ever being in the Humboldt house alone. It made his skin tingle to think of listening to the music box without the presence of someone hovering over his shoulder. For a brief moment the box was all his, and he could savor the music undisturbed. He could let the face of the woman come to him, the face that always appeared when the music box played. It gave him a feeling of security and of having been loved once, though he wasn't quite sure whether the woman was real or whether he had made her up a long time ago.

He let the song play again a third time, and then a fourth, and then finally he reluctantly closed the lid and silenced the music at the pause. Next time he would have to remember to wind it first so that the song would start at the beginning and not be interrupted.

Roy yawned contentedly while scratching his chest, then walked back toward the hall. He moved sluggishly, as though trying to pull himself out of a dream. He slowly turned his thoughts from the music and the woman to the piles of junk that remained to be hauled up the stairs. The dust and the stair climbing weren't fun, but he thought it might be exciting to go through the boxes with Miss Mae later. They might be filled with all sorts of fascinating treasures.

When Roy reached the basement door and peered down the narrow staircase, he stopped short and caught his breath. Climbing up the handrail and lapping over onto the steps were flames of fire. Roy suddenly remembered the cigar he had left burning on the shelf and let out a cry. He had meant to leave the cigar on the shelf for only a moment while he looked at the cover of the magazine. He had intended to pick it right back up again, but he had forgotten. And then he had come upstairs and listened to the music box four times while the cigar had burned down and ignited the pile of old magazines on the shelf where he had laid it.

Roy gave out another animal-like cry as he turned and rushed to the kitchen. There was a fire extinguisher by the stove. Miss Mae had pointed it out to him numerous times.

"In case of fire, Roy, you know where this is."

"Yes, Miss Mae. I won't forget."

"And you're familiar with how to use one?"

"Oh yes, Miss Mae. Had to use one several times down at work when cigarette ashes made a fire in somebody's wastebasket."

Roy grabbed the red canister, pulled the pin, bounded back to the basement doorway, and sprayed the foamy chemicals down the staircase. But he might as well have been shooting a squirt gun at a forest fire. The flames, with too much to feed on, had spread too rapidly. When the canister was empty, the fire raged on, unperturbed. Within its roar was a smaller, quieter sound of crinkling, the resigned sigh of all that was being reduced to ashes.

Waves of heat rolled over Roy as he stood terrified in the doorway on that same threshold where Miss Mae had stood in horror five years before. His chest heaved as he gave out short, crisp cries of anguish, as though in his fear he had lost the ability to speak. His large, round, unblinking eyes mirrored the agitated light of the flames. Sweat rolled heavily down his face, under his arms, into the small of his back. He felt as though his skin itself were ablaze, as though all the hairs on his body were being singed, as though his lungs were drawing in flame instead of air, and yet for a long moment he could not turn away from the fire.

Finally Roy slammed the door shut and threw aside the empty fire extinguisher. He paced the hall a moment and wrung his hands, and his cries took on the sound of "Oh, Miss Mae. Oh, Miss Mae." He became confused and disoriented. He thought maybe Miss Mae would come home and take care of everything. He ran to the kitchen window and searched the alley, but there was no sign of Miss Mae, not even the sound of a distant car approaching the garage. When he returned to the hall, a creeping, foglike cloud of black smoke began to seep out from beneath the basement door and curl itself around his feet.

"Oh, Miss Mae," he cried, "I done something bad. I done something real bad, and I don't know what to do now." He paced the hall and wrung his hands, then stopped suddenly as an idea came to him. "Gotta save what I can," he muttered. "Gotta get everything out. Real fast . . . real fast . . . gotta carry this stuff outta the house so it don't get burned up . . . gotta get everything out. . . ."

He ran to the front door and flung it open, grabbed the overstuffed chair in the living room and carried it out to the front lawn. Then he went back into the house and, with trembling hands, collected the framed photos and the music box on the mantel and carried them to safety. Back and forth he hurried, alternately whimpering and crying out as he hauled furniture and lamps and wall pictures out to the grass.

As the minutes passed, the flames slithered like eels from the basement straight up through the outer walls of the house and into the attic. In a moment the attic was filled with smoke. A couple of cars drove by on Humboldt without stopping, the smoke not yet visible from the street, but the woman in the house across the street, alarmed to see Mrs. Demaray's possessions being hauled out to the front yard, rushed over to see what was happening. Eleanor Nesbitt knew Roy by sight, though she'd never spoken to him. When she saw the horror in Roy's eyes and heard his unintelligible muttering mingled with his quick gasps for breath, she became even more frightened.

"What are you doing?" Mrs. Nesbitt demanded. "Where's Mrs. Demaray? Does she know you're doing this?"

Roy turned his wild gaze on the woman but said nothing. He ran back to the house. When Mrs. Nesbitt's eyes followed him, she saw the smoke that had begun rolling out of the attic eaves. "Dear heavens, the house is on fire!" she yelled. "Don't go back in there! Do you hear me? Don't go in there!"

But Roy ignored her. "Gotta get Miss Mae's things out. Gotta get everything out," he repeated.

"Is Mrs. Demaray in the house?" the neighbor yelled, but Roy had already disappeared inside and hadn't heard. Ignoring her own advice, she ran to the open front door and called inside. "Mrs. Demaray? Mrs. Demaray, are you in there?" She saw no fire on the first floor but was repelled by the heat. She was just about to turn away when she heard several explosions come from the basement. "Mercy heavens!" Mrs. Nesbitt cried. "Something's blown up down in the cellar!"

She hurried back to her own house, dashed to the telephone, and dialed the emergency number with trembling fingers. After giving the dispatcher what details she could about the fire, she hastily scurried across the street again. As she ran, the combs that held back her graying hair came loose, and her uncropped bangs drooped about her flushed face. She plucked the combs from her hair and slipped them into her skirt pocket. It had been a long time since the boredom of her morning routine had been interrupted by anything as exciting as a neighborhood fire.

Outside the Demaray house a handful of passersby, seeing the smoke, had collected on the sidewalk to watch. A woman, clutching her yelping terrier's leash, ventured timidly, "Did anyone call 9-1-1?"

"I just called them," Mrs. Nesbitt boasted breathlessly. "I hope they hurry. There's a man inside. He's been hauling all this stuff out of the house. I told him not to go back inside, but he wouldn't listen."

"Where is he, do you know?" A young man wearing a pair of mirror sunglasses turned to Mrs. Nesbitt. Eleanor Nesbitt, instead of meeting the man's eyes, found herself staring at her own disheveled reflection in the glasses.

"How should I know?" she snapped, as though he had accused her of negligence. "I looked in the front door but wasn't about to go inside. The heat's unbearable."

The young man turned the annoying lenses toward the house and gazed at it briefly, assessing the situation. "I'd better go in after him," he said finally, half heroically, half reluctantly.

He took a step forward but was stopped by the firm grasp of an old man's hand upon his forearm. "I wouldn't go in there if I were you," the old man warned. "No use losing the both of you."

When the young man didn't protest, the old

man let go his grasp. Leaning heavily on his cane with both hands, the old man asked of Mrs. Nesbitt, "How long's the fire been burning?"

Mrs. Nesbitt shrugged. "I don't know that either. I saw the smoke coming out of the attic just a minute ago. That's when I ran over to call 9-1-1." She fished a comb out of her pocket and pulled her bangs back with it. She wondered whether one of the local news stations might show up with cameras. Wouldn't her husband, Lester, be surprised if her face showed up on the evening news?

Just then the sound of approaching sirens cut through the still air and reached the group on the sidewalk.

"Here they come now," said the timid woman with the terrier.

"Not a moment too soon," the young man remarked. "There goes the roof." The half dozen people on the sidewalk all turned their faces upward to see flames licking at the eaves and crawling over the shingles. "Maybe if they get those hoses on it right away, nothing'll burn but the attic."

The old man shook his head. "Not likely. This place is going to fall like a house of cards," he predicted. The handful of spectators turned their attention to the old man.

"How do you know?" asked the young man defensively.

"The lady here tells us it was hot on the first floor, isn't that right?" He looked to Mrs.

Nesbitt for confirmation. She nodded hesitantly. Satisfied, the man next pointed toward the chimney with his cane. "Smoke's coming out the chimney. Both those clues together tell us there's fire in the basement. No doubt it shot right up through the walls. This whole structure's on fire." Then, as though his audience needed an explanation, he said, "I used to be a volunteer fire fighter years ago."

"He's right," Mrs. Nesbitt agreed. "I heard something blow up down there in the cellar. . . ."

Her words were all but drowned out by the fire trucks that pulled up in front of the house, sirens wailing. The old man looked at the trucks. Three pumpers, two hook and ladders. Plenty of equipment and plenty of men, but he still thought the house — and most likely the man inside — would be lost. These old houses — balloon-frame homes was what the firemen called them — were a bonfire waiting to happen. They were built in such a way that fire could travel through them unimpeded. Not at all like the newer homes that had to be constructed to meet safety codes.

He watched as the firemen swarmed out of the trucks like bees out of a hive and immediately started pulling at the hoses. The huge hoses were flat like tapeworms but would quickly be round as snakes with gallons of water pumping through them.

The old man shuffled over to the fire chief, who stood by one of the trucks, holding a two-way radio in his hand and watching as his men took their positions around the house. "Morning, Harry," he said mildly, as though they happened to be passing on the street.

"Ben!" The fire chief looked surprised. "This your house?"

The old man shook his head. "I was just walking by. Fire's in the basement and attic both, and there's a man inside."

"You know where he is?"

"No idea. I suppose he's unconscious or he'd have come out by now."

The fire chief threw some orders at a group of men who began breaking in the basement windows and aiming the hoses at the flames that escaped. Two men carrying axes and wearing air tanks entered the house to search for the man inside. A second hose shooting water at the roof seemed to do nothing more than create huge black billows of smoke.

Mrs. Nesbitt joined the old man and the fire chief. "I told him not to go back inside," she said without introduction. "I saw him hauling all this furniture and stuff out on the lawn, and . . ."

"You a neighbor?" Harry asked.

"I live right across the street," Mrs. Nesbitt said, pointing toward a house hidden by the fire trucks.

"Is there anyone else inside?"

"I don't think Mrs. Demaray's home," said Mrs. Nesbitt. "I hollered in the door, but she didn't answer."

"That doesn't mean she's not inside," Harry said. "Any children?"

"No. I mean, her children are grown. I don't think her grandchildren are —"

Once again Mrs. Nesbitt was interrupted when someone in the crowd yelled out, "Look! The upstairs window. There he is!"

Everyone looked up. A gasp escaped the crowd when they spotted Roy wandering back and forth in front of the bedroom window as though he were lost in a maze and searching for a way out.

"Get the ladder up," Harry ordered. "We'll get him from the window. Joe, you and Dan get ready. You're going up."

Just as the two men put the air tanks on their backs, the roof collapsed into the attic with a monstrous groan. A second later, the first-floor windows were alight with fire, the lace curtains dripping to the floor in bits of flame. "It's gonna go," said Ben, tapping the sidewalk ardently with his cane.

While Joe and Dan scrambled up the ladder to the porch roof, the chief radioed to the two men inside, telling them to get out. In the next moment two figures crawled out of the smoke and over the threshold of the front door toward safety. They reached the lawn just as Joe on the porch roof was breaking the bedroom window with an axe. The room beyond was thick with smoke that had filtered down from the attic. Joe secured the air mask over his face before jumping into the room. Shattered glass crunched beneath his heavy boots as he landed. He immediately got down on the floor and put one foot up against the wall to orient himself. In a moment he was joined by his partner Dan.

Carefully but quickly crawling on their stomachs along the floor, they found Roy crouched beside the bed, his head resting against the mattress. Tears and sweat mingled on his plump cheeks and dripped from his chin. His eyes were half closed and his lips moved slowly, almost imperceptibly.

The two firemen laid him down flat on the floor. "He's conscious," Joe yelled, competing against the roar of the fire and the mask that covered his mouth. "But there's no way he can take the ladder."

Dan, by far the larger of the two, said, "I'll carry him down. You radio the chief and have an ambulance sent."

Joe yelled, "He's a big load. Sure you can handle him alone?"

Dan nodded. "I'm all right. Call that ambulance."

Joe spoke into his radio while Dan gently bent Roy's legs so that his knees were pointed toward the ceiling. As he grabbed Roy's wrists and started to lift him, Roy protested weakly, "Gotta find Miss Mae's letters. The letters and all those photos. Can't leave until I find them. . . ."

"Sorry, buddy," Dan said as he threw the semiconscious Roy over his shoulder. "It's too late for that."

As though to confirm Dan's observation, the ceiling of the bedroom burst into flame. Joe escaped out the window and waited at the top of the ladder to help guide Dan and Roy down. Dan, grunting, stepped heavily out onto the porch roof with his burden. Only seconds after they escaped the bedroom, flames burst out of the broken window, as though the window were the gaping mouth of an angry dragon. A hose was turned on the window, and Joe and Dan, making their way carefully down the ladder with Roy, were drenched with water.

Two of the fire department paramedics met them at the foot of the ladder and dragged the now unconscious Roy to the edge of the lawn. Covering him with a blanket, they checked his vital signs. Roy was breathing on his own but with difficulty. One of the paramedics slipped an oxygen mask over his face.

Mrs. Nesbitt ran to where the paramedics crouched over Roy. "Is he dead?" she cried.

One of the men looked up briefly. "No, ma'am, he's not."

"Is he gonna die?"

"Not unless the ambulance gets broadsided on the way to the hospital."

"Well, why's he unconscious?"

"Not enough oxygen. But he'll come around. You a relative?"

"Neighbor." Mrs. Nesbitt pointed yet again across the street. "I'm the one who called 9-1-1. Guess I saved this man's life. . . ."

From far away, Roy heard the voices. They reached him in the place of darkness from which he struggled to escape. Where were Miss Mae's letters and photos? They were family keepsakes, supposed to be passed on to Ellen and Christy and Amy. He couldn't let them be lost, he had to find them. . . .

The fire had reached its peak when Mae arrived seconds later, parking the Buick two houses away, blocked by the tumult in front of her own house. She stepped out of the car slowly and, not bothering to shut the door, stared at the scene in disbelief: the ambulance that came roaring up, screeching to a halt beside the fire trucks; the men wearing helmets and yellow rubber coats struggling to control the monstrous hoses; the water spewing fiercely toward the relentless flames; the ever enlarging group of gawkers on the sidewalk — like the morbidly curious at a circus sideshow — watching the destruction of her home.

She began to move like a sleepwalker through the crowd, feeling as though she were moving through the landscape of a bad dream. The stench of smoke grabbed her throat until she gagged and coughed. The heat of the fire reached her on the sidewalk. Its touch made her feel faint and nauseous. All the sounds around her — the voices of men shouting, the babble of the onlookers, the whooshing of water shot from hoses, the crackling of wood consumed by fire —

melted into one deafening noise that beat against her brain like a hammer.

Finally Mae came to where Roy was being lifted onto a stretcher. She was startled by Mrs. Nesbitt, who cried, "Oh, Mrs. Demaray! Thank God you weren't in the house! I called for you but I didn't think you were inside. I saw your hired man here" — she nodded toward Roy — "go into the house even though he knew full well it was dangerous, so I called 9-1-1 and two of these brave men climbed right up to the porch roof and through the upstairs window and hauled him out of there. They said he's going to be okay, isn't that right?" She turned to the paramedic who'd been talking with her, and he nodded absently.

Mrs. Nesbitt continued. "I saw him out my front window. He was hauling all this stuff out of your house." She swept an arm toward the pile of furniture and other items that the firemen had dragged off to one corner of the yard. "They said he was trying to find something in the upstairs bedroom when they discovered him there half unconscious from the smoke. He would have been a goner if the firemen hadn't gotten to him when they did. Of course it's a good thing, too, I made that call when I did. But this man of yours must be real loyal to you, Mrs. Demaray, risking his own life like that just to save some of your furniture and things. Can you imagine?"

Mae looked down at Roy on the stretcher, a white sheet tucked up under his chin. The paramedics were just about to lift him into the ambulance when Roy, somewhat revived by the oxygen, tried to speak.

"You know him, ma'am?" one of the paramedics asked of Mae.

Mae looked at the man quizzically, trying to comprehend his question, then nodded her head once.

The paramedic continued. "He'll be all right, but we'd like to get him to the hospital right away."

Mae lowered her eyes again toward Roy. He was trying to lift his head to speak to her. "I'm real sorry, Miss Mae," he moaned, his words muffled by the mask. "I didn't mean to leave that old cigar down there. I'm real sorry. Miss Mae, you'll forgive old Roy, won't you? You'll tell old Roy it's all right, and we'll go on being friends just like before?"

Mae continued to stare while her face registered no emotion at all. She could say nothing, even when Roy's blue eyes became glassy and magnified by tears. The paramedics lifted the stretcher into the back of the ambulance. "Come on, fella," one of them said. "Time to take a little trip to the doctor."

Roy's eyes and Mae's locked on each other, and just as the paramedics reached for the door handles, Mae heard Roy speak again, but the words were lost inside the ambulance, and she didn't understand. Then the doors were shut, and Roy was whisked away in the blaring whirlwind of the flashing siren.

An hour later the flames had been quenched, but too late. The gutted remains of the house on Humboldt were nothing but charred and blackened wood dripping with water. The firemen were rolling up the hoses. Two were sifting through the ruins looking for clues to the fire and making sure there were no hot spots left that could later reignite. A few of the passersby lingered to give statements to the firemen, then drifted off to go finally where they had been going when waylaid by the fiery show. Mrs. Nesbitt ran home to call her husband and tell him what had happened.

Mae stood motionless on the sidewalk, as though her feet had melted into the concrete. She couldn't turn her head away from the dripping ruins. She hadn't been gone long. She hadn't even finished running her errands. She was still at the gas station when she realized she'd forgotten her bank book, and so headed home to get it. She had only been gone thirty minutes when she returned home for the bank book and found instead a burning house. Only half an hour, maybe less. Such a short time in which to lose everything. Such a very short time, she thought over and over, in which to lose everything.

Chapter 11

The first days of July were heavy with heat even before the morning sun appeared on the horizon. Minneapolis was in the midst of one of its hot spells when the daytime temperature didn't drop below ninety degrees.

Sam and Ellen had central air conditioning in their home but seldom used it during the day. Normally no one was in the house anyway; Sam was down at the office, Ellen was either working at the publishing house or was busy with her volunteer tasks, the girls were taken to day care or, for a couple of weeks during the summer, Vacation Bible School. When Ellen came home in the afternoon, she shut the windows and turned the air on again so that the family could sleep comfortably at night.

Now that Mae was staying in the spare bedroom Sam said they ought to go ahead and leave the air on all day. But Mae insisted that they not leave it on just for her. She knew their electric bill, already high enough, would soar with the extra usage. She claimed that the ceiling fan and a bottomless glass of iced tea were enough to ward off the worst of the heat.

By ten o'clock on the morning of July sixth, however, Mae was tempted to turn on the air conditioning and slip Sam a little money to help cover the cost. She sat at the desk in the spare room, her face moist with perspiration, her cotton sundress clinging to her back and thighs. A pad of stationery paper lay open on the desk in front of her, and she held a pen in her moist hand but couldn't quite bring herself to write. She felt light-headed from the heat. The ceiling fan turned overhead but did little more than circulate hot air. Even the glass of iced tea appeared to be sweating. It was covered with beads of condensation that ran down the sides and collected in puddles on the leather coaster.

Mae knew, though, that Sam wouldn't accept any money from her. She had been staying with her daughter and son-in-law since the fire, and to her annoyance, they wouldn't take the check she offered for room and board. "Don't be ridiculous, Mother," Ellen had said a dozen times. "It's only a temporary situation until you get settled somewhere else."

It was the when and where of that move that was bothering Mae.

She got up from the desk and wandered listlessly down the hall to the bathroom. Moistening a washcloth with cold water, she patted her face and neck and ran the cloth up and down her bare arms. She had experienced many sweltering days in Minneapolis, but she couldn't remember one that was as bad as this. She held the cloth under the cold water again, wrung it out, and took it back to the desk with her. Sighing as she sank into the chair, she lay the cloth across the back of her neck. The cold helped to revive her a bit. She took a large swallow of the iced tea, then squeezed a napkin to rid her fingers of the moisture of the glass. Picking up the pen again, she forced herself to write.

Dear Evelyn,

You must find it odd to receive a letter from me in the middle of the year, as Christmas is our usual time to correspond and catch up on news, but I'm writing because I'm afraid I must ask a rather odd favor of you.

You see, last week I lost my home to a fire. Little was salvaged, save a few items of furniture and so forth that were dragged out of the house by a man who was at that time working for me.

Mae stopped writing and thought of Roy. She hadn't seen him in the week since the fire. She knew he had been treated for smoke inhalation and a few minor burns but had been released from the hospital the same day. Ellen had gone to see him that night and had been back a couple of times since. But Mae didn't ask Ellen about her visits with Roy, not even to inquire as to how he was.

She was angry, and the anger gripped her and held her immobile. She couldn't bring herself to see Roy, to talk with him and tell him everything was all right. Everything wasn't all right. She had lost her home and everything that was in it, and the loss had come because of Roy's carelessness.

The previous evening, when Mae and Ellen were folding towels and linens together in the laundry room, Ellen had said cautiously, "Mother, it's been a week since the fire. Don't you think it's about time you see Roy?"

Mae had lifted a towel from the laundry basket and snapped it briskly in the air. "I need time, Ellen. I'm really not up to seeing anyone right now." She had taken a few calls from friends at the church but had given false assurances that she was fine and had hung up quickly. When her pastor came to visit, she listened politely while he spoke about God having a reason for everything, nodded when he asked if he could pray, and shook his hand when he rose to leave. She closed the front door behind him hoping he felt he had done his job and wouldn't bother to return. Seeing people meant having to feel something, and she didn't like the feelings inside of her.

Ellen continued. "Roy's really not doing very well. He feels terrible about what happened. I've never seen him like this. When I try to talk with him he just sits on the edge of the couch and mumbles. He won't even look at me."

Mae drew a pillowcase out of the laundry basket and smoothed it out with her hands, all the while giving little indication that she was listening.

Ellen waited for a response from her mother, but receiving none, she went on. "You've suffered a big loss, Mother. Believe me, I know that. But so has Roy. He loved that house — maybe as much as you did."

Mae's eyes darted at Ellen and narrowed in disbelief, but only for a moment. She looked away again and pulled another pillowcase from the basket.

Ellen clenched her jaw a moment, then pushed ahead against the older woman's unyielding stubbornness. "More than that, Mother, he thinks he's lost you, his best friend. That's almost more than he can bear. He needs you to come and tell him you're not angry with him. If you don't, he's just going to go on blaming himself."

Mae knew she couldn't tell Roy she wasn't angry with him — because she was. She wasn't about to go over there and lie just to appease him. She wasn't about to let him off the hook so easily. But to cut the conversation short, she said abruptly, "I'll go."

"When?"

"When I'm ready."

Mae didn't know when that would be. How long would it take for the anger to dissolve? How long before she could come to terms with the loss enough to forgive the one who had caused the fire?

Mae continued writing.

At the moment I am staying with my daughter, Ellen, and her family. I'm fortunate to have their generous hospitality, but I'm anxious to have my own home again. Ellen and Sam are trying to persuade me to sell the lot and move to Florida, but I am not yet convinced that that is the best thing to do. It's difficult to pull up roots and leave one's home of more than fifty years.

Mae had lain awake every night since the fire wondering what to do. Before the fire, moving to Florida had not been a consideration for her. She simply had no intention of going, but she was beginning to think that Ellen and Sam might be right. Even Mike, when she had called him the day after the fire, tried to talk her into moving.

"You know, Mom," he'd said, *"I've lived where it's cold and I've lived where it's warm, and I can tell you from experience that life is much better when you don't have to put up with ice and snow."*

Ice and snow — that's what most people thought about when they thought of Minnesota. For Mae, there was so much more to her home state than that. But even she had to admit that there seemed little reason to stay now. She loved her family and wanted to be near Ellen, Sam, and the girls, but it wasn't as though her daughter were begging her to stay.

The trip to Florida in December should help her decide. Christmas was still six months away, and she thought perhaps she ought to make a decision before then, but she didn't want to move to St. Petersburg without visiting the city first. And the family couldn't make the trip any sooner than Christmas. Ellen and Sam both insisted that Mae stay in their home for as long as she wanted and needed. They urged her, in fact, to stay until they could all make the trip together.

At the moment I'm overwhelmed with endless insurance forms. The insurance companies certainly do their best to make it as difficult as possible for people to make claims for their losses. I suppose they don't like the thought of paying out large sums of money, but, honestly, what else are they there for?

I'm having to make endless lists of everything I had in the house and to make all sorts of calculations concerning the value of the items lost to the fire. My head has been spinning with numbers as I've tried to determine what had appreciated in value, what had depreciated, what replacement costs would be. It is all a dreadful task and nearly as emotionally draining as witnessing the fire itself.

She wept every time she sat down to work on the forms. At first she had been overcome by the sense of having lost all. But when the "all" was broken down into specifics, the loss was even more difficult to face. As her mind traveled from room to room, it wasn't the large items that brought the tears, but rather it was the small things for which she longed: the wisps of hair saved from her children's first haircuts; the dried flowers that her mother had pressed between the pages of books; the black medical bag, worn and tattered, that her father had toted about for so many years; all the many little gifts George had given her over the years that she had kept and treasured.

As I think about what was lost, I realize that what was most precious to me can in no way be replaced. What price is there to old family keepsakes? There is no regaining those invaluable things that were once cherished by or used by or given to you by those you loved the most.

One of the things I'm most sorry to lose is the many family letters and photographs that I, and my mother before me, held so dear. That's why I'm writing to you today. A good number of the letters Mother kept were from your mother — hundreds of them! You know how they corresponded for so many years. Perhaps your mother also kept some of the letters she received from my mother.

If this is indeed the case, would you be so kind as to consider allowing me to have some of my mother's letters? It would mean a great deal to me to have them. Also, any photographs that Clara may have of Mother — if you can see your way to parting with them — would be gratefully received on this end.

I hope you don't mind my asking this of you. I know we met only once, and that save for the friendship of our mothers that ties us together, I'm practically a stranger, and yet here I am asking for these personal items. Please forgive me while at the same time you consider what is, I'm sure, an odd request.

I will be happy to reimburse you for any postage involved in sending me these items.

Mae reread the letter and considered how inadequate were words in describing the human experience. The words of a letter, of a newspaper article, of a biography or autobiography — they held the facts and maybe even attempted to describe the emotions, but no matter how talented the writer, it was all little more than a process of distilling the expansiveness of life into the narrowness of language. People's whole existence could be reduced to a few symbols on a page. In the space of a sentence, a person could be born, live, and die. But the essence of what happened couldn't be captured. *"Last week I lost my home to a fire,"* she had written. Distilled. Boiled down. All the life squeezed out of it. The words were a false front to a building filled with anguish, with sleepless nights, with days of grief.

Mae pulled the washcloth off the back of her

neck, snapped it open, and held it to her face. She pressed the cool cloth to her eyes with the tips of her index finger and thumb. Then she rubbed her neck and arms with it and took another swallow of tea. All the ice had melted and the tea had become lukewarm.

The heat was so oppressive she felt exhausted, though it was barely noon. Her temples began to pound until she wanted nothing other than to stretch out across the bed with the ceiling fan whirling above her at high speed.

But she had work to do. She signed the letter to Evelyn, addressed an envelope, and sealed it. Then she flipped through the address book that she kept in her purse, putting checks by the names of those she wanted to contact. Her brother Jim had died of a stroke some years back, but she would get in touch with her two remaining brothers, both of whom had long ago settled in California. They weren't very sentimental, but there was the chance that they had stashed away some mementos from the war years. Besides her brothers, there were a good dozen people from whom she might pry photos, letters, or other family keepsakes. Actually, she had been intending to write to these people for years, to see what she could gather. Now she was glad she hadn't, for it all would have burned in the fire.

That was some consolation, she thought. Perhaps her uncharacteristic procrastination was a blessing. Surely now, because of it, she might be able to gather a little bit here and a little bit there until finally she had a bouquet of keepsakes to help make up for what had been lost.

Chapter 12

Two weeks passed, two more weeks of relentless heat and humidity. When Sam finally insisted that the air conditioning be left on all day, Mae decided not to protest. She was thankful for the cool air circulating through the rooms. Now she could abandon the cold washcloths and cut back on the iced tea — the caffeine only made her more nervous anyway. She was much more comfortable in body now, if not in mind.

With the insurance forms completed and with what she called her "begging letters" written and posted to numerous friends and relatives, she didn't know what to do with herself. Waiting seemed the only activity left to her. Waiting to hear from the insurance company. Waiting for responses to her letters. Waiting, too, for her own mind to come to a conclusion about the future.

Mae had always been one to stay busy and to use her time wisely. Even during her episodes of deepest grief, she had tried to build some structure into her days. She was forever considering what needed to be done and then went about doing it. But now, suddenly, everything was different. She no longer had the familiar arena in which to organize her hours. Instead, she found herself in a strange environment, on a new stage with unfamiliar props. She didn't know how to play this role. She didn't know who her character was, nor what was expected of her.

She tried to make herself useful by doing the laundry and puttering around the kitchen, but Ellen was a disciplined housekeeper and there was little for Mae to do beyond the basics. When the dishes were washed and the occasional load of laundry was folded and put away, numerous empty hours remained. And so she spent a good portion of each day simply lying on the bed, anticipating the arrival of the mailman sometime in the midafternoon. She lay diagonally across the bedspread, watching the ceiling fan turn at low speed, listening to it whirl as it lazily dragged its arms in circles. It seemed to Mae that the arms of the fan turned only slightly faster than the hands of the clock, which moved so slowly and imperceptibly that Mae sometimes thought they weren't moving at all. She had never known time to pass so slowly. It was as though everything was trying to push against a great weight, as though gravity had gone wild and was bearing down on the earth, impeding all movement, stopping time, halting the rotation of the earth itself.

But outside in the streets and on the sidewalks, life moved along at its normal pace.

Children ran and skipped and jumped, and the balls that they threw soared skyward. Skaters rolled by and cyclists sped past, peddling furiously. Cars rumbled over the asphalt, motorcycles thundered through the streets, and the city bus chugged along, grinding its gears.

It was only Mae who was heavy, held down, and wearied not by an outer force but by the emotions that bound her more tightly than ropes.

Often in the empty hours she found her heart longing for that resting place that years ago had been so familiar — that green, still, quiet place. But when she thought about God now, she couldn't help but wonder whether He had allowed the fire as part of her punishment. If He had, then rightly so. She deserved His wrath, not His comfort. Her heart longed for something she couldn't have.

Ellen encouraged her mother to get out, to go shopping, call someone from the church for lunch, visit a museum, but nothing appealed to Mae. Eventually, Ellen brought up the subject of Roy again. "You know, Mother," she said gently, "I really don't think you're going to start feeling better until you talk with Roy."

Mae knew at once that Ellen was right. She wanted to talk with Roy; she missed him. She was fully aware, too, of how he must be suffering, and more than once tears pushed heavily at the back of her eyes when she pictured him alone in his room at the boardinghouse. Sometimes at night she dreamed about him, and very often in her dreams he was a young Roy all dressed up in a soldier's uniform going off to fight the war in place of her brothers. Always, watching as he boarded the train, Mae tried to call out to him to beg him not to go, but hard as she tried, she had no voice. She couldn't utter the smallest of sounds, and the train swallowed Roy up and carried him away.

When she awoke in the morning, she felt compelled to go to Roy at once and try to make amends, but time after time she didn't go as she reminded herself of what Roy's carelessness had cost her. She willfully pushed the image of his childlike face from her mind and refused to listen when memory played back his voice: *"Miss Mae, you sure are good to old Roy. Yessir, you'll always be my very best friend, Miss Mae."*

She couldn't quite understand herself the ambiguity of her emotions — her belief that the fire was just punishment and her anger at Roy for having started it; her missing Roy and her refusal to forgive him. She had the means to restore their friendship with a few simple words. She knew Roy would gladly pick up right where they had left off, yet she couldn't bring herself to form the words in her heart, much less say them aloud.

To Ellen, she said, "I'll talk with Roy when I'm ready, Ellen, but right now I just can't."

"Why, Mother? What has to happen before you'll be ready?"

Mae shook her head. "I don't know. I can't answer that."

Ellen hesitated a moment but finally said, "I think you're avoiding having to forgive him, Mother. You just don't want to do it. You're going to go on blaming him forever for starting the fire."

Mae surprised even herself by blurting out, "But he should have been more careful. His one stupid act cost me everything!"

Ellen nodded slowly in agreement. "Yes, he should have been more careful. Even Roy should have known better than to light up a cigar when he was going through all that flammable stuff in the basement. But we all make mistakes. Accidents happen."

Mae cast angry and despairing eyes on her daughter. "Do you think I don't know that accidents happen?" she wailed. "Do you think *I* don't know! I know very well that accidents happen, and those of us who are careless are to blame. *We're* to blame!" she said, hitting her chest with an open palm. Red-faced, she stared at her daughter, then took in a deep breath and said more quietly, "We are to blame, and nothing can change that."

That was it, Mae realized. The disturbing thought lurked somewhere in the back of her mind that if it were possible to forgive Roy for what he had done, it would only follow that it might be possible to forgive herself for what she had done.

And that she couldn't do.

Ellen, too, sensed her mother's inner struggle. She took a step closer to where her mother stood by the front window, a familiar pose now as Mae sometimes stood there in the afternoons searching the front street for the mail truck. Ellen wanted to throw her arms around her mother and comfort her, but at the same time she fought the urge to grab the older woman by the shoulders and try to shake some sense into her.

She did neither but chose to let her words quietly fill the distance between them. "Mother," she began, "last week on the final day of Vacation Bible School, I told the kids the story of Theodore Thimble. Do you remember that one? He was the thimble who took his share of the inheritance and ran away from the tailor's sewing box to find the good life but ended up on a scrap heap at the city garbage dump instead." Ellen chuckled briefly at the thought. "That was your version of the Prodigal Son. You were a good storyteller, a good teacher. But you never told me there's more than one reason people run from God. I always thought it was because they want to go their own way and have fun, but that isn't always so, is it, Mother? You never told me people sometimes run from God because they want to punish themselves."

Ellen had been talking all the while to her mother's back as Mae stood motionless by the window. After a moment when both women

226

were silent, Ellen asked, "Mother, did you hear what I said?"

Mae nodded. "Yes, Ellen, I heard you."

Ellen waited for her mother to say more, but she said nothing. In the next moment the mail truck rumbled to a stop along the curb, and the mailman hopped out with his heavy pouch to make his rounds on the Nollingers' street. "Well," Ellen sighed, feeling once again defeated in her attempt to reach her mother, "maybe he'll have something for you today. I've got to go pick up the girls from day care; I'm already late."

She left her mother to her solitary watch by the window, not knowing that Mae longed to call out to her, to tell her she was tired of running and wanted to come home, that in all these dreadful years she had heard God calling her, whispering, *"He restores my soul."* In Dr. Garrett's office, when she smelled the lilac blossoms, and countless times when she least expected it — when she was reaching up to put dishes in the cupboard, when she flung open a window on a summer morning, when she was winding the music box for Roy, she sensed His presence with her, comforting her, but always she had resisted. She resisted because she didn't deserve to be rid of her grief. Because of her, Sammy's body had been broken, and he had died. What right had she to think her own broken soul should be restored?

And yet He had pursued her tirelessly. He was

pursuing her even now as she wondered whether He might not have sufficient grace to heal the wound of so stubborn a heart as hers.

That afternoon the mailman did bring the first responses to Mae's letters, and after that more continued to arrive almost daily. Some of the people she had contacted had little to offer, including her own brothers. Ken said he had left all family keepsakes at the Humboldt house when he moved away, and Peter said he thought he had some letters somewhere, but it would take weeks for him to lay his hands on them. But others were able to send her bits and pieces of her mother's life. One cousin in New York had uncovered a half dozen pictures of his aunt Amelia, which he wrapped in tissue paper and sent to Mae in an oversized box. Another relative in Sioux Falls, a cousin on her father's side, dug up a few wedding pictures of Dr. and Mrs. Wollencott and said she would continue to scout around for more. Two nieces responded by sending a few photos as well as some postcards, birthday greetings, and notes they'd received from Amelia years before. A family friend offered a small book of poetry that Amelia had given her for a long-ago birthday. Inside, Amelia had written a birthday greeting and signed her name. Another family friend said she knew she had some letters from Amelia up in the attic, but because of her rheumatism she didn't anticipate climbing the attic stairs any time soon. Her son was supposed to visit over Labor Day weekend, however. When he arrived she would send him to the attic in search of the lost letters, then she would get back to Mae to let her know what the search turned up.

Mae was glad for even the trickle of mementos that came to her, and yet she couldn't help being somewhat disappointed. She had hoped for more. At this rate, she couldn't even begin to make up for what had been lost.

Finally, though, the mailman dropped off what she had most been hoping for — a package from Vermont. It was from Clara Reynolds' daughter, Evelyn. Mae rushed to the kitchen where Ellen kept a pair of scissors in a drawer by the sink. She set the package on the kitchen table and, with trembling fingers, cut away the string and ripped open the brown packaging paper. The box itself, about twice the size of a shoe box, had been taped together. Mae found that in her excitement she barely had the strength to rip off the masking tape.

When she got the box open and drew back the flaps, she discovered that it was filled end to end with musty, tattered envelopes. Mae held the box up to her face and breathed deeply. She thought the musty odor of those old envelopes the most wonderful fragrance she had ever known. She let herself drop into one of the kitchen chairs, the box of letters landing placidly in her lap.

Lying lengthwise across the top of Amelia's

correspondence was a crisp white envelope with Mae's name on it — a letter from Evelyn. Mae laid it on the kitchen table for a moment as she sifted through her mother's letters. There were dozens of envelopes, stiff and turning brown, the black ink across their faces fading with age. Each envelope was nearly identical to the others: Clara's name and address in the center in Amelia's neat handwriting, and in the upper left-hand corner, in the same neat handwriting but penned more tightly, Amelia's name and the Humboldt address. The address that Mae had all her life called home. "How sorry Mother would be to know that the house is gone," Mae said aloud to herself. But even that couldn't dampen her excitement at the treasure that had found its way to her from Vermont.

Mae looked at the postmarks on the envelopes. The first letter in the box had been sent from Minneapolis in 1925; the last had been sent in 1947. That didn't quite span all the years the two women had corresponded, but Mae imagined Clara had received many more letters than what was in this box. Mae smiled when she noticed the stamp on the first letter. It was a red stamp with a profile of George Washington, worth two cents. Amelia could have sent ten letters for what it now cost Mae to mail only one.

She sat for a long time with the box on her lap, touching the envelopes, smelling them, tracing her mother's handwriting with her index finger. Finally she picked up Evelyn's letter and carefully sliced open the envelope with one blade of the scissors. Inside were two pages of yellow notepaper covered with Evelyn's sprawling script.

Dear Mae,

You are more than welcome to the letters in this box. I also intend to send some photos of your mother, but I must go through Mom's photo albums, as she has many photos of our own family that I would like to keep for myself. I'll send the photos along separately as soon as I've picked out the ones you might want. I don't know that there's many of your mother, but I know there are some. I'll see what I can find.

Mom has held on to these letters for years, but she'll never miss them now. In her condition there's scarcely a day she even recognizes me, her own daughter. When I go to get her up in the morning, she invariably asks me who I am and says she wants to speak to Henry, whoever that is. Dad's name was Arthur, as you probably remember. I am rather glad Dad isn't around to see Mom like this. It would break his heart.

Mom was already showing the first signs of Alzheimer's some eight years ago when Dad died. I don't think he ever imagined how bad it would be. Neither did I. It's like caring for a baby, only worse. Instead of growing up, Mom deteriorates. Ned has been patient, more than most husbands would be, I think, though sometimes he suggests we move her into a nursing home. But I can't stand the thought of putting Mom in a home because even at the best of them she wouldn't get the care that I can give her here.

Well, enough of that — I'm getting sidetracked from my point, which is why there aren't twenty-five years' worth of letters in this box. When we took Mom in just after Dad's death, it took months to clear out her home and get it sold. Mom was always what you might call a pack rat. The attic was stuffed to the rafters with junk that most people would have hauled away to the garbage dump. Even the most sentimental of persons would think Mom had gone overboard in her keepsakes. In addition to decades' worth of unusable items that Mom had tucked away in the attic for posterity, she had accumulated countless boxes of letters from relatives and friends — most, in fact, were from your mother. I told her she couldn't keep them all, as we simply had no place to store them. My own attic was — is still! — filled to the rafters with who-knows-what. I guess I'm just a chip off the old block and probably had no right to ever chastise Mom for her tendency to horde things.

Anyway, Mom carefully — and tearfully — went through all her letters and saved certain ones that were meaningful to her. And probably some that weren't so meaningful, too, judging from the number she claimed she simply couldn't throw away. "You can have a lovely bonfire after I'm gone," she said, "but until then, these letters stay with me."

Well, she isn't gone yet, though her mind is certainly somewhere other than here. She does remember your mother and converses with her on occasion. I'm not sure whether she is remembering things that actually happened or whether she is making things up, but at least she and Amelia still seem to be enjoying a pleasant companionship.

She hasn't looked at these letters in five years or more, I'm sure. They just sit in her closet taking up space. I'm sorry to say I've never read them myself — I just never found the time — but I'm happy to send them off to someone who will enjoy reading them. And as I say, I'll get some photos to you soon, though how soon I'm not sure, since taking care of Mom demands a good portion of my time and energy.

You have my deepest sympathy over the loss of your home. I can well imagine that it is a painful loss to you. I'm sure Mom would also grieve for the house where she spent so many pleasant hours with Amelia were she capable of understanding what has happened.

If there is anything else I can do to help, please be sure to let me know.

Sincerely,
Evelyn

Mae read the letter through twice, immensely thankful for the sentimental streak in Clara that had preserved, in the form of letters, a little bit of her mother. These letters were even more precious than the collection of letters from Clara that had been destroyed by the fire, for these were not *to* her mother but had been written *by* her. No doubt her mother had poured out her heart and soul onto these pages.

Mae closed the box and leaned forward to let her cheek rest against the cardboard flap. Sam and Ellen and the girls would be home soon. Pans would be clanging as dinner was made, and the girls would be chattering and vying for their parents' attention. That would be the end of Mae's solitude for the day.

As much as she longed to read the letters, Mae didn't want to begin only to be interrupted. She wanted it to be a placid ritual, this meeting of past and present, this reunion of mother and daughter. She carried the box to her room and didn't touch it again until morning, didn't even tell Ellen it had arrived.

At breakfast the next morning, Ellen told Mae she didn't have to go in to work, but after she took the girls to day care, she was going to come home and hole up in her workroom downstairs. She had just started taking a class in painting with watercolors, and she had an assignment to complete before the next session. "I've just got to get something halfway decent on paper, or the instructor is going to wonder why I signed up for the class in the first place," Ellen said. "Sorry to ignore you this morning, Mother, but maybe in the afternoon we can take a little walk. It's supposed to be cooler today."

"That would be nice, dear," Mae said, swallowing the last of her orange juice. "And don't worry about me. I have plenty to do to keep me busy this morning."

If Ellen was curious as to Mae's sudden busyness, she didn't ask, and Mae was thankful. She still wanted to keep the treasure to herself until she had read through all the letters. Then she would share them with Ellen.

After Sam left for work and Ellen rushed out the door with the girls in tow, Mae carried a glass of iced tea to her room and settled into the easy chair. The box of letters sat invitingly on the small table beside the chair. Mae felt as though it were a living companion, waiting to walk with her into the past. She placed the glass of tea on the table beside the box, propped her feet up on the footstool, and straightened her cotton skirt. It was going to be a long journey, and she wanted to be comfortable.

She pulled the first envelope from the box and unfolded the letter. It was dated October 13, 1925, and from the opening sentence, Mae could tell that it was the first letter Amelia had sent to her friend after Clara's move to Vermont.

My dearest friend,
We have only just returned from the train

station after seeing you off, but already I feel the emptiness of a separation of years. I will never forget how you looked, framed in the train window, waving good-bye. . . .

The tea was left untouched. The ringing of the telephone was not heard. The rattle of dishes in the kitchen as Ellen got herself a cup of coffee and a bran muffin went unnoticed. All sights and sounds of the present faded and became unreal as the past emerged to take its place. With each letter, Mae sank further and further into the memory of her mother's life.

Mae was anxious to read the letters written in 1930, the year she was born. She wondered what Amelia had told her best friend about the arrival of her only daughter, but when Mae reached the letters from that year, she found the first one postmarked September 16. By then, Mae would already have been almost five months old. With a twinge of disappointment, she wondered whether there had been earlier letters that Clara had thrown away, letters that might have been written just before and after her birth. She would have liked to have had them. *Well, I should be glad for what I have,* she thought. *If Clara weren't such a keeper, I might have ended up with nothing.*

She opened the letter with a hint of a smile on her face, anticipating the joy her arrival had brought. Indeed, the letter was filled with joy and an abundance of exclamation points. However, as Mae's eyes moved across the first page and then the second, her smile faded and the color drained from her face. Her breathing quickened, and the stationery trembled in her fingers. With her heart pounding hard against her ribs, she tried to grasp the meaning of what she read. She couldn't quite understand, couldn't quite believe what her mother had written, and when she finished she got up from the chair to start walking — though she didn't know where it was she wanted to go. It didn't matter, because in the next moment her mind shut itself down, and the letter dropped away from her hands as she fell unconscious to the floor.

Chapter 13

Her first sensation was of the scratchy tendrils of the carpet against her cheek, then of a tingling in the arm wedged between her body and the floor. A certain vague darkness pulsated around her, broken only by a weak finger of sunlight reaching in through the window and touching her eyelids. She felt drained and dizzy, as though the floor were tilting back and forth while she floated up through layers of consciousness. She heard a distant, disturbing sound that she couldn't identify until she realized it was a moan crawling through her own throat.

Before she could move or even open her eyes, her mind scrambled to make sense out of the confusion. What had happened? How did she come to be lying here on the floor, her cheek pressed against the scratchy carpet? Was it night or day? Was she sleeping or ill or hurt?

Her mind tugged at her, trying to pull her up out of the darkness, trying to bring her again to the place of awareness. But as she reached forward toward consciousness, she couldn't think back to what lay before the blank, couldn't put her finger on what it was that had caused her to escape into this shelter of numbness. She wasn't sure she wanted to know. For the moment, she wanted only to lie quietly until the dizziness passed and the floor became still again.

But she was jolted by a cry that broke through the fog of semiconsciousness. She heard a voice above her and knew she had to respond.

"Mother! What happened?"

She felt gentle hands turning her over, relieving the weight on the arm that had been pinned beneath her when she fell. She hadn't known how stifling hot she had been until the air of the ceiling fan blew across her face like a lake breeze. The cool air refreshed her, and she took deep breaths of it.

Now, with her head in Ellen's lap, she was able to focus on her daughter's face. She saw at once the look of questioning and fear in Ellen's eyes. Mae lifted a hand to her moist forehead just as Ellen was saying, "Mother, what on earth happened to you? How did you fall? Are you hurt anywhere?"

So many questions at once. Mae struggled to sort them out, then replied tentatively, "I'm all right, I think."

"Let me help you to the bed," Ellen offered. She gently eased her mother up, guiding her to the floral-patterned bedspread on which Mae had lately spent so many hours.

Mae sat down heavily on the edge of the bed and rubbed her tingling arm. No bones broken, it appeared. Just a bit sore. She waved a hand at Ellen. "No need to make a fuss," she said mildly. "I'm all right." But a wave of dizziness hit her, and she clutched the edge of the mattress to support herself.

"All right?" Ellen exclaimed. "I come up here and find you unconscious on the floor, and you tell me you're all right? Dear heavens, Mother, you're as pale as a ghost."

Mae inhaled deeply, then patted nonchalantly at her hair and smoothed her skirt. "I just got up too fast," she said. "I got dizzy — must have lost my balance."

Ellen reached for the still untouched glass of iced tea and offered it to Mae. "Here," she said, "drink some of this. It might make you feel a little better."

Mae took the glass without protest and took several generous swallows. She nodded as she placed the glass on the bedside table. "Yes, that does help. Thank you, dear."

"Now you lie down while I call your doctor," Ellen insisted.

Mae waved her hand again and tried to shake her head, but the movement only made her more dizzy. "No, no, no," she said, "There's no need to bother the doctor. I'm fine. I just need a minute to catch my breath."

Ellen had made a move toward the door but came back again to her mother's side. "I don't think it's wise to ignore this. People just don't go around blacking out for no reason. I really insist that we call Dr. Brinkman."

Mae reached out and squeezed Ellen's hand reassuringly. "Please, dear," she said. "Just let me rest for a while. I'd really prefer that you not call the doctor right now."

Mother and daughter looked at each other for a long moment. Their eyes were placid, yet they both knew they were locked in a clash of wills.

"I don't understand," Ellen said finally. "Why don't you want me to call the doctor?"

"There's nothing wrong with me," Mae insisted. "Dr. Brinkman would only tell me I've been under too much stress lately, and I don't think I need to pay anyone to tell me that."

Ellen sighed. She always felt tired when she came up against her mother's stubbornness. "All right, Mother, I won't call. But if you still feel like this tomorrow, will you let me make an appointment?" she asked.

"Yes, yes, all right, but I'm sure I'll be fine. Now stop worrying and go on back to whatever you were doing. I think I will lie down after all, though — just for a bit." Mae propped the pillows up against the headboard of the bed and eased herself back against them.

Ellen hesitated another moment before relenting. "All right," she said. "I'm almost finished painting for today. Let me get that mess cleaned up, and then I'll bring you some lunch. Would a tuna fish sandwich be okay?"

Mae shut her eyes and nodded absently. "Fine, dear." She folded her hands across her stomach and breathed deeply. With some relief she heard Ellen head for the door, but then suddenly she remembered the letter. Feeling too weak to retrieve it herself, she called out just as Ellen was shutting the door. "Ellen, dear, would you please —" Then she changed her mind, afraid that Ellen would ask about the letter, or even begin to read it. "Never mind, you go on."

Ellen turned back toward her. "What is it, Mother? Can I get you something?"

"No, nothing. Nothing, really."

Ellen shrugged. "All right, then. I trust you'll stay in bed for a while and not try to get up and putter around." She started to shut the door, then opened it again. "I'm going to leave the door open. You holler if you need anything."

"I will. Thank you, dear."

Mae waited until she heard Ellen reach the bottom of the stairs before she quietly eased herself off the bed and picked up the letter from the floor. She lay back down then against the pillows and pressed the letter to her chest with the fingertips of both hands. The stationery was a delicate parchment, cream colored, with Amelia's initials embossed along the top. The letter itself was only two small weightless pieces of paper, but to Mae it felt uncannily heavy. She had to gather all her strength to lift the pages up to where she could see them. She took a deep breath and started to read slowly and deliberately, thinking that if she read each page carefully and studied every word, she would discover she had been mistaken, that the letter did not say at all what she thought it had said the first time she read it.

But when she came to the end, she found that the letter hadn't changed, and that she had not been mistaken. Every word was the same, sprawled across the pages in her mother's delicate handwriting.

September 16, 1930
Dearest Clara,

My heart overflows with thanksgiving to God — our baby girl has arrived! After so many years of unanswered prayer (you, Clara, are one of the few who knows how long I've prayed for this), I can scarcely believe that God has graciously fulfilled the desire of my heart and made me the mother of a little girl! Of course it did not happen as I had originally hoped or expected, but God knows what is best. I don't feel the least bit disappointed by the manner in which He has answered my prayer. I am filled with far too much joy and contentment for there to be room for anything else.

On the 22nd of this month, our little darling will be five months old. She is so sweet and all I ever dreamed of! We have had her for a full five days now, and I would have written to you, my dear friend, the very first day except that now that I have her, I've scarcely been able to let her out of my arms.

243

Even now as I write she sleeps in her cradle beside me — I can't bear to let her out of my sight. Frank fears that I am going to spoil her, and the boys think it is of no great consequence to have a little sister, but I suppose I can hardly expect them to appreciate a mother's joy!

I can in no way describe my excitement of the afternoon that Mrs. Elsbree called and said that they had a baby girl available and she could be ours if we wanted her. I wanted her even before I laid eyes on her! Of course it is terribly tragic about her parents. They were both killed outright in an automobile accident only weeks after the birth of the baby. I can scarcely bring myself to think of it, as at times I feel I have gained only because of their great loss, but I will try to make it up to them at least a little by raising their daughter — my daughter — with the greatest of love and devotion. Perhaps I will tell you more of the story in a later letter, but today I don't want to taint my joy with thoughts of tragedy. I am selfish, God forgive me, but I can't help the way I feel.

She is the dearest little angel, so good-natured — she hardly ever makes a fuss and sleeps soundly through the night. Not at all like the boys, each of whom suffered colic and gave me many a sleepless night. Not that it wasn't worth it, of course, but it is so much nicer to stand over the baby's crib in the morning refreshed and ready to greet the day.

I believe she knows me already, for she smiles a big smile when I come to pick her up from the crib. She even puts her chubby little arms around my neck when I carry her, and she squeezes my finger when I lay it across her palm. We've been out walking — I push her about the neighborhood in her carriage to show her off to the neighbors, and they all declare she is the loveliest child they've ever seen.

I intend to have her portrait made very soon. I will send you a copy, I promise, as soon as I get them.

Frank suggested that we call the baby Amelia, but I didn't particularly want to name her after myself. I decided rather that she should be called Mary; though to compromise we settled on Amelia as a middle name. I chose Mary from the passage in Luke that talks about the two sisters, Martha and Mary. You'll remember that when Jesus came to their house, Martha stayed busy in the kitchen while Mary sat at Jesus' feet to listen while he talked. Martha complained to Jesus that she had to do all the work alone. "Tell Mary to come help me," Martha requested. But Jesus said (and I paraphrase, as I haven't my Bible at my fingertips), "Martha, you're troubled about so many things. But only one thing is needful; Mary has chosen the good part, which shall not be taken away from her."

Oh, I see that little Mae — as I like to call her — is awakening from her nap. I must prepare a bottle, and then we will see about getting lunch for the boys. She loves to sit in the kitchen and watch me as I go about my work.

To think that I finally have a daughter. Oh, my dear, I am infinitely happy!

Your loving friend,
Amelia

It didn't seem possible, but it was all laid out right here like a criminal's confession: Mae Demaray was adopted. Mae examined the idea as though it was something distasteful, a jar of moldy food in a refrigerator or a pile of discarded trash by the side of a country road. There was nothing good about it. To be adopted meant to have parents other than one's own. To be adopted meant that one had come from an orphanage — like Roy Hanna. Mae thought of her childhood horror of the orphanage where Roy lived, her thankfulness that she had never had to live in such a place. But now that childhood nightmare had suddenly come true.

A scientific theorem that she had learned in high school but had long ago forgotten came back to her now: "For every action there is an equal and opposite reaction." It seemed to Mae that for every ounce of joy once contained in Amelia's heart, there was now an equal amount of pain in her own.

All the days of her childhood that had brought happiness while she lived them now brought confusion. Security melted into deception. All the words and actions of love that she had known became quiet lies. All the faces that were so familiar — her mother, father, brothers — were now the faces of strangers because they were not who she had believed them to be. And the love, the devoted love, she had felt for her mother now turned to anger.

Why did she never tell me? Mae wondered. *Why did no one ever tell me?*

As she lay there, her mind furiously searching all the corridors and tangents of her life, she came upon one hint of the adoption, an incident that her child's mind had long ago tucked away. She was about six years old at the time, and her eldest brother, Peter, was upset with her for something. It might have been the time she spilled paint on his collection of baseball cards, though she couldn't be sure. She did recall, however, that Peter had been angry enough to knock her down and scream, "I hate you. I wish Mom and Dad had never adopted you!"

Mae had been horrified. What was Peter saying? That she had come from a place like that orphanage where Roy lived? That she didn't really belong to her mother and father?

She ran to her mother in tears and, in between sobs and hiccoughs, told her that Peter had said she was adopted.

Amelia had taken Mae into her lap, wiped

away the tears with the corner of her apron and said, "Now, don't you worry. That's what my brother used to say to me, too, when he got angry with me. Big brothers can be mean and unthinking."

Mae had looked at her mother with saucerlike eyes, sniffed heavily, and tried to stifle her sobs. When she had caught her breath, she asked timidly, "Then I'm not adopted, Mama?"

Amelia had laughed and stroked her daughter's hair. "Don't listen to Peter," she had said soothingly. "You're Mama's own little darling, and I love you very much."

Peter had been severely punished. He had, in fact, been whipped with his father's belt for the first and only time in his life and had not been allowed to eat dinner with the family for several days. After a time Mae no longer thought of the incident, and no one ever mentioned adoption to her again.

But why? Mae wondered. *Why was it — how could it have been — kept from me all these years? Everyone must have known, everyone but me.*

Mae thought of all the letters from Clara that her mother had saved. Mae herself had read them dozens of times. Not a mention of the adoption — but then, there was that yearlong gap in the correspondence in 1930. Her mother, knowing that Mae might one day read the letters, must have destroyed any that talked about the adoption.

Mae thought of her surviving brothers and

wondered what they knew, what they might be able to tell her. Peter obviously knew something about the adoption, but since the topic had been taboo in the family, she suspected he didn't know much. Ken, who was barely three when Mae was brought into the Wollencott home, probably hadn't been aware of anything unusual about her arrival. He too might have thought all these years that Mae had been born into the family.

Perhaps the orphanage . . . but there were no more orphanages in Minnesota. The facility where Roy grew up had merged with another orphanage back in the early 1960s and was now being run as a home for the temporary care of children until foster homes or adoptive families could be found for them. Besides, Mae had assumed that her adoption had been processed at the facility where Roy lived, but she realized that wasn't necessarily true. She didn't know where she had come from, or whether the adoption had even taken place in Minneapolis.

Mae looked at the box of letters sitting placidly on the small end table. What had only hours before looked so inviting now appeared as perilous as Pandora's Box. She had opened the box and everything had changed. All that she had believed to be true wasn't true at all, and suddenly she was stripped of her identity and was left wondering, after half a century of life, who exactly she was. She wanted to shut the flaps of the box and seal it with yards and yards of tape so that no more horrors could come out of it. Yet she knew she would have to read the letters because one of them might hold a clue as to who she was and where she had come from. She would read them all, but not today. She didn't have the strength today.

Mae barely touched the tuna fish sandwich Ellen brought on a tray shortly after noon. Until early evening she lay on the bed, her body immobile while her mind raced through all the years of her life, trying to seek some understanding, trying to make sense of what she had learned. But she could make no sense of it, and the hours left her feeling only more lost and confused. She felt disconnected from herself, as though not only her life but her own mind and body were something other than what she had always known them to be. Questions tumbled through her head, angry questions that she wanted to hurl at those who could give her the answers. But those people were dead and had carried away the answers with them.

In the midst of all the scattered and fragmented thoughts, two things suddenly and for the first time became clear to Mae. She understood now her father's awkwardness with her, his subtle aloofness. It wasn't because she was a girl, but because she wasn't his. He hadn't quite been able to regard her as one of his own. Perhaps that had changed when she had grown into womanhood. She had been the one, after all, who had stayed with him after his wife died and after the boys all married and left the house. Maybe he had finally taken her into his heart, as evidenced by the gift of the house when she and George had married. Even so, the acceptance had taken years and had cost a little girl many hours of wondering why her father preferred his sons.

And she now understood, too, why she bore no physical resemblance to her mother — nor to her father, for that matter. Two of her brothers had had Amelia's red hair, and two were dark like the doctor, but even the dark-haired boys had carried their mother's features and more closely resembled her than had Mae. Only a few people — strangers and casual acquaintances, mostly — ever remarked on how little Mae favored either parent, and when they did, her mother always brushed off the comment with, "Well, everyone's unique, you know." That had satisfied Mae. She hadn't spent much time wondering at the dissimilarities between herself and the rest of her family. She simply accepted herself as unique.

Now, suddenly, she knew why she was different. It wasn't that the family genes had played a trick by casting her into a peculiar mold. She undoubtedly looked like someone. She simply had no idea who.

When Ellen returned with a dinner tray in the evening, she found her mother pale and still, lying against the pillows with her eyes shut.

"Mother?" she said quietly. Mae opened her

eyes. Ellen thought she had never looked so weary. "I've brought you some broth and crackers. Do you think you can sit up and eat?"

Mae lay quietly a moment as though considering the question. Then she said, "I'm afraid I'm really not very hungry right now."

"But you hardly touched your lunch. You've scarcely had anything to eat all day," Ellen said. "Is your stomach upset or are you in pain somehow?"

Pain, yes, Mae thought. *But I can't point to it or tell you how it feels.* Finally she said, "I'm just tired."

"I really think you ought to see a doctor today," Ellen insisted. "Why don't you let me take you to the after-hours clinic? Maybe you have a simple virus or something, but we might as well find out and put our minds at rest. Please, Mother, don't be obstinate. Please let me take you to the clinic."

Mae shook her head while trying to lift herself up on the pillows. "No, I don't need a doctor," she replied. "Please, dear, put the tray down on the desk and come sit with me. I have something to tell you." She patted the bed beside her and waited for Ellen to sit down before she began to talk.

Chapter 14

Mae studied her daughter's face while Ellen read the letter. Other than a slight frown of concentration, there was little there to let Mae know what her daughter thought or felt. Mae's first intention had been to explain to Ellen herself that she was adopted, but when Ellen sat down and waited for her to begin, Mae discovered she couldn't find the words. Instead, she said simply, "This is a letter your grandmother wrote. It reveals something — very important."

Ellen's frown deepened as she finished reading and folded the two pages of stationery. Mae waited expectantly for her daughter's response. Only after a moment did Ellen finally raise her eyes and say, "Well, that is something of a shock, isn't it? Is this what you were reading when —"

Mae nodded. "I couldn't take it in. I guess my mind more or less just shut down on me."

"Well, now I can understand —" Ellen took a deep breath and placed the letter on the bedside table. "Never having known Grandma Amelia, I don't know why she never told you about something like this. It seems a little" — she paused and looked away, as though searching the room for the right word — "well, it just seems a little odd, though I've heard of other people discovering as adults that they were adopted."

"I never thought . . . never would have imagined . . . it changes everything. Everything!" Tears gathered in Mae's eyes, and she was glad in the next moment to accept her daughter's comforting hug.

"Oh, Mother," Ellen said, holding her mother close, "I know this is difficult for you. I can only imagine how difficult. But it doesn't change who you are. Not really. You're still the same person."

Mae pulled back and gazed anxiously at Ellen. "But, my dear," she whispered, "who is that?"

Ellen took one of Mae's hands and held it between her own. "You're my mother, whom I love. Mae Demaray. That's who you are."

Mae shook her head sadly and squeezed Ellen's hand. "I feel lost," she said, "as though my whole life has been a lie."

"You shouldn't feel that way," Ellen said gently. "You've had — and still have — a good life. You were a wonderful wife, and you're a wonderful mother." She reached for the letter again and shook it a moment above the table, as though she were ringing a bell. "This doesn't change that. This doesn't change your marriage or all the years you were raising Mike and me. It doesn't change all the good you've done in your life. Maybe you don't know who your real par-

254

ents were, but that doesn't change who you are inside."

"But doesn't it bother you, all of this?" Mae asked.

Ellen thought a moment. "Well, I'm not sure how to answer that. It was a well-kept secret, that's for sure. But bother me? No, I don't think so."

"But this is *your* family, too," Mae pointed out. "Whoever my parents were, they were your grandparents. We don't know the first thing about them — who they were, where they came from, what they were like. Worse than that, I don't know what to feel for my parents — that is, the people who raised me."

"You loved them. You can love them still. Why should that be any different?"

"I did love them, yes; I loved them deeply. But I believed they were my mother and father."

"They *were* your mother and father. Not just legally, but because they were the ones who gave you a home, gave you the chance to be part of a family."

"But they should have told me the truth. I should have known the truth from the beginning."

"Granted, they probably should have told you about the adoption. Heaven only knows why they didn't, but it was their choice not to. I think what matters was that they loved you. Maybe you should consider yourself fortunate that they took you as their daughter. Who knows where you might have ended up otherwise?"

"Someone else may have been honest with me. Maybe I wouldn't have had to discover the truth by accident."

Ellen sighed and put her hands on her mother's shoulders. "Oh, Mother, I love you so much, and I hate the unhappy things that have happened to you. The fire, and now this. It seems more than anyone should have to face. All I want is for you to be happy. What can I do to help? Tell me what I can do."

Mae lifted her arms, and mother and daughter hugged again. Both faces were moist with tears when they pulled apart. Mae took a deep trembling breath and lay back against the pillows. "I wish you could tell me who I am. I feel so . . . disoriented, as though I've suddenly become someone else. I'm afraid I'll never really know the truth about myself."

Ellen raised her fingertips to her lips thoughtfully. "If it really matters to you, there must be ways of finding out where you came from, who your family was."

Mae shook her head in defeat. "Who's left alive who could tell me anything?"

"Aren't records kept somewhere for adoptions? Don't you think the county or the state —"

"I suppose," Mae interrupted, "but — I wouldn't even know where to begin."

They were quiet for a moment; then Ellen asked, "Where'd you get this letter of Grandmother's, anyway?"

Mae pointed to a face in the framed photograph on the bedside table. It was her favorite photo of her mother — the photo of Amelia and her friends that had once had a place on the mantel in the Humboldt house. Roy had rescued it from the fire when he carried it out to the lawn along with the music box and some other photos. "Clara Reynolds," Mae said in answer to Ellen's question. "Mother's friend who moved away to Vermont."

"She's still alive?"

"Yes."

"Well, couldn't she tell you something?"

"She might have been able to once, but she has Alzheimer's now. She's not a bit aware of what's going on around her. It was her daughter Evelyn who sent the letters on to me. There's a whole box of them over there by the chair, all from Mother to Clara."

Ellen turned to where her mother was pointing, then looked back at the photo. After a moment, she tapped the glass in the frame with an index finger. "This one's Helen Lewis, right? Isn't she still alive? I think you mentioned some time ago that she was in a nursing home somewhere around here."

Mae sat up straighter and looked at Helen's young face in the photo. "Of course," she said, suddenly remembering, "you're right. Helen is still living. I don't know why it didn't occur to me. She still sends out Christmas cards every year, and I got one last Christmas. Her daughter writes the cards because poor Helen is practically paralyzed with arthritis, but I suppose I could call Joyce and ask whether I might visit Helen." Mae looked at Ellen hopefully, then glanced again at the box of letters. "But first I think I'll finish reading those to see what other surprises they might hold."

Mae spent the next several days reading the letters. There were no more surprises, but one letter in particular disturbed her. It was a letter that she read many times and thought long and hard about. She put it aside from the rest, along with the letter revealing her adoption.

As for the remainder of the correspondence, Mae found it difficult to work her way through it. Instead of the joy the box had promised when it arrived, it produced only anxiety and a profound sense of sadness. All sorts of childhood memories and feelings were awakened, and the long-ago days that had once been so happy now held ghosts of untruths and deception. Often the page in her hand became blurred, the words running together as her eyes filled and spilled over with tears.

Finally Mae called Joyce Hoffmann, who reported that her mother would love a visit, and yes, of course, Helen would remember Mae. "She's past eighty now, but her mind's as sharp and alert as it ever was."

If that was so, maybe she could give Mae a clue as to who she was.

The two corridors of the low one-story building stretched out from the central lobby like the wings of a bird in flight. Nestled in those wings were the elderly living out their final days — nodding in wheelchairs, shuffling along on slippered feet, lying in hospital beds, dreaming their last dreams before death.

This was probably how Sophie Mills had pictured retirement, Mae thought, before she stepped into her Floridian wonderland. But being retired and being decrepit, though often considered synonymous, were two very different things. Mae would never be retired; she had nothing to be retired from. Yet as she walked the corridor in search of Helen Lewis's room, she felt as old and weary as some of the octogenarians she passed. Sometimes it isn't the years that wears a person down, she decided. Sometimes it's what happens in those years.

At the end of the corridor, Mae found Room 21 and in it she found Helen Lewis — a small, wizened patch of flesh in the center of a bed hemmed in by railings. She was a pale figure lying between plain white sheets. Her snowy hair, loose and disheveled, was as white as the pillowcase against which her head rested. Her once brown eyes were clouded and milky, her lips blanched, her cheeks waxen. Mae decided that as Helen's health faded, all her color was draining away with it.

As Joyce had predicted, Helen recognized Mae as soon as she slipped on the horn-rimmed glasses that hung about her neck on a chain.

"Oh, my dear!" Helen said, lifting one twisted hand from beneath the sheet and offering it to Mae. "How good it is to see you. Joyce said you planned to stop by sometime. So kind of you to come visit an old woman. Please have a seat. Make yourself comfortable, and we'll have a nice chat."

Mae suffered a pang of guilt, knowing that her visit had nothing to do with kindness, that she had come for reasons having to do only with herself. She tried to remember the last time she had visited Helen and couldn't recall when it was. Years ago, no doubt, and even then only briefly.

She settled herself in the stiff vinyl chair and fumbled for words. Before she could say anything, Helen said, "Such a lovely Christmas card you sent last year with the manger scene on the front. I save them all, you know." Helen smiled placidly at Mae, then pushed the control button on her bed to elevate the head. It seemed to take forever for the mattress to inch itself upward, but finally Helen was satisfied that she had reached the proper height. "There, I guess that will do." She then reached for a blue knit sweater that lay across the far railing and attempted to wrap it about her shoulders. Mae stood and helped Helen with the sweater. "Thank you, dear," Helen said.

Her voice was shaky and weak, but Mae could tell that Helen's mind was indeed sharp.

"There we are, I think I'm all set now and ready to receive my visitor."

The aged woman offered another serene smile as her eyes traveled over Mae's face. "Oh, my dear, it *is* good to see you," she said cheerfully. Then, in the habit of the elderly, she slipped at once into reminiscing. "How you used to tickle me so when you were a child. I remember when you were, oh, maybe three years old, you used to wander up to where your mother and I were drinking afternoon tea on the couch, and you would say to me quite primly, holding out your little arm, 'Please have a seat, Auntie Helen!' And I would say, 'Thank you, Mae dear, but I already *am* having a seat.' And your mother and I would giggle behind our teacups" — Helen giggled as though she were even now sitting on the couch with Amelia drinking tea — "and when you saw that you had amused us, you clapped your little hands and yelled, 'I'm so happy!' You did so love to make people laugh, even when you didn't know exactly why they were laughing.

"You were such a delightful child — always, all the years you were growing up. I'm afraid my gravest mistake as a mother was comparing my Joyce to you and placing her in a rather unfavorable light at times. Sometimes when she wearied me or made me angry, I'd say to her, 'You could take a lesson or two from Mae Wollencott, you know. Why, she's always happy and polite to everyone!' I shouldn't have done it, I suppose. It wasn't fair to Joyce; she was such a good girl in her own way. But back then we didn't have all the books that young women have today to tell

261

them how to be mothers. We just lived and learned, and very often it was our mistakes that taught us.

"Well, Mae, I'll just lie quietly now and let you catch me up on all the news. Tell me about Ellen and the girls. How is everyone?"

"Everyone's fine, just fine, thank you, Helen," Mae said, flustered. She hadn't come for small talk, but she supposed it was the expected threshold to any conversation.

"I imagine the girls are growing up fast," Helen sighed. "You can't keep them little for long, can you? Of course, I can hardly believe that Ellen's a mother already. Seems like only yesterday . . . my, time does fly. . . ."

Helen's words faded and Mae could see that she was again traveling into the past. Mae wanted Helen to go back in years but to find something specific, not to wander aimlessly. Mae decided she might as well do away with pleasantries and get right to the point.

"Helen," she said softly but firmly, "I came to speak with you about — my mother."

Helen looked at Mae quizzically for a moment, then laughed lightly. "Amelia? Why, certainly, dear, I'd be delighted to reminisce with you about your mother. You know how she was always one of my best friends — beginning way back in our girlhood when we were assigned seats next to each other in the first grade. I've always been glad for that bit of good luck that seated us side by side." Helen, her head resting in the center furrow of the pillows, stared at the ceiling as though a movie of her early life were playing itself out overhead. "We had many happy times together, your mother and I. We shared the tough times too, mind you. We spent many an hour crying on each other's shoulders for one reason or another. But when you grow old, you tend to forget the bad times. What you find yourself remembering is the good. I do wish your mother could have grown old with me. Oh, I know, it's terrible to *be* old." She held up both arthritic hands, as though presenting evidence. The knuckles were swollen and the fingers gnarled. "I wouldn't wish this upon Amelia. But if anyone was entitled to her seventy years, it was your mother." Helen moved her head from side to side and clicked her tongue. "So young when she died. Just in the prime of life. Well" — she smiled — "your mother certainly squeezed every drop out of the years she did have. I've never known anyone to appreciate life more than your dear mother."

Suddenly Helen lifted her head weakly and turned her faded eyes toward Mae. "But I mustn't ramble or I'll keep you here for a week. Was there something in particular you wanted to talk about?"

Mae unsnapped her purse. Her hand disappeared in the hollow of white leather for a moment, then reappeared with the letter Amelia had written to Clara more than fifty years before. "Helen," Mae said, "I don't quite know exactly what I want you to tell me but . . . well, let me just ask you directly. Did you know that I was adopted?"

Helen's eyes widened and became almost clear for a moment as surprise replaced age. She drew in a gasp of air and held it, made immobile by a sudden fear. Crimson crept into her cheeks, and she looked like a child about to be scolded for having misbehaved. "Oh, my dear!" was all she said, and that in a whisper.

Without emotion, Mae asked, "Will you tell me what you know, Helen?"

Instead of speaking, Helen reached for a Styrofoam cup of water on the nightstand. Mae grasped it first and handed it to Helen. After the old woman had taken a few shaky sips, Mae replaced it on the stand. She waited for Helen to speak.

When Helen had finally composed herself, she said, "Amelia had so hoped . . . well, you were never to know. She said you were never to know about the adoption. Oh, my dear, how did you find out?"

"Mother told me herself, so to speak," Mae said. She held up the letter so Helen could see it. The old woman tried to focus her eyes on the handwriting. "It's from Mother to Clara Reynolds, written in 1930," Mae explained. "The letter makes it clear that I was adopted."

Helen shut her eyes a moment and nodded, then took a deep breath. "Ah yes," she sighed. "She and Clara were great friends. Your mother told her everything, even after Clara married and moved away."

"But you knew too?"

"Yes, of course. She could hardly hide it from me or from any of her friends. Now, not everyone knew, mind you. Not everyone. Some people at the church, some neighbors even, people like that — they thought you belonged to Amelia and Dr. Wollencott. When a couple already has several children, people begin to lose track. They just assume the couple will have another child every two or three years — or at least they did in those days. That suited Amelia just fine. She wanted people to believe you were her own. She herself wanted to believe you were her own. But, as I say, she could hardly hide it from her closest friends."

Mae sat up straighter in the chair and tried to stifle the annoyance she felt rising inside of her. "So all of you knew, but no one told me."

Helen gazed at Mae, her eyes heavy with compassion. "Believe me, Mae, we thought you should be told. Edna and I had some candid talks with Amelia — oh yes, it was our opinion that you should be told. Even Clara said as much in one of her letters to your mother. But Amelia wouldn't hear of it. She wouldn't listen to any of us. And it was hardly our place to tell you. There was nothing more we could do."

Mae considered Helen's position, then said, "I can understand the predicament you were in. I'm sorry for that. I appreciate your trying to persuade Mother to tell me." Then more quietly, she added, "Still, it seems inexcusable for Mother to let me live a lie."

Helen cocked her head and leaned closer to Mae. "I'm sorry, what was that last thing you said?" she asked. "My hearing's not what it used to be."

Mae repeated more loudly, "I said, Mother let me live a lie. She lied to me."

Helen lifted one hand wearily and shook her index finger like a schoolteacher. "Now, now, you must understand, Mae. Your mother did not lie to you," she said. "She merely didn't tell you the truth."

"It amounts to the same thing."

"Not at all."

"I don't see how you can say that."

"Amelia didn't want the adoption to be an issue in your life."

"Not an issue! It's no small fact that she was hiding."

"No, no. I agree. It's no small fact."

Mae sighed, trying to calm herself. She didn't want to take out her pain and frustration on this tiny ailing woman who had at one time, unknown to Mae, tried to help her. She replaced the letter in her purse and said quietly, "I'm sorry, Helen, if I seem angry. I'm not the least bit upset with you, of course. I just don't understand Mother's reasoning. Why didn't she want to tell me?"

Helen was quiet a moment, as though searching her mind for any reason that Amelia might have given long ago. Finally she said, "You have to understand your mother's desire for a daughter. Even when Amelia and I were little children playing with our dolls, her make-believe children were always girls. All girls. She loved the thought of frilly dresses, plaits with ribbons, shiny patent leather shoes. Even when we were teenagers swooning over young men and dreaming of our future role as wife and mother, Amelia always pictured herself surrounded by daughters. She wanted at least three, she said. She was constantly thinking of names. 'What do you think about such-and-such a name?' she would ask. She must have come up with hundreds of names for her little girls.

"Well, she had four sons, you see. And then when my Joyce was born shortly after your brother Kenny, it was something of a blow to Amelia. Not that she wasn't happy for me; of course she was. But here I was with a brand-new daughter, a beautiful little girl, while Amelia had been warned not to have any more children. They'd almost lost her and Kenny both when he was born — I don't suppose you knew that. So when the attending doctor said no more children, of course your father agreed. He was quite satisfied himself. Four boys. What else could a man want? But a hole was left in Amelia's heart, a terrible hole she thought would never be filled. The one thing she had wanted and planned for all her life — now she couldn't have it.

"Now don't get me wrong; your mother loved her sons. Loved them with every ounce of her mother's heart, but it wasn't the same. She felt she couldn't have the relationship with them that she could have with a daughter. I have a son and a daughter myself, and I can tell you it's true. A mother's relationship with a son is different from her relationship with a daughter. Not that one is necessarily better than the other; they're just different. Mother and daughter can share together all the wonders of a woman's world. And men, fathers and sons, they have their own world. Your mother believed — and rightly so, I think — that she couldn't really share her woman's world with her sons, and she felt her beautiful world becoming a lonely place when there was no more hope for a daughter.

"But Amelia was always one for making the best of a situation, so she decided that if she couldn't have a daughter of her own, she would adopt one. Your father was against it at first. He said there was a depression and they had four children already. He couldn't see his way clear to taking on the added expense of a fifth child. But Amelia didn't give up, and Dr. Wollencott finally relented.

"They began talking with a social worker at that children's home — I forget the name of it, but you know the place. And it wasn't long before they got the call that you were available. You were practically a newborn. Your parents had been killed in an automobile accident. The other car was speeding and ran right through a stop sign."

Mae, who had been listening intently, interrupted at this point. "But what about other relatives?" she asked. "Why wasn't I sent to live with an aunt or a grandmother?"

Helen shrugged weakly. She was obviously getting worn out from so much talking. "I don't know all the details, dear," she said. "But, as your father was known to say, there was indeed a depression on. Everyone was desperate for work, and families were scattered all over the country. It could have been that there were no relatives or that the authorities just plain didn't know where to find them. Those were hard times you were born into."

"Well," Mae said, then paused a moment. Her eyes fell to her lap, then traveled the room as though she didn't know what to rest them upon. She was afraid of the emotions and the tears that might well up if she looked at Helen's sympathetic face. Finally she managed to say, "I guess I still don't understand why Mother felt she had to keep the adoption a secret."

"Yes," Helen nodded, "that's a difficult one. I never fully understood her reasons myself. But, you see, whether she was mistaken in her thinking or not, Amelia felt that the bond between the two of you would be stronger if you believed she was your real mother. She thought if you knew about the adoption, she would appear to be somehow not quite real as a mother — just a substitute of sorts. She thought you'd be forever wondering about the woman who had given you life. And she was afraid her relationship with you would be diminished by your curiosity about your real mother."

Mae clasped her hands together in her lap and took a deep breath. "Oh, I see," she said. "I —"

Before Mae could say more, Helen interrupted. "My dear," she said gently, "your mother loved you so much. You have to understand that. She wanted only your good. No daughter has been more wanted or more loved than you. Perhaps you feel cheated for having been adopted, but there are many natural children who don't receive the devotion you received. Life could have been very hard for you had you ended up somewhere else."

Mae squeezed her hands together and pursed her lips as she felt the conflicting emotions of gratitude and grief tumbling through her chest. She looked at Helen's sallow face at rest against the pillow, small and weak as an infant's. She understood the desire to take care of the helpless. "Yes, I know, Helen," she said. "I know I'm fortunate that good people took me in as their own. But I only wish Mother had told me."

"But she didn't, and you can't change that now," Helen said gently.

No, Mae thought, *we can't change the past, no matter how much we might want to. I know that only too well.*

For a moment, neither woman said anything.

Then Helen continued. "I believe Amelia would have completely forgotten herself that you were adopted, if she could have. But she was never able to, of course, because of the boy."

Mae waited for an explanation, wondering which of her brothers Helen might be referring to. It had to be Peter, she decided. She thought of how Peter had told her she was adopted, of how he had almost given away their mother's secret. Maybe Peter was a constant threat to Amelia. He had been old enough to understand. The younger boys might have been fooled — Mother went away and came back with a child. That was all they knew and all they needed to know about babies. But Peter knew the truth, and he had blurted it out once in anger. Maybe Amelia lived with the fear that he would do it again — and that this time Mae would believe him.

When Mae saw that Helen needed prodding to continue, she asked, "Are you talking about Peter?"

"Peter?" Helen said. "Oh no, my dear, not Peter. I mean Roy, of course."

Mae frowned and stared hard at Helen. She leaned forward in the chair so that she could hear and be heard clearly. "What about Roy?" she asked.

"Why, I assumed it would be in your mother's letter," Helen said.

Mae patted the side of her purse. "Not in this one. She mentions him in later ones, of course.

He was at our house all the time."

"Then you don't know?"

Mae's arms and legs went weak, and she was glad she was sitting down. She clutched at her purse until her fingers ached. "I can't know, Helen, unless you tell me," she said evenly.

Helen shut her eyes a moment, then opened them and looked directly at Mae. "May Amelia forgive me," she said firmly, "but this is something else you should have known long ago. Mae dear, Roy Hanna is your brother."

Mae could not take her eyes away from Helen's face. She could not move. Roy, her brother? It wasn't possible, it wasn't —

She felt as though what she had just heard, all that she had recently learned, was a story belonging to someone else. It couldn't possibly be *her* story. She had always somehow pictured a far different unfolding of the years and a different ending. Just as, before it happened, she could not have imagined the accident that took Sammy's life, neither could she imagine afterward that her life would take on so many twists and turns. She had resolved to live out the remaining portion of her life quietly and more or less alone, treading carefully so as not to bring about any sudden changes or interruptions.

But now, after a series of upheavals, everything was different. Not just the future, but the past and the present too. Her home was gone, her possessions destroyed, and the people she had always known were suddenly different people altogether. Her family wasn't really her family. And Roy wasn't just a friend — it was *he* who was family. She could not make sense of it. It was like walking into a house she thought she had always known and finding that she didn't recognize it at all. The furniture was completely new; the wallpaper that of odd colors and patterns; unfamiliar paintings and photographs of strangers hung on the walls. How was she to live here? It wasn't home. It wasn't *her* home.

"My dear, are you all right?"

The voice came to her from far away, and Mae slowly became aware that Helen was speaking. She tried to focus on the mouth that was forming the words.

"Would you like me to ring for a nurse? You look terribly pale."

Mae managed to shake her head. Her mouth was dry. She moistened her lips with the tip of her tongue and said, "No. No, Helen, don't call a nurse. I'm all right."

"It's a terrible shock, I'm sure."

Mae sat back in the chair. "Perhaps I ought to be used to such shocks by now," she said, trying to smile. "I am surprised, of course. Roy Hanna, my brother." She shook her head again slowly in disbelief. "But then, I suppose I should have known. I always sensed — I don't know what — something. I can't explain it."

Helen laid her head back and shut her eyes. "Well, Mae, I've lived long enough to know that life is constantly surprising us. Now, not everyone has quite as many surprises as you've had, but we all have our share."

Mae thought a moment, then asked, "Why weren't Roy and I adopted together? Do you know anything about it?"

"Not everything, of course, but you see, Roy being what he is, that is, not very bright, he was not a good candidate for adoption. He was already five years old when the two of you arrived at the orphanage and his — handicap, I guess you might say — was already apparent. The people there knew it wasn't likely that he'd find a home. But you were different. You had a chance. A healthy baby girl, and an infant at that. They had the perfect family for you — the Wollencotts."

"Mother and Dad never considered adopting Roy as well?"

"Amelia might have adopted him if your father had been willing. But the doctor put his foot down, saying it was out of the question. They had all the sons they needed, he said."

"So that was why Mother was so kind to Roy, always having him over to dinner, always trying to include him in our lives."

"Yes. I think she nursed a sense of guilt that they had given you a home while Roy was left to grow up in the orphanage. It didn't seem quite fair to Amelia. She was so softhearted, you know. Kind to everyone, especially children. She did the best she could for Roy under the circumstances."

"And since he was so often at our house, Mother could never quite forget that I was adopted."

"No. She wanted to forget, as I said. And might have, too, if it hadn't been for Roy."

"Yet she always insisted that he come. She welcomed him."

"Yes, well, that was Amelia."

A few minutes passed in which the women were lost in their own thoughts, their own memories of Amelia. Then Helen asked, "The music box that used to sit on the mantel — was it lost in the fire?"

Mae found it curious that Helen should mention the music box. "No," she said. "It's one of the items Roy managed to get out of the house before it burned."

Helen smiled and looked satisfied. "I think that box might have belonged to your family — your natural family, that is."

Mae cocked her head and looked at Helen quizzically. "Why do you think that?" she asked.

"You and Roy arrived at the orphanage with one small suitcase of clothes and that music box."

Mae frowned. "Seems like an odd combination," she said.

"Yes, it does. Nevertheless, when you were adopted the box was given to Amelia, rather as though it were a baby gift from the orphanage."

"I wonder why it didn't stay with Roy?"

Helen lifted her shoulders, then let them drop

wearily. "Who can understand why people do what they do? Amelia told me that Roy loved that music box, that he listened to it whenever he visited your house."

Mae almost said, "He still does," but stopped herself when she remembered that the house was gone and she hadn't seen Roy since the fire. Instead, she replied, "Yes, he did. It seemed to remind him of something, or someone. He mentioned a woman once. I wonder whether she might have been . . ." Mae's voice trailed off as her mind wandered. After a few minutes her eyes settled on Helen, who was staring at her.

"You were saying, dear?" Helen asked.

"Nothing," Mae said, flustered again. She rose to leave. "I'm afraid I've tired you. I'd better go now and let you rest." She reached out and gently took one of Helen's hands. "Thank you, Helen, for what you've told me."

Helen squeezed Mae's hand weakly. "My dear Mae," she said, "of all that I've told you, remember this above all else: Amelia loved you. She *was* your mother in the most important sense of the word. And she was a good mother, wasn't she?"

Mae smiled. "Yes, Helen, she was a good mother."

"Then you mustn't blame her for the decision she made, even if you can't understand it. Perhaps she was wrong not to tell you, but her intentions were only good. If she's hurt you, see if you can find it in your heart to forgive her."

Mae smiled again, but sadly this time. She said

good-bye and turned to go. Her heels tapped out her retreat on the linoleum floor of the corridor as she walked. The hall was long and straight and led finally to only one place, but Mae felt as though there were a hundred corridors before her veering off into different directions, leading to as many ends. And she would have to decide which one to take. There were choices to be made, so many choices.

She passed an old woman restrained in a wheelchair, her head bent in sleep, a stream of drool dripping from her chin and onto the bib that covered her chest. Mae envied the old woman. She had only to stay put in this narrow hallway where she had been placed. She had nowhere else to go and nothing else to do. Mae thought it must be a great relief to reach that place where there are no more choices to be made, and all a person had to do was sleep or wait for sleep and, either way, to lose oneself in dreams.

Chapter 15

Mae stood on the sidewalk in front of the lot where her home had once been. It was her first visit since the fire, and the first thing she noticed was how strange the view was that formerly had been obstructed by the house: the detached garage that remained intact, the alley dotted by an odd collection of trash cans, the fenced-in yards and garden plots across the alley, the backs of the houses that faced the opposite street.

Along with George in their Pontiac station wagon, she had traveled years ago through all the wide-open spaces of Minnesota, South Dakota, Wyoming, and Montana, but no space seemed wider or more open than this empty plot of land on Humboldt Avenue. Her mind didn't want to believe what her eyes could see. It seemed like a magic trick or an optical illusion. She *knew* there was a house here somewhere, behind some invisible veil. She'd lived in it her entire life. She knew every inch of it — the way the floor creaked in the upstairs hallway, how the scent of cigar smoke lingered in the drapes, how the glass in some of the windows was rippled with age. What she needed now was a magician or a special effects expert from Hollywood to come along and lift the veil so the house would reappear.

Men had come, at some time in the past few weeks, but not magicians or Hollywood experts. Plain workingmen in denim clothes, wearing heavy boots and gloves, who pulled apart the remains of the house and carried away bits of charred timber, twisted and melted, and scorched furniture and piles of all sorts of unidentifiable debris. Fresh dirt was hauled to the lot to fill in the basement, and then the dirt was covered with rolls of sod so that when the men were finished there was not one trace left of the house that had sat on this patch of land for the better part of a century.

Mae walked up the front walkway, still slicing its way through the overgrown lawn but leading nowhere. She stopped at the end of the last square of concrete where the first porch step had been. All that met her feet now was the newly laid, dew-moistened grass.

More than a month had passed since the fire, but whenever a breeze rolled through the leaves of the trees and drifted across the grass, it lifted with it a faint odor of smoke. Mae breathed deeply. The ashes in the soil were like a phantom pain, the aching of a limb that had been removed.

Mae folded her arms against the chill and rubbed the goose bumps that prickled her flesh. It was early August, still the height of a hot summer, but the morning breeze was deceptively cool, and the sun certainly didn't offer the warmth it seemed to promise when Mae left the house without a sweater. She had left too without breakfast, or even a cup of coffee, and her stomach felt hollow and growled for food, but she didn't want to go back to her daughter's house yet. All those corridors that had rolled themselves out at her feet in the nursing home were still stretched out before her, and she knew she had to choose one to go down. No one was going to do it for her. No one was going to tie her into a wheelchair and roll her into place and leave her there for the remainder of her years.

Not that some wouldn't try to point her in a particular direction. Only the day before, she had received a long, dramatic letter from Sophie Mills, filled with profuse condolences about the fire but ending with the advice, "Now you really *must* come to Florida. You simply have no reason not to." Sam and Ellen, she knew, were anxious for Mae to sell the lot. They were still planning the trip to Florida so that she might become enamored with the palm trees and the warm temperatures and the senior citizens center. Mae knew they all meant well, and as she looked around at the empty grounds, she wondered briefly whether they may even be right.

But she continually came back around to the thought that whatever she did with her future, it wouldn't change the past. A decision to settle here or there wouldn't unravel the huge knotted skein of pain and confusion that her life had become. What should she do with all of the questions for which she would never find answers? What should she do with all of her anger and frustration? How should she think of herself? How should she view her life now that everything was different from what she had always believed?

Ellen and Sam had simply been amused to think that Roy was Mae's brother and Ellen's uncle. "Imagine!" Ellen had cried. "Maybe that's why he always seemed like family — because he is."

Sam added, "I think it's great. All the time we thought Roy was alone in the world, he was actually a part of us. Wait till we tell the girls."

"Let's not tell them quite yet," Mae suggested. "Nor Roy either."

"But why not, Mother?" Ellen asked.

"I just need some time to think," Mae answered lamely. "We can tell everyone when the time is right." First, though, she wanted to make some decisions about her future. There was the question of where she would live now that the house was gone. But perhaps more important, she thought, was the question of how she would live, what kind of person she would choose to be after what her mother's letters had revealed.

Mae's eyes followed the trunk and branches of a tall cottonwood tree until she was looking straight up at the expanse of sky overhead. There were no clouds, only a saucer of unbroken blue hanging over the world. Mae wondered whether Amelia was out there somewhere, and whether, if she screamed loud enough, her voice might travel undisturbed until it reached her. She had always considered a relationship over once one of the people involved had died. She didn't know that new feelings could come along, that new situations could arise, that a relationship could go on living though one of the members was long buried. She wanted to cry out, "You left some unfinished business here, Mother! You somehow failed to tell me I was adopted, and I want to know why."

But she knew why, really. Helen Lewis had told her. It hadn't mattered to Amelia Wollencott that her daughter was adopted. All that mattered was that she finally had a daughter after so many years of longing for one. What mattered was a mother's great love for her little girl. What more could Amelia add to what Helen Lewis had already said? Mae had the answer; the question now was, would she accept it? Would she try to understand and forgive her mother for not telling her the truth?

Mae slipped her hand into the roomy pocket of her skirt where, before leaving the house, she had tucked away two of her mother's letters to Clara. One was the letter that revealed the secret of her adoption. Though it had left her shocked and wounded, it also reminded Mae of why she had been named Mary. Her mother had taken the name from the Scripture she loved so much, the passage where Jesus said, "Only one thing is needful; Mary has chosen the good part, which shall not be taken away from her."

Choices. Here Mae stood at a many-pronged fork in the road, knowing that in her lifetime she had not always chosen the good part. Instead, she had sometimes made unwise choices, choices influenced by anger, stubbornness, pride.

A good example was in the second letter in Mae's pocket, the one that had disturbed her so when she first read it. She didn't take it out to read it again. She knew well enough what it said. Besides, every time she read it, she felt the words needling themselves into her anger, trying to change it into something else — and she was resisting. Nevertheless, the letter her mother had written haunted Mae, and she couldn't put it out of her mind.

At five years old Mae is already more stubborn, and in some ways, more strong willed than the boys. My mother's pride is loath to admit that sometimes my little angel is transformed into a little devil at the mere pulling of her plaits or the wagging of a tongue by one of her brothers! She retaliates by kicking shins and hitting as hard as her little fists are able. I admit that the boys shouldn't provoke her, but their deeds are done mostly in fun, I think, whereas Mae is angry to the point of tears. When I have the provoker (whichever one of the boys that may be) apologize, Mae won't accept it. She stamps her foot and cries, "Never! Never! Never!" I have plenty of scuff marks on the hardwood floors around the house to prove it.

A good case in point is what happened with Roy the other day. The two of them were on the front porch playing with Mae's marble collection when Roy accidentally dropped Mae's favorite marble down a knothole in one of the planks. I was alerted to the situation by Mae's ear-splitting screams. I found her crying alone on the porch, and when I asked her what had happened and where Roy was, she answered — without the slightest interruption in her wailing — with one index finger pointed downward. Sure enough, when I got down on hands and knees in the yard, I spotted Roy beyond the lattice of the porch, crawling around on his stomach in the dirt in search of Mae's marble. He was unsuccessful, and it took me twenty minutes to convince him to give up the search and come out. He was covered head to toe with dirt, and you can be sure I had to get him in the tub and give him some of Jimmy's clothes to wear before sending him home again, or he'd never be allowed to visit with us in the future.

I told him not to worry, that Mae would forgive and forget. She had locked herself in her room, and when I tapped on the door and Roy called out that he was sorry, Mae's angry little voice greeted us from the other side with the warning that Roy had better not ask to play with any of her toys ever again. Roy left with his head hanging down, and I felt so sorry for him. He tries so hard to be a good boy. He's just clumsy and awkward sometimes, but what he lacks in intelligence, he makes up for in kindness — and I don't wonder that the latter is the more important anyway.

Mae is really a happy and loving child most of the time. She's pleasant to people — until she's crossed or hurt in some way. I fear I will have a difficult task when it comes to teaching her about forgiveness. If she doesn't learn now, I'm certain she will face untold heartache in the future. How do I convince her that holding on to her anger only makes for a bitter heart and an unhappy soul, and that only by forgiving can she be at peace?

Mae had, in fact, completely forgotten the incident with the marble until Amelia's letter jogged her memory. Even then, she had only a faint recollection of being on the porch with Roy and watching her favorite green marble disappear down a knothole in one of the planks. She didn't remember the tears or the screams of rage, nor did she recall locking herself in her room. All of that had vanished for Mae, but when she read her mother's account of the incident, she felt ashamed. Though she had been only a child, the five-year-old Mae was nevertheless an intimation, a foreshadowing, of the fifty-two-year-old woman.

Mae didn't know how long she had mourned that lost marble, but she imagined it had been only a short time. She had soon grown tired of her entire marble collection and traded it to a neighbor girl for a pair of rusty roller skates.

And yet she had never told Roy that it didn't matter about the marble. She had chosen not to acknowledge his apology, even though she was always aware that, unlike her four brothers, Roy never did anything out of malice. He was the only one who didn't tug at her hair or wag his tongue at her, and where one of her brothers might have purposely tossed her green marble off the porch, Roy had lost it accidentally.

And she knew now that Roy, the one who was kindest to her, was the only one of the five boys who really was her brother. He was the only one who shared with her the same mother and father, whoever those people might be. Mae remembered how as a child she had imagined invisible ropes running from each member of her family to the other, so that they were "connected." An invisible rope connecting her to her mother. An invisible rope connecting her to her father. And a much smaller rope — thinner, like a piece of string — connecting Roy to her mother and father and to herself. Just recently she had tried to sever that tie with Roy, only to discover that it wasn't a bit of string at all, but a thick cord, tough and swollen like the rope on a ship that has been through many storms. He was her brother. No matter what she might do, nothing could change that.

Mae wondered at her mother's prescience. It was as though Amelia had somehow seen the road ahead of Mae and had wanted to prepare her for what was to come. To survive inwardly, Mae would need to learn how to forgive. *"If she doesn't learn now,"* Amelia had written, *"I'm certain she will face untold heartache in the future."*

"And apparently, Mother," Mae said aloud, "I didn't learn." She carried inside herself the heartache that her mother had predicted. She was aware of every weighty pound of it. Her heart grieved the loss of Sammy, the loss of her home, the loss of her identity. But the ache came not just because of what had happened, but because of how she had reacted to what had happened. Much of the pain in her heart was there because she hadn't learned to forgive. She had so far refused to forgive Roy for the fire. She hadn't forgiven her mother for not telling her about the adoption. And in five years, she hadn't forgiven herself for leaving the basement door open and making a way for Sammy to fall to his death.

Mae wished she could start all over again, the way an actress is allowed to redo a scene if she doesn't get it right the first time. She wished she could reach back even through half a century and open that bedroom door and tell Roy that it was all right, that it was only a silly marble after all. But she knew only too well that no matter how much a person desired it and wished for it and tried over and over again to change the course of one event or another, there was no reaching back in time to alter what had happened. There was no reaching back to open doors that should have been opened, and there was no reaching back to close doors that should have been closed. There was only the present, and only in the present moment could she act and make choices and open and close all the doors that at this minute needed opening and closing.

What choice am I to make now? she wondered.

She had come to realize that the house as it appeared after the fire was a good picture of her own self. Sammy's death had left her life in ashes the way the fire had razed the house, left it a pile of charred wood, melted glass, blackened remnants of furniture. But while the ruins of the house had been cleared away and fresh sod laid on the ground, she had refused to let anything be changed within herself after the accident. Every time God had come to clean up the mess, she'd turned her back and told Him to leave her alone.

Yet tirelessly the truth had come to her again and again over the years: *"He restores my soul."*

"I had to ask my Mom about the 'He restores my

soul' part. I didn't really understand it, but I guess I do now."

"And what did your mother say?"

"She said it means I might not get fixed up on the outside, but God will make sure I'm always all right on the inside."

"That's right, Alfie. Our true self — what's inside of us — is always safe with God."

Alfie had gone to heaven; she did believe that. She smiled even now as she pictured him playing with the stars. He was safe with God.

But she herself was not "all right on the inside," and that, she knew, was by her own choice. She had made a little shrine of her grief, and she wanted not one charred piece of it to be taken from her.

Until now. She was tired of the ashes, tired of living among the black and gray of burnt wood. She wanted color in her world again, and beauty, and goodness. The goodness that her mother had shown her and told her always to hold fast. From the tangle of feelings hanging heavy inside her — the anger, frustration, grief — one rose above the others, overshadowing them all. She was homesick, and of all the paths that stretched out before her feet, only one led home.

That was the path she wanted to choose, and she knew what she'd have to do if she expected to walk down it.

The thought came to her then from somewhere beyond herself: *Even a house can be rebuilt, and that by human hands. How much more can the hand of God restore a human soul.*

Mae lifted her head and breathed deeply, taking in again the odor of ash. "But I have to let you do the work, don't I, Lord?" she asked. "Forgive me, dear God, for all these wasted years. And help me to forgive, because it's hard for me — especially to forgive myself." These were the first words she had said aloud to Him since the accident five years earlier. And now, as she spoke, a burst of hope rose within her that God would restore her.

Just as she decided to leave, she became aware of a noise that she'd been unconsciously listening to for several minutes, a steady whisk-whisk reaching her from somewhere. She turned to see her neighbor across the street, Lester Nesbitt, sweeping the sidewalk in front of his house with a large broom, gathering up the freshly mown grass along with bits of trash that had been blown there by the wind. She smiled to herself as she realized that, just for a moment, she had thought the sound of sweeping was coming from somewhere inside her own heart.

Chapter 16

When she pulled up in front of the boardinghouse the next day, Mae cringed at the sight of the shutterless second-floor window. One shutter had blown away in a windstorm. The other had simply come loose over the years, and then one day it finally let go of the house altogether and tumbled over the porch roof, dropping into the bushes below. It remained there still, a permanent part of the shrubbery. Miss Pease, the owner of the house, hadn't bothered to replace either shutter, and Mae thought the old Victorian looked like an aging woman who had lost one of her false eyelashes. What had once been a fine home for a well-to-do family was now a run-down cluster of rooms for a series of transient residents. The boarders who lived there didn't care about the missing shutters, the sagging porch, the peeling paint, the untrimmed bushes that overgrew the windows and kept the sunlight out. The rent was right, the rooms furnished, the terms reasonable. You could stay for only days or weeks, maybe a few months, if you wanted, and move on again without worrying about breaking a lease. Only a very rare few, like Roy, stayed for years. It was a house that wasn't a home, and no one worked to make the place more inviting or cheerful. Not even Miss Pease. Especially Miss Pease, who complained continually about her arthritic knees. Her brother had once looked after the upkeep of the house, but he'd died some years before. Roy had tried to take over, doing what he could, but that was relatively little when Miss Pease refused to buy new shutters, new paint, new tools with which to do yard work and routine maintenance.

Mae stepped out of her car and looked up at the unadorned window. The room beyond it was Roy's room. The shade was up, but Mae saw no light or movement beyond the glass, no sign that Roy was there. She wondered whether he might have taken the bus downtown to Loring Park where he often went to toss peanuts to the squirrels. Mae felt a momentary pang of disappointment. She should have called ahead to let Roy know she was coming. She should have made sure he would be there, because she was anxious to see him. She had put it off for far too long already.

She hurried along the walk and up the porch steps, as though by hurrying she could catch him at home rather than downtown. She suddenly couldn't bear the thought of going away without talking with him.

Mae took a deep breath and rapped loudly on the front door with her knuckles, the doorbell having given out long ago. After a moment, she heard heavy footsteps in the hall. They stopped abruptly on the other side of the door, and for a moment Mae sensed herself being eyed through the peephole. Then the door flew open and Miss Pease, stone-faced and perspiring, appeared like an angry vaudeville performer throwing back the stage curtain to stare at a hostile audience. She was a large woman, nearly six feet tall, with broad shoulders and heavy jowls. Her upper lip sported a visible mustache while a few curly whiskers dangled from a double chin, begging to be plucked. Her graying hair was pulled straight back into a tight French knot, and her cold blue eyes peered over the tops of a pair of half glasses that sat slightly lopsided on the tip of her wide nose. She always wore dark dresses, the seams of which were stretched to the limit around her thick waist. Her clothes gave her the appearance of being ready to explode.

When she opened her mouth to speak, a dark hole appeared along her upper gum where one of her teeth was missing. "Mrs. Demaray," she said as she stepped aside to let Mae in. "Haven't seen you around here for a while, though your daughter's been by. Come in. Take a load off your feet. By the way, sorry to hear about your house."

The tone of her voice left Mae wondering about the sincerity of Miss Pease's words. Mae nodded but didn't bother to acknowledge the condolence beyond that. As she entered the front hall, Mae noticed the odor of cooking grease and musty furniture that was an identifying trait of the house. The same odor had drifted through the rooms for the past decade or more that Roy had lived here.

"Come to see Roy, have you?" Miss Pease asked. She shut the door and walked past Mae toward what she called the parlor.

Mae found herself talking to the back of Miss Pease's head. "Yes. Is he here, by chance?" She followed Miss Pease into the parlor, where she found the large woman plumping up the pillows on the ancient couch with her man-sized fists.

"Where else would he be?" Miss Pease replied abruptly. She gave one of the pillows a final whack and motioned for Mae to sit down. "He's hardly set foot out of his room since he managed to set your house on fire. You sit yourself down right here, and I'll go call him. Don't mind Emmett over there." She tossed her head in the direction of an elderly man slumped in a low-backed chair by the vacant fireplace. "He's harmless."

Mae studied Emmett while she lowered herself onto the couch. He was a thin-faced, toothless old man whose round brown eyes seemed to be staring at something far beyond the confines of the room. He was rather like the elderly residents she'd seen in nursing homes, only he managed to keep himself propped up in the chair without having to be tied into it. That he was harmless didn't seem to Mae to be in question.

By the time she turned back to Miss Pease to

thank her, the large woman had disappeared. In a moment Mae heard a shrill voice calling up the stairs, "Roy Hanna, you come down here! You got company in the parlor."

Mae shook her head and wondered why Miss Pease couldn't have climbed the stairs and politely tapped on Roy's door. But then she remembered about Miss Pease's arthritic knees and her oft-repeated comment, made with conflicting overtones of pride and self-pity, "I haven't climbed a staircase since 1965, and I suspect I never will again."

In a moment Miss Pease stuck her head in the parlor doorway. "He's coming," she announced. "Can I get you something to drink? Coffee or milk is about all I got. I don't care for any of them carbonated drinks myself."

"No," Mae said. "No, thank you, Miss Pease."

All she wanted was for Miss Pease to go away before Roy arrived. She was relieved when the other woman said, "Well, if you'll excuse me, I got lunch to be worrying about. Emmett there don't like it when lunch is late." She nodded again at the old man, who appeared to Mae incapable of caring about much of anything.

"Of course," Mae said. "Thank you for calling Roy."

Miss Pease turned her large body away from the door and lumbered down the hall toward the kitchen. Mae listened to the heavy footfalls that were gradually replaced by a lighter tapping in the hall. Mae knew that the quieter footsteps were Roy's. Even here he walked lightly so that less dirt would fall off his shoes and onto the floor.

Suddenly Mae's heart raced and her breath became shallow. *That is my brother in the hall,* she thought. *If it hadn't been for the accident that killed our parents, I would have always known him as my brother. We would have grown up in the same house, we would have known our mother and our father, we might have had other brothers and sisters. My last name was Hanna once too, like Roy's, and I would have known the first name that my parents gave me, had it not been for the accident. . . .*

Mae considered again the twists and turns of life, of how its course is knocked first one way and then the other by all the seemingly senseless and unexpected events that buffet it. Her parents riding in a car and reaching death before they ever reached their destination. The doorbell ringing and Sammy falling down the stairs. Roy leaving his lighted cigar on a shelf in the basement. All of these had changed her life completely, sending it reeling in a whole new direction.

Mae took a deep breath and tried to calm herself. When Roy appeared in the doorway she rose without thinking, as though she were meeting him for the first time.

She had thought he might look different somehow. Roy, the friend, she was well familiar with; she knew his every feature, every gesture. But

Roy, the brother. How would he appear? Would she see him as someone completely changed from the Roy she had always known?

He stopped on the threshold between the hall and the parlor and stood quietly, making no move to step farther into the room. As the two looked at each other, Mae saw that he had not changed at all. He was still round-faced, over-weight, wearing his usual cotton shirt and jeans. The only difference was that he appeared not to have shaved for a couple of days; a brief stubble of beard shaded his face. She wondered that he and she should look so different from each other. *It may be that he looks like our father, and I like our mother,* she thought, *though I'll never really know.*

Finally Mae said, "Hello, Roy."

Roy opened his mouth, but no words came. His large blue eyes were round with surprise and fear. He pulled a crumpled handkerchief from the pocket of his jeans and swiped at the back of his neck.

Mae sat down again and patted the couch beside her. "Please come sit beside me, Roy," she said.

Roy looked at the couch where Mae's hand lay, then his eyes traveled back to her face. His own face was ashen as he whispered her name, "Miss Mae."

To Mae, he looked like someone facing a ghost, or a person come back from the dead. She didn't know how she had expected him to react, but she hadn't thought he'd be afraid. His reluctance to enter the room made her realize he thought she had come to confront him, perhaps to reprimand him for his carelessness.

Before she could assure him, he said, "I done real bad, but I didn't mean it, Miss Mae. Old Roy sure didn't mean to burn down your house." He dabbed at his face with the handkerchief, and Mae noticed that it wasn't sweat he was wiping away, but tears.

She held out her hand to him then. "Please, Roy, come sit beside me," she invited again, smiling this time. As she sat with her hand extended, she could hardly believe that she had ever been angry with Roy. All the anger was gone now; she could barely remember it. She felt only tenderness and a kind of protectiveness toward Roy, not unlike those feelings of a lifetime ago when she stared at him from across the dinner table and felt a deep compassion for the boy from the orphanage.

Roy hesitated, then stepped lightly over to the couch. As he sat down, Emmett let out a moan. Mae and Roy looked at the old man by the fireplace. "That's Emmett," Roy said. "He don't say very much, but he's a nice enough person."

"Yes, we've met — sort of," Mae said as she gazed at Emmett. After a moment, she turned on the couch so that she was facing Roy. His eyes still mirrored his fears. "You see, Roy," Mae said kindly, "I've come to tell you that I know the fire was an accident. It was just an accident, that's all. I don't blame you. I came to ask you to forgive me for being angry and for staying away so long."

Roy stared at Mae, seemingly unable to comprehend what she had said. His forehead creased and his lips moved as though he wanted to respond, but again there was no sound.

Mae was concerned by his silence. "Do you forgive me, Roy?" she asked. She waited for him to say something, wondering for the first time whether she was too late, whether she had lost his friendship for good. She had simply assumed he would forgive her for staying away for more than a month, but maybe she had assumed wrong.

Just when she thought Roy was not going to answer, his eyebrows went up suddenly, and he moved his head from side to side. "Oh no, Miss Mae. Old Roy don't need to forgive you. You gotta forgive old Roy. It's you who's gotta forgive old Roy. I'm the one that did bad."

"No, Roy, I shouldn't have acted —"

"But I left that cigar down there on the shelf and went upstairs to listen to the music box, and when I went back to the basement stairs, next thing I knew there was flames all over the place."

"Oh," Mae said quietly, "is that what happened? You went upstairs to listen to the music box?"

"Yes, Miss Mae," Roy confessed. "Musta listened to the box three, maybe four times. I shouldn'ta done that, when you told me to clean out the basement. Shoulda just done what you told me to do."

Roy wiped at two fresh tears coursing down his cheeks until Mae took the handkerchief from his hand and dabbed at the tears herself. "Now, no more tears, Roy," she said gently. "I forgive you for starting the fire."

Roy continued to shake his head as he mumbled, "But all your pretty things, Miss Mae —"

"It doesn't matter," Mae assured him. "They were just things, after all."

"But the photos and the letters — I know how you cherished them. I tried to find them, tried to get them out, but they all got burned up."

"It's all right, Roy. Really it is. In fact, maybe what happened was all for the best."

Roy looked stunned. "All for the best, Miss Mae?"

Mae nodded and smiled. "People have been sending me family photos and letters to replace the ones that were lost. And the new letters — well, I've learned a lot of important things from them. Especially about forgiveness. Which brings me back to my point. I really came here to ask you to forgive me, and so I'll ask you again. Do you or do you not forgive me?"

The look of sorrow on Roy's face was replaced by one of disbelief, but even that evolved into a smile of joy and relief as Roy began to understand. His smile finished stretching itself across his face until all his tobacco-stained teeth were fully exposed. "Oh, Miss Mae!" he said, jumping up from the couch. "Oh, Miss Mae! Miss Mae! I don't know what I'm forgiving you for, but yes, I forgive you. I forgive you!"

Mae couldn't turn her eyes away from Roy's own violet-blue eyes, so childlike, so filled with unclouded joy. So much like Sammy's blue eyes. *But why shouldn't they be?* she thought. *Sammy was related to Roy too. Sammy has — had — Roy's eyes.*

Just then a great snore escaped Emmett's lips. Mae and Roy again looked over at the old man, who had fallen asleep in the chair by the fireplace. His head had fallen backward and his toothless mouth was wide open. His mountainous Adam's apple slid along his throat, and his lips and nostrils quivered as he struggled to pull in air.

Mae and Roy looked at each other and burst into laughter. Roy laughed so hard he clutched at his stomach and had to sit down again. When he had finally managed to subdue the laughter, he asked eagerly, "Can I come work for you again, Miss Mae? Just like before, every Tuesday morning?"

"Well, that's another thing I came to tell you," Mae began.

"Miss Mae, are you gonna be moving to —"

"Now hear me out, Roy. You can't come work for me anymore. Everything's changed now. Everything's completely different from what it was before. Well . . . I mean . . . what I'm trying to say, Roy, is . . ." She paused a moment, wondering at the palpable fear that had settled again over Roy's face. Roy must think she decided to move to Florida! "Oh, I'm not moving, Roy, if that's what you think. I'm going to rebuild. Ellen and Sam did want me to sell the lot and move to Florida, and I seriously considered it, but it just didn't seem right. I'm going to rebuild the house to look very similar to how it looked before, though perhaps it'll be a bit smaller. I haven't quite worked out all the details yet, but at any rate, there'll be plenty of space for the two of us. Upstairs you'll have your own bedroom with a connecting bath. Would you like that?"

Roy looked puzzled. He pulled his handkerchief slowly across his forehead while he thought. Finally he said, "You want me to live there instead of here, Miss Mae?"

Mae nodded emphatically. "Yes, that's what I want."

"You gonna give me a room?"

"Of course, your own room."

Roy stuck out his lower lip and absently scratched at the stubble on his cheek. Then he cocked his head and asked, "You opening a boardinghouse, Miss Mae?"

It was Mae's turn to look puzzled. "A boardinghouse? Oh no, no, Roy, you don't understand," she said, waving one hand in the air as though to wave away any confusion. "I'm not opening a boardinghouse. I'm building a home. Our home. We're going to be a family now, Roy."

Roy sat motionless, his blue eyes searching Mae's face. By the fireplace, Emmett let out several more loud snores, but both Roy and Mae ignored him. Roy scarcely heard the snoring as he tried to comprehend the meaning of Mae's words.

"A family, Miss Mae?" he asked quietly.

"Yes, Roy. You see . . ." Mae paused, stumbling over her answer. She hadn't been sure when she arrived what she was going to say, how she was going to explain her plan. As she gazed into Roy's wide, innocent eyes, she suddenly made her decision. "Well, Roy," she said, "you've been a dear and faithful friend to me all my life, and you were as much a son to Mother as any of her own boys. I think she'd be pleased for you to come live in the house on Humboldt once it's rebuilt. You've lived in boardinghouses long enough. It's time for you to have a home."

Roy inched himself forward to the edge of the couch and rolled the words around on his tongue, as though they were new to his vocabulary. "A home. A home," he repeated. "A home and a family." Then, as though he suddenly understood the meaning of the words, he smiled broadly and, jumping up, ran over to Emmett. "Emmett!" he said, grabbing the old man's hands. "Emmett, wake up! I'm gonna have a home and a family! A home and a family!"

Mae watched in amusement as the old man drew in one last interrupted snore, then with great effort lifted his head and stared wide-eyed

303

at Roy. Emmett looked dazed, as if emerging from a coma. But he slowly must have caught on that Roy was delighted about something, and instead of objecting to a loss of sleep, the old man laughed and swung his arms and tapped his own slippered feet. He smiled merrily, revealing his naked gums. What a pair the two men made, Mae thought, celebrating what neither of them really understood.

In a moment, Miss Pease appeared in the doorway, wiping her hands on an apron that was tied snugly around her waist. "Roy Hanna!" she exclaimed. "Just what do you think you're doing to poor Emmett?"

Roy paused in his impromptu dance with Emmett and, still holding the old man's hands, turned to Miss Pease and said, "We're celebrating, Miss Pease." Emmett nodded and emitted a moan of affirmation. His toes were still tapping weakly on the hardwood floor.

"And what in the world are you celebrating?" Miss Pease asked. She had finished wiping her hands and now held her arms akimbo, her fat fists on her ample hips.

"Gonna have a real home, Miss Pease," Roy explained. "Gonna have a home and a family. Miss Mae and me, we're gonna be a family now."

Miss Pease turned her steely eyes on Mae. "That so?" she asked, her tone suggesting she wasn't happy about losing one of her long-term residents.

"Yes," Mae replied evenly. "That's so."

Miss Pease slowly turned her head from side to side. "Roy here's been living in boarding-houses some forty years and going to your fancy house every week to work for you for just as long, and now you say you're going to be family?" She clicked her tongue. "Seems more than a little strange to me."

"Yes, Miss Pease," Mae agreed. "It has all seemed rather strange to me too. It'll take some time to rebuild the house. I don't expect to be able to move in until next spring. But when the house is completed, Roy will be moving in with me. So perhaps you can consider this as his official notice, though it's being given far in advance."

Miss Pease shrugged and dropped her hands to her sides. "Suit yourself," she said. "There's always someone else to come along to take the room." She turned and wandered off as though she didn't care, though a moment later Mae noticed an inordinate amount of pot banging coming from the kitchen. Well, let Miss Pease stew about it, Mae decided. It was time for Roy to have a home.

Roy gently replaced Emmett's hands in his lap and walked back over to Mae. "I'm going to like living with you a whole lot more than living with Miss Pease," he said.

Mae nodded and pulled one corner of her mouth back in a half smile. "I'm only sorry you've lived here for so long," she said. "Well,

I'll say good-bye for now. I've a great deal to do, so I'd better get started."

Mae rose to go, then impulsively she stood on her toes and lifted her arms about Roy's great neck. Roy's arms remained at his side for a moment. The last person to hug him, besides Christy and Amy, was Amelia, and that had been decades ago. Slowly he lifted his arms and settled his hands clumsily on Mae's back.

After a moment, they stepped back from each other. Roy tried to mirror Mae's smile. He was happy but also confused.

"Well, I'd better go," Mae said again. She started toward the door, with Roy following. Emmett, having decided the party was over, was already asleep and snoring again in the chair by the fireplace.

On the porch, as Mae began to descend the few steps to the sidewalk, Roy called out to her. "Miss Mae," he said, rubbing his whiskered cheek again with his grease-lined fingernails. "Why?"

Mae didn't need him to elaborate on his question. She knew what he was asking. She stopped and looked down the long narrow street of apartment buildings and boardinghouses. After a moment, she turned to Roy and said, "Some of the things we think are such treasures turn out to be only silly green marbles after all. You find out after a while that there are much more important things in life than green marbles."

Roy cocked his head, more confused than

ever. He couldn't imagine what green marbles had to do with anything. "Miss Mae?" he asked, hoping for an explanation.

Mae only smiled again. "Never mind, Roy," she said. She was halfway down the walk when she turned and asked, "Do you want to come to dinner tomorrow night? The girls have been begging for spaghetti and meatballs, so Ellen and I are planning to make a big batch of it. Sam's out of town on business this week, and there'll be plenty to go around with just us ladies at home. You like spaghetti, don't you?"

"Like it?" Roy grinned. "You know it's my favorite, Miss Mae!"

"Yes," Mae said with a laugh. "I thought it might be." She waved, slid into the car, and drove off down Pillsbury Avenue.

Roy stood on the porch in the warm summer sunlight, watching the Buick until it was gone and rolling the words around on his tongue again. "A home. A home and a family."

Chapter 17

That evening when Mae and Ellen were clearing the dinner dishes from the table, Mae said casually, "I invited Roy to share our spaghetti dinner tomorrow night."

Ellen stopped abruptly, as though her shoes had suddenly stuck to the linoleum floor. "You what?" she asked, turning toward her mother wide-eyed.

"I invited Roy to dinner. We'll probably have to double the batch; you know how Roy likes to eat." Mae was trying hard to keep up an effortless front, but her heart beat rapidly, and her hands trembled as she gathered up silverware on the table. All through the meal she'd been debating how to talk with her daughter about her recent decisions, her thoughts at the empty lot, her prayer for forgiveness. She was finding it hard to admit she'd been wrong, even to Ellen.

"When did you talk with Roy?" Ellen asked, setting a pile of plates gently into the sink.

"I went to see him this afternoon."

"You did?"

Mae nodded. "At the boardinghouse. Dreadful place," she added, muttering.

"Why didn't you tell me? I thought you were out running errands."

Sighing, Mae put the handful of forks and knives into the sink beside the dirty plates. "I don't know, Ellen," she admitted. "I really don't. Maybe I was afraid of the outcome. Maybe I had an unconscious fear that Roy wouldn't forgive me."

"You asked him to forgive you, Mother?"

"Yes, for being angry and for staying away so long."

"And of course he did," Ellen said positively.

"Of course. I don't suppose dear Roy could do otherwise. It isn't in him to hold a grudge."

"Hold a grudge? Roy was never angry that you stayed away, just sad and afraid he'd lost your friendship. He was waiting for you to come back — hoping you would. And, Mother, I'm so glad you did! But what made you decide —"

The shrill ringing of the telephone interrupted Ellen's sentence. Ellen frowned as she looked at the extension by the kitchen door, seemingly hesitant to pick it up. After the second ring, she said, "Well, it might be Sam. I'd better get it. Excuse me just a minute, Mother." As Ellen reached for the receiver, Mae went back to clearing the table. She couldn't help but overhear her daughter's side of the conversation.

"What do you mean, he changed the deadline to noon tomorrow?" Ellen said. "The deadline was supposed to be next Monday. . . . Well, that's a fine thing for Mr. Parkins to do. Didn't Harry try to explain . . . ? Well, honestly, I just don't see how Parkins can insist. . . . But what about Grant? After all, he's your full-time artist. He's the one who's supposed to be designing. . . . Sick *again?* Well, listen, Marie, my husband's out of town on business, and I've got two kids here to look after. I can't just come running down there. . . . Sure, I've got a regular sitter, but I don't generally call her at the last minute on a weeknight and expect her to be available. I just really don't see how I can —"

Mae pursed her lips, pushed against her fears, and forced herself to tap on her daughter's arm. "Honey, I can —"

"Listen, Marie, can you hold on a minute?" Ellen put her hand over the receiver. "What is it, Mother?"

"You go on," Mae said. "If they need you at work, you go on. I'll look after the girls."

Ellen seemed to consider her mother's offer for a moment, then said, "No, Mother, I know how you feel about being alone with —"

Mae waved a hand in the air to silence her. "I don't want to hear any arguments. If they need you at work, then you'd better go. And don't try to get a sitter — it'd be foolish to call anyone else when I'm right here. Now, you tell whoever's on the phone that you're on your way."

Two lines formed between Ellen's eyes as she frowned. She let her hand drop and opened her mouth to speak, but then she covered the receiver again. "Mother, are you sure?" she asked.

"Perfectly sure. Now, go on."

Ellen told Marie she was on her way. After kissing the girls good-night, she stood at the door to the garage and fumbled through her purse, mumbling about her keys but appearing to Mae to be reluctant to leave. Mae wondered if Ellen was afraid to leave the children in her care.

Finally, Ellen pulled the keys from the purse and said, "If you have any problems, call me. You know the number."

"Of course, dear," Mae assured her. "We'll be fine."

Ellen stepped into the garage but turned again and sighed heavily. "Mother, if you're not comfortable with this —"

"Don't you trust me with the girls, Ellen?" Mae asked quietly.

"Of course I do," Ellen insisted. "But you've always said you won't stay with them alone."

Mae felt the fear inside of her fluttering about like a giant moth trying to get out. She *was* afraid to stay alone with her granddaughters. But she simply smiled and said, "Well, it's a woman's prerogative to change her mind, isn't it?"

Ellen returned her mother's smile and opened the car door. "I'll be home late. Don't wait up. But — I want you to finish telling me what happened with Roy."

"We'll talk all about it later, dear. Right now I want to check on the girls."

Mae wasn't going to let them out of her sight

the whole evening, not even for a minute.

Mae was curled up in an overstuffed chair in the living room, drinking herbal tea and listening to the stereo, when Ellen arrived home at two o'clock. As her daughter appeared in the archway between the front hall and the living room, Mae felt a sense of accomplishment. Ellen was home, the girls were safe in bed, she had gotten through the evening without mishap. She had stayed alone with her grandchildren and had taken care of them — something she never thought she'd be able to do again. When she looked up at her daughter's weary face, she thought, *I should have got back up on the horse a long time ago. What a stubborn, foolish old mule I've been.*

"You still awake, Mother?" Ellen asked. She tossed her purse onto the couch, then plopped herself down on the inviting cushions and stretched out her legs in front of her. "I thought you'd be in bed long ago."

Mae set the cup and saucer onto the coffee table beside the chair. "No," she said. "I'm wide awake for some reason, even though this chamomile tea is supposed to make a person sleepy." She smiled mildly and nodded toward the cup.

"I hope you weren't anxious about the girls."

"Of course I was," Mae admitted. "Every minute."

Ellen sidled up to the edge of the couch and leaned toward her mother. "I'm so sorry,

Mother. I shouldn't have left you alone with them. I could have tried to call Marsha. She might have been able to come."

Mae shook her head adamantly. "No, I wanted to stay and I'm glad I did. I wanted to prove to myself that I don't have to live in fear."

A long silence followed, broken when Ellen asked, "Mother, what made you change your mind about Roy and about staying with the girls?"

Mae laced her fingers together in her lap and gazed across the room. "So many things, really," she began. "The letters. My mother's words. You." When Ellen looked puzzled, she continued. "You were right about that silly story I used to tell about Theodore Thimble." Both women smiled at the mention of the name. "I suppose most people run from God because they think they can have a better time without Him. But I was running because I didn't think I should accept His grace. I didn't think I deserved to be healed of the grief."

"Were you angry with God for what happened to Sammy?"

"At God?" Mae shook her head. "No, not at God. Only at myself. I've always had a hard time forgiving, Ellen. All these years, I just couldn't forgive myself for what happened. If I could have forgiven myself, had I even tried, the Lord would have helped me to heal. He wanted to, I believe, but I wouldn't let Him."

"Will you let Him now, Mother?"

Mae nodded. "You see, I've come to understand something. All these years I thought the thing I did wrong was leave the basement door open. Well, that was carelessness, but what was really wrong was the way I acted afterward. Not forgiving myself, not accepting your forgiveness and Sam's forgiveness, turning my back on God. But something has followed me all these years, and that something is four little words: 'He restores my soul.' "

"From the Twenty-third Psalm?"

Mae nodded. "Yes, that very familiar Scripture. Too familiar, maybe, so that we miss the meaning of it. Just tonight as I was sitting here thinking about everything that's happened, I came to see that the Bible doesn't say He restores my soul if I do this or if I do that. He just does it because that's the way He is. He doesn't want us to stay in" — she paused a moment and thought of the house after the fire — "in ruins. That's grace, Ellen, undeserved grace. For the first time in my life, I'm beginning to understand the extent of God's grace. Even though I closed my heart to Him, He continued to pursue me."

Ellen slipped over to the footstool of the overstuffed chair and took her mother's hands. "Oh, Mother, I'm so glad."

Mae squeezed her daughter's hands. "I want you to know that I accept your forgiveness, and Sam's. I should have done it a long time ago. I'm a stubborn old woman, Ellen."

"Old, no," Ellen said, laughing. "Stubborn,

314

yes. But that's all right, Mother. It can be a good trait, too, if you decide to be stubborn about the right things."

Mae sighed, but smiled even as her shoulders sagged. "I've been stubborn about all the wrong things, but I don't want to live that way anymore. I want to start over with a clean slate. I've even decided to rebuild the house."

"You have?"

"Yes, and I've invited Roy to live there with me. After all, he's my brother. We ought to be together."

"I can't believe it! This is wonderful news. I'll just bet Roy was thrilled."

"He was pretty happy, I think." Mae remembered Roy's impromptu dance with Emmett.

"Did you tell him he's your brother?"

"No." Mae shook her head. "No, I didn't. I thought I might, but at the last minute I couldn't do it."

"But why, Mother?" Ellen exclaimed. "Don't you think he ought to know?"

Mae thought for a moment. How could she explain it?

Before she could speak, Ellen added, "Just think how upset you were that Grandmother never told you about the adoption. Why would you turn right around now and do the same thing to Roy?"

Mae smiled pensively. "Because I love him," she said, "and I want to protect him."

"And?" Ellen pressed.

"I had to consider how it might make him feel to know Mother and Dad had chosen to adopt me but not him. I don't want Roy thinking they were willing to offer him home-cooked meals but weren't willing to offer him a home. He could so easily get the wrong idea and think they didn't adopt him because he wasn't good enough, wasn't bright enough, and that's not true. They *did* love Roy, especially mother, but as Helen Lewis said, they had four sons and that was enough. But I'm not sure Roy would understand. He has such happy memories of our family. I don't want to risk spoiling that for him."

Ellen nodded her understanding. "You're in something of the same position Grandmother was in when she adopted you."

"Yes," Mae sighed, "I've been thinking about that. For some reason Mother thought it would harm our relationship if I knew she wasn't my real mother. I can't imagine I would have loved her any less if I had known, but she didn't want to take that chance. Right or wrong, she made her decision out of love. I think I can understand that now."

"I'm glad you see it that way, Mother. I'm sure Grandmother did what she thought was best for you. It was probably a tough decision for her too."

"No doubt," Mae agreed. "Life's never very easy, is it?"

"No," Ellen said with a laugh. "You can say that again."

"Do you understand why I'm not telling Roy?"

"Yes, I can see your point."

"So let's just keep it between you and me and Sam. We can explain everything to the girls when they're older, but right now I don't think they need to know."

"Afraid they'll spill the beans to Roy?"

"Well, not on purpose, but they're so young —"

"I understand, Mother. Mum's the word for now."

"Thanks, honey," Mae said. "Thanks for understanding."

After a moment, Ellen frowned and said, "Speaking of understanding, what do you think the neighbors will say when Roy moves in with you? After all, they won't know he's your brother."

Mae looked startled and almost laughed. "I never even thought about it," she admitted. "Imagine tongues waving over me and Roy! Well, I don't know, honey, Roy's been hanging around the house for so long that I don't think anyone will think much about it. Do you?"

Ellen shrugged. "I guess people would have to be pretty hard up for gossip if they thought the two of you were carrying on an affair."

Mae did laugh then. "At least it'll give Eleanor Nesbitt something to occupy her days, wondering whether Roy and I are an item. Otherwise, most of the neighbors know Roy and like him. I

317

think they'd realize our relationship is perfectly respectable."

Ellen smiled contentedly. "Things have really turned out for the best, Mother. You've made the right decisions."

In spite of Ellen's confidence, Mae's eyes filled with tears. "There's still one thing I'd like to change. After all this time, I'd still like to go back and shut that basement door and keep Sammy safe. I miss him so much."

"I miss him, too, Mother," Ellen said quietly. "We all do. We'll always miss him."

"I often wonder what he might have done with his life had he been able to grow up, what he might have become. All of that was taken away."

Ellen dropped her eyes, but not before Mae saw the tears. After a moment, though, she lifted her head again, and the tears had been replaced with a brave smile. "Well, you remember what Roy said on the way to the funeral, how he believed Sammy was up in heaven eating peppermint-stick ice cream?"

Mae nodded. "I remember."

"Well, I can't be certain about the ice cream, but I do believe Sammy's in heaven. That's what gives us hope, isn't it?"

Mae managed a smile. "Maybe he *is* eating peppermint-stick ice cream. Maybe he's playing with the stars. I guess we'll find out when we get there."

The next morning the two women stumbled

upon each other in the kitchen at six o'clock. Ellen, who had to go back to work, had already made coffee, and both women poured themselves a steaming hot mug and sipped it greedily. They looked exhausted, both in floral cotton robes with uncombed hair and dark circles under their eyes.

"Short night, wasn't it, Mother?" Ellen mumbled. She stuck her head in the refrigerator to see what might be there for breakfast.

Mae looked out the kitchen window, holding the coffee mug in both hands to warm them. The day was just beginning to break. A hint of light was rising in the yard as though gently lifting upward on the wings of the morning. Mae recognized an odd feeling hanging about inside of her, an unfamiliar yet strangely familiar feeling. She was glad to be greeting the day. Glad as she had not been glad since her old life, her life before Sammy's accident. And she felt somehow that the gap between that old life and this new life had been removed, that her life was a solid whole again, not truncated, not broken, not divided in two.

She thought of all the dark years, more than half a decade now. But as she looked back over her life as though from an aerial view and saw the whole of it, the bright whole of it, the dark part seemed to have been only a short night.

She turned to Ellen, who was breaking eggs into a bowl. "Yes, dear," Mae said. "A short night. But I'm really very glad that it's finally morning."

Chapter 18

Mae met with an architect, described the old house, and was soon presented with a blueprint for the new one. Sam hired a contractor, a friend of his whom he knew he could trust, and before autumn was in full color, the foundation of the new house had been completed and the walls were going up.

While the building progressed, Mae and Ellen put hundreds of miles on Mae's Buick, visiting all the antique shops they could find, not only in Minneapolis but also in the smaller outlying towns of Stillwater, Red Wing, Excelsior, Northfield. Not all the furnishings would come from these shops, but Mae decided to take this opportunity to indulge her love for antiques. She still winced when she thought of what had been lost to the fire, but she decided to enjoy the chance to decorate, something she had never done before, having inherited a furnished house. Everything she and Ellen hauled home — or had delivered, if it was too big for the Buick — was kept in storage, awaiting the day it would take its place in the new house.

One early December afternoon Mae and Ellen were browsing through a shop in Stillwater and talking about their upcoming trip to Disney World when Ellen suddenly blurted out, "Oh, Mother, I'm so glad you're not moving to Florida!"

Mae couldn't help but laugh. "And you were the one who tried so hard to get me to go."

"But I didn't want you to," Ellen said, shaking her head. "Not really."

"Wasn't this Christmas trip planned so that I could visit St. Petersburg?"

Ellen picked up a veiled hat from a dresser and pretended to inspect it. "Well, partly, I guess," she said as she fingered the plastic daisies that adorned the hat's broad brim. "But the only thing I really wanted was for you to make a fresh start, and now you've done that without moving all the way down there."

Mae nodded and smiled. "I really don't think moving was what I needed."

"No," Ellen agreed. "And I would have missed you more than I can say, had you gone."

"And I would have missed you and the girls and Sam. It wouldn't have seemed right at all to be so far away."

"Well, we don't have to worry about that now. You made the right decision to rebuild the house. It's the best thing for all of us, for Roy too. I've never seen him so happy in his life."

Mae smiled at the thought of Roy. Occasionally he joined the women on their shopping

321

trips so he could pick out items for his room, and to Mae he appeared like the proverbial kid in a candy store. He walked around the shops wide-eyed, wanting everything, gazing in fascination at the old toy train sets, the cathedral-style radios, the jukeboxes and cash registers and hand-wound phonographs. "I don't really think those are the things you need for your room," Mae would advise, though she let him linger as long as he wanted, glad he was having fun.

"Well," Mae said to Ellen, "I'm glad I finally made a good decision. It's about time, wouldn't you say?"

Ellen waved a hand. "Don't berate yourself, Mother. I'm just thrilled to be antique shopping with you again. It's just like old times, before —"

Ellen stopped abruptly, but Mae finished the sentence for her. "Before the accident. I know, Ellen. I haven't been very good company for you these past few years. But that'll change, I promise."

"Things already *are* changing. It's like — I don't know — like I've got the old you back again." She put on the hat she'd been inspecting and pulled the veil down over her face. "What do you think?" she asked.

"Ghastly," Mae replied. "Though it looks like something Sophie Mills could use to keep the sun off her nose while she's hunting for seashells. Why don't we send it to her?"

"A splendid idea," Ellen said, laughing, "un-

322

less you'd like to use it yourself while we're at Disney World."

Mae pretended to consider the offer. "Well, it's tempting," she replied, "but I think I'll pass. I never did look good in plastic daisies."

Mae and Ellen laughed as Ellen took off the hat and laid it on the dresser where she'd found it.

Sam suggested that Roy be allowed to help with the work on the house, and Mae agreed that it was a wonderful idea. "He still feels guilty that it was his cigar that started the fire. It would probably do him a world of good to help with the rebuilding."

Sam spoke with the contractor, Joe Henderson, and it was agreed that Roy could lend a hand wherever possible, assisting the carpenters, doing odd jobs, helping with cleanup at the end of the day. "He's really quite skilled with his hands," Sam had assured his friend, "and can follow directions to a *T*. Let me know if you have any problems, but I don't think you will."

"Miss Mae!" Roy cried when Mae told him of the plan. "I'd be honored to help build your house!"

"Our house," Mae corrected. "Don't forget."

"I won't, Miss Mae," Roy said. "Our house. You bet, Miss Mae. I'll work real hard to make our house the best on Humboldt. You can count on me, Miss Mae."

Most days found Roy on the building site, and

Mae tried to visit the site herself about every other day, both to check up on the progress of the work and to take donuts and hot coffee to the workers. Winter had settled in and the men were working in some brisk temperatures made worse by the wind chill, but, as Roy put it, "a little bit of cold don't stop a Minnesotan."

On a cold but sunny day in mid-December, Mae noticed as she approached the house that the workers had hung a wreath on the door frame. Christmas carols played on the radio that kept the men entertained while they worked. The ground was covered with a couple inches of fresh snow, but someone — probably Roy, Mae decided — had shoveled the walkway that led up to what would be the new front porch.

Mae stood on the walkway for a moment, clutching the box of donuts and the Thermos of coffee against her heavy winter coat. She liked to pause from time to time to listen to the sounds of the work, the hammering of nails into wood, the occasional buzzing of the power saw, the voices of the men as they spoke among themselves. It was as beautiful as music, these noises that meant her home was being built.

How the scene had changed since she stood on almost this exact spot in June, the day of the fire, and then again in August, when she came to visit the empty lot. Now it was December, and the house was taking shape, and more and more the scene of the summer that had passed was becoming vague, less defined, replaced by something new. A picture of restoration. *Kind of like me,* Mae thought, as she considered how, since her prayer for forgiveness, little bits of guilt and bitterness had been swept away daily, to be replaced by a fresh joy, a new hope.

"Miss Mae!" Roy called, coming around the side of the house carrying a two-by-four. A red knit hat with a pompon was pulled down over his ears, and a blue scarf was wrapped around his neck and tucked into his coat. He wore a pair of heavy work boots that were tied with a set of mismatched laces. Clenched in his teeth was the stump of an unlit cigar. He took it out and stuffed it into his coat pocket as he said, "See the wreath we put up? Looks like Christmas around here now, don't it?"

"It sure does, Roy. And the house looks more like a real house every day. You fellows are doing a great job. How about a break? You hungry?" She held up the box of donuts for Roy to see.

"Sure am, Miss Mae," Roy said. "Could use a little coffee to warm up the insides too." His breath came out on little clouds of fog in the cold air.

After Mae passed around the donuts and poured coffee into the men's seldom-cleaned mugs, she and Roy walked around the house to view the progress. Much of the frame was complete, and the wiring and plumbing were being installed.

"It's coming along real good," Roy said.

"Won't be long now before we'll be ready to put in the insulation."

"That'll be a messy job, won't it?" Mae offered.

Roy nodded. "I never done it before, but Joe — he's going to let me help out anyway. He says I'm real good at building stuff. Says I have a job waiting for me if I ever want to go to work for him."

"Think you will, Roy?" Mae asked, chuckling, expecting a quick negative reply.

Roy was thoughtful a moment. "I don't know, Miss Mae. If I were young I'd sure jump at the chance. I like putting things together, working with wood. Remember when we was just kids in school and I was taking that shop class and my teacher Mr. Thomas said I was real good at it?" When Mae nodded, Roy continued. "Maybe I shoulda listened to him and become a carpenter. But then the war came along and I got that job at Honeywell and just never left. I been wondering whether I did the wrong thing. Maybe just because there was a war I spent my whole life as a janitor when I shoulda been a carpenter. Do you think so, Miss Mae?"

Mae's heavy sigh was visible in the frigid air. "It's terrible to carry regrets like that, Roy — always wondering whether you should have done one thing or another when it's too late to do anything at all." She looked at her old friend — her brother — and offered him a smile. "I really don't believe you did the wrong thing, Roy. You were happy at Honeywell, and you did a good job. That's what matters."

Roy shrugged. "Yeah, I guess so. I tried to be the best janitor I could be. But sometimes these past few weeks I been wishing I'd become a carpenter, not just because I like the work but because of another reason too."

"And why's that, Roy?" Mae asked kindly.

"Because Jesus was a carpenter, and I'd kinda like to be in the same profession as He was. While I been working on the house here, I been thinking about Jesus and trying to do a job that would make Him proud."

Mae patted Roy's arm with one gloved hand. "Oh, I'm sure He's very proud of the work you're doing."

"I hope so, Miss Mae. It's funny, you know. You think about Him going around preaching and healing the sick and all that, but you never really think about Him doing everyday stuff like working in His carpenter's shop, just like a regular person. Least I never thought much about it, anyway, till I started working on the house. But He did, didn't He? He worked with wood, and He liked to build things and fix things up that were broken and give them back to the owner all polished up and like new. Do you ever think about that, Miss Mae?"

Mae was quiet a moment. The men were back at work after their break, and the sounds of hammering had started up again. "To tell you the truth, I never thought about that much before, Roy," she said finally. "But you're right, you know. If He didn't start preaching until He was thirty, then He must have spent plenty of years just quietly working in His shop. But you know something else, Roy?"

"What's that, Miss Mae?"

"Fixing things that are broken is what He does best. He's still a carpenter, Roy. It's just that He no longer works with wood."

Roy looked up at the house thoughtfully. After a moment, he shrugged. "Well, whatever kind of material He works with, Miss Mae, I'm sure He still does a good job."

Mae took her brother's arm. "That He does, Roy," she said as they went on walking together around the new house, their home.

Chapter 19

On a May morning filled with the flowering of spring — daffodils and tulips, lilac bushes and crab apple trees in full bloom — Mae drove to the boardinghouse on Pillsbury one last time to pick up Roy.

Miss Pease, in her usual tight black dress and thick-soled shoes, met Mae at the door. "Come to get Roy, have you?" she remarked, not bothering to offer a greeting. "He's so excited he couldn't eat any breakfast. He'll be famished way before noon, if I know Roy. I hope your refrigerator's full."

"That it is, Miss Pease," Mae said confidently, still standing on the front porch and wondering whether or not she would be invited in. "I'm well prepared and looking forward to cooking for a grateful eater."

"I don't know how grateful he is," Miss Pease interjected, "but he's an eater all right. I've run this house for more than twenty-five years, and I've never quite seen the likes of —"

"Good morning, Roy," Mae said cheerfully, interrupting Miss Pease. Roy had descended the stairs while the two women were talking and stood quietly in the hallway, half hidden by his landlady.

"Morning, Miss Mae!" Roy responded eagerly. Mae saw his head bobbing as he moved this way and that in an attempt to get around Miss Pease and out the front door.

"Are you all ready to go?" Mae asked, leaning slightly to one side and throwing the question over Miss Pease's shoulder.

"Oh yes, Miss Mae! Been ready for a long time."

Miss Pease finally stepped aside and said to Roy, "I trust you left your room clean and in order?"

Roy nodded emphatically. "Cleaned it the best I could. Even scrubbed the floor. I know how to do that kind of stuff — that was my job, you know. The boss said I was one of the best janitors the company ever hired on."

"Yes, well, I'm glad for that, then," Miss Pease said stiffly. "I can't abide a dirty room, not when I'm in the position of having to find a new tenant. You know that every time a tenant leaves I have to have my niece show the room until it's rented, seeing as how I can't climb them stairs myself. Haven't climbed them since 1965, but Eliza Sue, she lets me know if the rooms are clean or not and ready for a new tenant to move in —"

Mae, interrupting Miss Pease for a second time, tossed another question to Roy. "Can I help you carry anything, Roy?"

"Nope," Roy said. In one hand he clutched the handle of a large suitcase, which he held up for Mae to see. Draped over his other arm was his heavy winter coat. "Got everything right here."

Mae looked at the suitcase. "That's everything?"

"Yup," Roy said. "All I own."

"What about your radio?"

Roy dropped his chin toward the suitcase. "In there," he said.

"You're sure that's everything?"

"That's it, Miss Mae."

"Well, okay, then. Let's go home."

"Let's go, Miss Mae." Roy squeezed past Miss Pease and hurriedly slipped out the door.

"Roy Hanna!" the large woman called to him. "I guess you packed away your manners. After living here more than ten years, aren't you even going to say good-bye to me?" She stood in the doorway in her tight dress, her arms akimbo like bat's wings.

Roy smiled sheepishly and said, "Sorry, Miss Pease. Guess I was so excited I forgot. Good-bye, and take good care of Emmett, okay?"

During the drive to the house on Humboldt, Roy talked nonstop, his hands flying animatedly in all directions. He talked about how he was anxious to get out the lawn mower to give the grass its first trim of the season. He wanted to keep the yard free of dandelions and weeds so that it was perfectly smooth and green, like a golf course. Maybe, if Miss Mae wanted, he could dig out a garden over near the garage where Miss Wollencott used to have her garden. He had always wanted to try his hand at growing tomatoes and cucumbers and radishes and maybe even rhubarb, and he would be glad to pull all the weeds himself if that was something Miss Mae didn't want to do. As for the front porch and the walkway, he intended to sweep them every day in good weather, and when it snowed, he'd be the first one on the block out shoveling. And maybe he would polish all the windows in the house once a week so that no dirt would build up on them and interfere with the view outdoors. He'd also be sure to keep the bushes trimmed so they would never grow up over the windows and keep the sunlight out the way they did at the boardinghouse. And if ever a shutter fell off in the wind, he would be out there quick as a flash to hammer it back up again. "Gonna take good care of our home, Miss Mae," Roy said. "Yessir, you can count on old Roy to take good care of our home. And I don't have to do the chores just on Tuesday mornings, either, like I done before. I can work every day of the week, if I want, because I'll already be right there all the time."

Mae laughed. "You have free run of the house, Roy," she said, "and you have my permission to do whatever you want, whenever you want to do it. As for Tuesday mornings, you'll be on your own. Thursdays too. I'm afraid you won't find me at home those two mornings."

"Where will you be, Miss Mae?"

"I'll be helping out at the children's hospital, working as a volunteer."

Roy's eyebrows went up. "You mean, just like you used to do?"

"Yes, just like I used to do."

"Well, now, that's real nice, Miss Mae. I remember those couple of times you took me with you, like that time it was close to Christmas and I dressed up like Santa Claus and handed out presents to the little ones. You remember that, Miss Mae?"

"Oh my, yes! How could I forget?"

"I remember how excited those children were at seeing Santa Claus, but you know, I always thought the children were even happier just seeing you. Remember how they used to call you Mother Mae?"

Mae nodded and replied quietly, "Yes, Roy. I remember."

"You suppose you'll be Mother Mae again, just like before?"

Mae sighed wistfully. "I don't know, but I hope so."

Roy was confident. "Oh, you will, Miss Mae. I'm sure you will. If ever there was a Mother Mae in this world, it's you. Not one bit of doubt about that."

Mae had never heard Roy talk so much, nor so excitedly. But the moment they pulled up in front of the house, he fell silent. He got out of the car and stood on the sidewalk, clutching his suitcase and coat. He stood stiffly, staring at the house but making no move to walk toward it.

Mae took his arm. "Come on inside, Roy," she said gently.

But still Roy didn't move. "Looks just like it did before," he said quietly, with something like awe in his voice. "Only this time it's my home too. I can't hardly believe it."

Mae turned her eyes from Roy's face and looked at the house. "In a way it was always your home," she said. "I think Mother wanted you to feel that it was, anyway. She wanted you to feel like part of the family."

Roy nodded. "Miss Wollencott — she was real good to me, always inviting me over and all. I guess I did feel like I was part of your family, even though I didn't really live here."

"I don't suppose it's living in a certain house that makes a person part of a family, Roy. I think it has more to do with just being loved for who you are."

"I guess I been real lucky all my life. I was an orphan and a spinster, but I never been alone because of you and Miss Wollencott."

Mae tried to hide her smile. "You were a bachelor, Roy, not a spinster. But anyway, I suppose we were the lucky ones really, having you as our friend."

Roy sighed contentedly as his eyes surveyed the house again. "I'm real happy, Miss Mae," he said simply.

"So am I, Roy."

Roy dropped his eyes to meet hers. His face was filled with questions. "Are you, Miss Mae?" he asked. "You know, for a long time I prayed that something would happen to bring your joy back after little Sammy fell and all. But the last time I prayed that prayer was the day I burned your house down. I didn't think you could ever be happy again after I did that."

Mae shook her head slowly and offered Roy a smile. "You know, Roy," she said, "in an odd sort of way, I think the fire might have been the answer to your prayer."

Roy's brows went up in surprise. "How could it be? I wanted something good to happen, not something so terrible."

"Well, Roy." Mae pursed her lips a moment before going on. "Sometimes what appears to be bad is really good in the end. Because of the fire I learned some things I wouldn't otherwise have known, and I had to do a lot of thinking and make some important decisions. I might not have made those same decisions had it not been for the fire."

Roy was quiet and pensive but finally said, "If you say so, Miss Mae. I'm just glad everything's all right."

"Everything," Mae added, "except that we're standing out here on the sidewalk when we should be inside enjoying our new home. Come on inside now."

Mae led a smiling Roy up the walkway and onto the porch. She reached into her purse for her keys, but instead of retrieving one key ring, she fished out two and handed one to Roy. "Here's your set of keys," she instructed. "One key is to the front door. That's this one. And this one's to the back door, and this one is to the garage. Do you think you can keep them straight?"

Roy nodded and stared wide-eyed at the keys in the palm of his hand as though they were jewels. Mae unlocked the front door and the two of them stepped inside. Here, just as before, was the hallway that stretched from the front of the house to the back, leading to the kitchen in the rear. And there was the staircase with a sleek new banister similar to the one the Wollencott children had slid down for years. Leading off the hallway to the left was the dining room and to the right, the living room, just as the layout had been in the old house. But most of the furniture was what Roy and Mae had bought at the antique shops, not what Mrs. Wollencott and the doctor had bought decades ago. And the smell — it smelled new, like freshly cut wood, not musty and smoky as the old house had smelled. The glass in the windows was clean and clear, not old and rippled, and the shiny hardwood floors were as yet free of the scuff marks of a million footfalls.

"Looks real nice, Miss Mae," Roy commented.

"Well, thanks to you, since you helped build it. It has the marks of your handiwork now." The two gazed about them in silence. Then Mae said, "I just finished getting everything in place yesterday — everything we have so far, that is. We still have plenty of things to buy before we're through, but there's lots of time for that. Take a look around, Roy. See what you think."

Roy stepped lightly into the living room and let his eyes wander from floor to ceiling. He was glad to see that the furniture wasn't completely different; there were the two chairs and the coffee table and the lamp he had carried out of the house on the day of the fire. And on the mantel were the framed photographs he had gathered into his arms and removed from the threat of the flames. There was the photo of Mrs. Wollencott and her three friends that Mae loved so much, sitting on the mantel just as it had been before.

Roy smiled widely, but as he continued to search the mantel, the smile slid from his face and was replaced by a look of concern.

When Mae noticed the change in Roy's expression, she asked, "What's the matter, Roy? Don't you like the room?"

Roy looked around a moment longer, then answered tentatively, "Oh yes, Miss Mae, I like the room. But I thought I took the music box outta the house before the fire got it. I coulda sworn I carried that music box out, but I guess I only thought so."

"You did, Roy," Mae assured him. "The music box is safe. I just put it somewhere else. Come upstairs and I'll show you."

Mae led the way up the newly carpeted staircase, through the upper hall, and past her own room to Roy's room. It was the first room in the house that Mae had completed. She had let Roy pick out the furnishings, but she didn't want him to see the room until the day they moved in. She wanted him to be surprised, and she wanted to enjoy the look on his face when he saw the room for the first time.

She wasn't disappointed. When Roy stepped into the room, his face fairly glowed. He said nothing, but his mouth hung open as though he were trying to find words to describe his joy. His eyes traveled the room, moving from one object to the next, resting on each a moment to take it in. There was the antique bed with a walnut headboard that Roy had found in Stillwater, the garage-sale dresser and chest of drawers that he had stripped and repainted over the winter, the bedside table that Ellen had donated, a recliner and lamp that Mae had bought new at Sears, and on the walls, three Maxfield Parrish prints that had caught Roy's eye in a shop down in Red Wing. And, of course, on the wall was his Disney World pennant, and on the dresser, his souvenir hat with the Mickey Mouse ears, brought home from their trip to Florida over Christmas.

But Mae had added one more thing to the room just that morning. "There it is, Roy," she said, pointing to the music box on the bedside table. "I thought you might like to have it beside your bed. That way you can listen to it anytime — even in the middle of the night if you want."

Roy put down the suitcase and coat that he'd carried from the car, then moved across the room to the bed. Sitting, he carefully cradled the music box in his hands for a moment before turning the key and lifting the lid. When the box was opened, the old familiar tune greeted him like a friend. He hadn't heard it in nearly a year, since the day of the fire.

The notes, clear and sweet, drifted through the room. Roy breathed deeply, as though taking them in like a scent. Mae saw him leave, his eyes wide, staring, as he returned to the place where the music always took him. The song played twice, three times, and then the box began to wind itself down. Roy slowly turned the key again and sat motionless, listening, as the song continued to play.

Finally Mae asked quietly, "Was she very beautiful?"

For a moment Roy didn't answer, and Mae thought perhaps he hadn't heard. Then, without looking at her but staring as though seeing only the image that was inside, he said, "Oh yes, Miss Mae. She was beautiful. And real nice too. Just like you."

Mae took a step closer to Roy. She was eager to know more but didn't want to frighten Roy or confuse him. She tried to keep the emotion out of her voice as she asked, "Do I remind you of her, then — sometimes?"

Roy cocked his head in thought. "I don't know. Sometimes, yes. I think so."

"What do you remember, Roy?"

Roy creased his brow, as though it were painful to think. More than a minute passed as he considered Mae's question. Then he said, "Not very much. Just a face. Me, lying in bed or something, and her face above me. Sometimes she would sing, sometimes she'd just talk to me. 'My own sweet boy,' she used to say. I remember that. 'My own sweet boy.' And I remember her hand on my cheek." Roy lifted one rough hand to his cheek, as though to touch the hand that had once rested there. "She had soft skin. She was real nice, Miss Mae. I think you might have liked her."

Roy finally turned his eyes toward Mae and smiled. She smiled in return. Roy closed the music box and replaced it on the nightstand.

"Well," Mae said, "Miss Pease told me you didn't have any breakfast. You're probably starving."

"Yeah, guess I am," Roy said with a chuckle. "Didn't notice it before, but now my stomach's beginning to rumble."

"How about if I go fix a midmorning snack, maybe some toast and coffee, and I'll put lunch in the oven at the same time. We can eat an early lunch, around eleven-thirty or so."

Roy smiled broadly. "That sounds real good to me."

"You just stay here a few minutes, then, and enjoy your new room while I get that bread in the toaster," Mae said, heading toward the door.

"I'll call you the second it pops up."

She had nearly disappeared into the hall when Roy called after her. "Miss Mae?"

Mae reappeared in the doorway. "Yes, Roy?"

Roy, still sitting on the bed, struck a match and began lighting a cigar. When he had taken enough quick puffs to get the end burning, he took the cigar out of his mouth and asked, "Will she be there too?"

Mae laughed and gave Roy a curious look. "Will who be where?" she asked.

Roy nodded toward the nightstand. "The lady in the music box. Will she be up there at the banquet table with Miss Wollencott and the doctor and Willie and George and little Sammy and Jesus too? Think she'll be there when we get there?"

Mae stood silently. Roy's question was something she had never considered. She was surprised at the unexpected hope it brought. "Yes, Roy," she said quietly. "I think she may very well be there too."

Roy nodded and looked satisfied. He took a long pull on his cigar and blew the smoke out the side of his mouth. "I'll be glad to see her," he said.

Mae looked at her brother and smiled. "So will I," she said.

As she walked down the hall toward the stairs, the notes of the music box followed her and spoke less of what had been than of the possibility of what was to come.

Ann Tatlock is a full-time writer who has also worked as an assistant editor for *Decision* magazine. A graduate of Oral Roberts University with an M.A. in Communications from Wheaton Graduate School, she has published numerous articles in Christian magazines. This is her second novel. She makes her home in Minneapolis with her husband Bob and their daughter Laura Jane.

The employees of G.K. Hall hope you have enjoyed this Large Print book. All our Large Print titles are designed for easy reading, and all our books are made to last. Other G.K. Hall books are available at your library, through selected bookstores, or directly from us.

For information about titles, please call:

(800) 257-5157

To share your comments, please write:

Publisher
G.K. Hall & Co.
P.O. Box 159
Thorndike, ME 04986